Praise for

ANN TATLOCK and

EVERY SECRET THING

"Intelligent, introspective, and beautifully, hauntingly written, *Every Secret Thing* deals with tough issues in a manner that underlines Ann Tatlock's stature as a rising master of Christian and crossover fiction."

—Tom Morrisey, author of *In High Places*

"A hint of romance, a puzzle from the past—*Every Secret Thing* has it all . . . and more. Anyone who has ever had a favorite teacher will identify with the impact one person can have. Ann Tatlock has written a lovely story."

—Roxanne Henke, author of *After Anne* and *The Secret of Us.*

"Ann Tatlock has proven her powerful, gentle skill of sculpting words with *Every Secret Thing*. She made me smile, made me cry, and warmed my heart, all in one well-crafted novel as she reminded me that even our smallest actions have eternal consequences."

—Hannah Alexander, author of the *Hideaway* novels

"*Every Secret Thing* by Ann Tatlock is a warm, honest, intimate story of many hearts entwined. PLUS the story had enough of the unexpected to keep me turning the pages and wanting to get back to the story when life interrupted my reading time. Touching and unpredictable."

—Lyn Cote, Author of *Blessed Assurance*

"*Every Secet Thing* is a profoundly beautiful and moving novel. Ann Tatlock's words paint a tender metaphor of lives divinely intertwined for reasons we can't always see or understand."

—Deborah Raney, author of *A Vow to Cherish* and *Leaving November*

"A hauntingly beautiful story that carries you along until the last page. I loved it!"

—Elizabeth Musser, author of *The Swan House*

THINGS WE ONCE HELD DEAR

"[Tatlock] creates a vividly immersive world. . . . The background detail is immense and well-crafted. . . . It's beautiful, amazing writing. . . . a truly enjoyable and refreshing experience."

—Tim Frankovich, *Christian Fiction Review.com*

"Ann Tatlock's work is consistently an engaging and enticing read. Her dialogue is fresh and inviting, and her characters are disarmingly genuine as they struggle to contend with emotions and difficulties so common to the human heart."

—Michele Howe, *FaithfulReader.com*

"Tatlock does an admirable job of creating resolution without resorting to stock solutions that a lesser writer might have chosen . . . [She] is a superb storyteller."

—Susan Meissner, *Armchair Interviews.com*

". . . a treasure for people who enjoy a literary yet unpretentious read."

—RT Bookclub

I'LL WATCH THE MOON

"Tatlock continues to weave 20th-century history into absorbing, finely crafted literary tales with issues of spirituality springing naturally from the text."

—*Library Journal*

"This is a moving and wonderfully encouraging novel . . . one of the most realistic and significant ones I've read, and one that leaves a great inspiration and message of trust in God for the outcome of all things . . . I highly recommend it."

—*Renownmagazine.com*

EVERY
SECRET
THING

ANN TATLOCK

BETHANYHOUSE
Minneapolis, Minnesota

Every Secret Thing
Copyright © 2007
Ann Tatlock

Cover design by Studio Gearbox
Cover photography by Getty Images/Will and Deni McIntyre

Published by Bethany House Publishers
11400 Hampshire Avenue South
Bloomington, Minnesota 55438

Bethany House Publishers is a division of
Baker Publishing Group, Grand Rapids, Michigan.

Printed in the United States of America

ISBN-13:   978-0-7642-0005-2
ISBN-10:   0-7642-0005-4

Library of Congress Cataloging-in-Publication Data

Tatlock, Ann.
    Every secret thing / Ann Tatlock.
       p.   cm.
    ISBN-13: 978-0-7642-0005-2 (pbk.)
    ISBN-10: 0-7642-0005-4 (pbk.)
    1. Women teachers—Fiction. 2. Preparatory school teachers—Fiction.
I. Title.
    PS3570.A85E84   2007
    813'.54—dc22   2007023748

To
my English teacher at
Sanford School, Hockessin, Delaware
Bea Cope
because I think you too
have known those
moments of being.

Books by Ann Tatlock

ABOUT THE AUTHOR

ANN TATLOCK is the author of the Christy Award-winning novel *All the Way Home*. She has also won the Midwest Independent Publishers Association "Book of the Year" in fiction for both *All the Way Home* and *I'll Watch the Moon*. Ann lives with her husband and daughter in Asheville, North Carolina.

Visit Ann's Web site: *www.anntatlock.com*

PROLOGUE

The first thing I want you to know is that there really is a state called Delaware.

You see, when I left home to go away to college in the Midwest, I discovered I had spent my whole life in a place that most people were only vaguely aware of. "So where are you from?" I was asked time and again, and time and again when I replied, "I'm from Delaware," the response I got was, "What state is that in?"

No, no, no. You see, Delaware isn't *in* a state; it *is* a state. It was and is, in fact, the First State—so says the license plate of every car owned by every Delawarean. One of the thirteen original colonies, Delaware earned its rank as number one when, on December 7, 1787, it was the first state to approve the United States Constitution. Now, there's something to be said for that, isn't there? Delaware was a state before most other states were so much as a twinkle in the government's eye.

So, you might ask, if it led this country into nationhood, why is it we never hear anything about this state called Delaware? Good question. One I've often pondered myself. Did it accomplish this one historic act, and then sit back to rest on its laurels? I mean, let's face it. Delaware seldom makes the headlines, seldom makes the national news at all, save for those instances when a certain senator stirs up the waters in Washington with one biting partisan remark or another. But most people just ignore that kind of thing. I know I do.

When I was a child, a Bible passage I heard in Sunday school always made me think of Delaware. It was the story in the Gospel of John where Philip goes and finds Nathanael to

9

tell him they've found the Messiah, the one Moses and the prophets wrote about. This should be good news for a couple of Jewish fellows, right? But oddly enough, the man is Jesus of Nazareth, son of Joseph. Instead of rejoicing because the Messiah has come, Nathanael is appalled to think he came from Nazareth, that haven for the Roman army, persecutors of the Jews. And so Nathanael cries out, "Can any good thing come out of Nazareth?"

Those words stuck with me until my impish mind tweaked the question, turning it around to become, "Can anything *at all* come out of *Delaware*?"

While growing up, my best friend Natalie and I dubbed our home state Dullaware. To us it was The Place Where Nothing Ever Happens. We did, however, think that people outside our state at least knew we existed. That crushing realization was saved for later.

It might be that Delaware is largely overlooked because of its size. In spite of the idealistic promotional slogan selling the state as a Small Wonder, the epithet nevertheless exposes Delaware for what it is: just a little slip of land, too pint-sized a place even to have its own commercial airport. To fly to Delaware you have to land in Philadelphia, or maybe Newark, New Jersey, or even Dulles Airport in Washington, but you don't land in Delaware proper unless you're in a private jet or a military plane. It might be said—only partly in jest, I suppose—that there is simply no place to put the runway. Consider the old joke of road travelers: "Delaware. If you blink, you miss it."

It's true that lengthwise, Delaware measures only eighty-five miles. And the width—well, the southern end of the state is the widest part and that's only thirty-five miles. Farther north, just below Wilmington where I grew up, the state is eight miles wide. Eight miles!

"Hey, want to hike across the state?"

"Sure. There's nothing better to do until supper."

I know, I know. It doesn't look promising. You just don't hear of people saving up for their dream vacation to Delaware or grabbing up land to retire there. You don't hear of people talking up its splendors in such a way that everyone longs to experience the place for himself.

When it comes to Delaware, you don't really hear much of anything.

But then, you have to consider, the state itself is not so different from most of us, is it? Think about it. You, me, that person down the street—we're all here, just as real as the next person, living out a life as real as any other life, and yet, unless you're as influential as New York or as big as Texas, very few people know that you exist, or that I exist, or that anyone exists beyond a vague knowing that there are "other people out there."

Can anything good come out of such a life?

In the same way Philip answered Nathanael's question about the good that can arise out of so doubtful a place, I can only invite you to come and see.

CHAPTER 1

I have lived in half a dozen states—in the Midwest, the South, along the Eastern Seaboard—but nowhere have I seen the evening light the way it appears on summer nights in Delaware. I struggle to tell you what it looks like, and chances are I won't succeed. That light is one of the few things I've come across that may actually be ineffable—that is, beyond the scope of human language. And that's because it doesn't appear to be light at all so much as it seems simply to be a sigh of contentment, as though the earth itself has let off a breath of satisfaction.

Wherever I went, wherever I lived over the years, I remembered that light. As a child, I let it cover me with its warmth, and in that light I first sensed the very real presence of the eternal.

Within the first week of my return to Delaware, that particular light showed up to welcome me. I was sitting at the dining room table in the faculty house called Pine Glen on the campus of Seaton Preparatory School. Books, index cards, loose papers, and piles of lesson plans covered the length of the table as I prepared for the classes that would begin in a few days. I had been teaching for years, and yet the mounds of paper in front of me appeared as insurmountable as a range of snowcapped mountains. Not only was I nearly overcome by feelings of inadequacy, but just being back at Seaton—now as a teacher rather than a student—flooded me with a confusing ambivalence. This was a place that I had once so loved and yet so hated, a place that had once so kindly nurtured me, yet filled me with an agonizing fear.

I was feeling some of that same fear—and it was leaning toward regret at having come back—when I lifted my face toward the breeze drifting in through the open window. That certain familiar twilight was circling the pine trees outside like a contented cat, and as had happened before, something broke in upon my dread, and I was comforted. For several minutes I didn't move because I didn't want that feeling to fade. I had not known it for a very long time.

When I was young, I called such instances my *moments of being*. I stole that expression from the novelist Virginia Woolf, and I admit that I did so without compunction. For one thing, no one knew about my moments of being, including Virginia Woolf herself, who was dead. And for another thing, and maybe more importantly, what she and I meant by moments of being were two entirely different things.

I lowered my head to the papers again. Before I could get back to work, though, my thoughts were interrupted by a car pulling up in front of the old clapboard house that was Pine Glen. I wasn't expecting company and couldn't imagine who might be stopping by past eight o'clock in the evening. I stepped uneasily to the window and peered out at a pale blue Honda Accord coming to a stop in the circular drive. The front door of the car eased open, and the driver emerged, and in the moment of recognition I felt as though I really had finally come home to Delaware. Walking up the pebbled path to my door was my lifelong friend Natalie Primrose. *No,* I thought, shaking my head, *it's Natalie Fraley, remember?* Twenty years since I was her bridesmaid, and would I still not remember to call her by her married name?

I met her at the door, arms wide, and we laughed as we greeted each other with a long and joyous hug.

"I can't believe you're here, Beth," she cried as she pulled back to look at me.

"I can hardly believe it myself," I said. "Come on in."

She stepped inside and looked around. "Imagine you living in Pine Glen. I can't believe it," she said again.

"Well, it's true. Believe it or not, here I am. Teaching English at Seaton Prep."

"Teaching? You look exactly the same as when you were a student here!"

I laughed out loud. "Except that I've got twelve fewer inches of hair and several dozen wrinkles that I didn't have then."

"No way, Beth. You look great—"

"So do you, Nat—"

"—and I like your hair shorter and wavy like that. How do you stay so thin? Look at me, carrying twenty pounds more than I should."

"Yeah, well, you've had three kids. I haven't."

"Still . . ." She shook her head. "How long has it been since I last saw you? Fifteen years?"

"Something like that. Maybe more. Way too long, that's all I know."

"I hope you don't mind my just dropping by. Maybe I should have called ahead—"

"Of course not!"

"—but I couldn't wait to see you. Figures we'd be out of town with the in-laws when you arrived—"

"When did you get back?"

"Just this afternoon. I told Ron and the kids they were on

their own for the rest of the evening, and I jumped in the car and took off."

"I'm glad you did. Come on in and have a seat. Can I get you anything to drink? Coffee? Soda?"

"Nothing, thanks. I won't stay long. Hey, it looks like you've lived here for years. How'd you get unpacked so fast?"

"Well, I've been here for almost a week already. Still, you should see the upstairs. Boxes everywhere."

I motioned her into the living room, but before she had gone three steps, she stopped. "Wow," she said. I watched her eyes move across the bookcases that lined the walls of the room. "This isn't a house; it's a library. I've never seen so many books all in one place."

I shrugged. "Yeah, I guess I've picked up a few over the years. Once I have them, I can't seem to part with them."

"You always did like to read, I know, but . . ." She stopped and offered me a lopsided smile. "Well, books are probably more useful than my collection of ceramic cows. All they do is sit there looking silly. But I can't help it; I like them."

She took a seat in the wing chair by the fireplace and used the footstool to prop up one foot while the other foot stayed on the floor. I sat down on the couch across from her and tucked my feet beneath me.

"I have to say, Pine Glen looks a whole lot better than when the Buckleys lived here," she said. "Remember all that black suede furniture and those fuzzy psychedelic glow-in-the-dark posters they had on the walls? Talk about a lack of taste. And him an artist! This room looked like a cross between a funeral parlor and a really bad acid trip."

"How could I forget!" I laughed.

We were familiar with the Buckleys' décor because they

had often hosted groups of students in their home on week-ends. We all pitched in for pizza, then sat around talking about art and pop literature and the tunes of the Top 40 Count-down. Sometimes some of the kids brought their guitars, and we sat around singing songs by Cat Stevens and Jim Croce and Dan Fogelberg. Natalie and I came to these gatherings occa-sionally because her first love was art and Mr. Buckley was the upper school art teacher. His wife taught social studies and history in the middle school. Those were the daytime school-approved get-togethers at the Buckleys'. What the school authorities didn't know about were the late-night unauthori-zed get-togethers that Natalie and I only heard rumors of through the student grapevine. Apparently the Buckleys grew their own marijuana on a windowsill in one of the upstairs bedrooms, the yield of which they shared freely—if quietly—with certain members of the student body.

"But then, good grief," I went on, "it was the seventies! When you think about it, the Buckleys were really just a cou-ple of hippies trying to make a living."

"Sure, I know. I liked them—I'm not saying I didn't—I just think, in hindsight, that Stan Buckley wouldn't have been my first choice for a high school art teacher. What were they thinking when they hired him? Talented or not, if any of my kids' teachers invited them over for late-night pot parties . . ." She finished the sentence by shaking her head.

"Yeah, pretty wild, I know. But the kids would have been smoking pot anyway, with or without the Buckleys' home-grown stash. There was plenty of that stuff around."

"No kidding. And somehow we missed it all and had a good time anyway."

I smiled at my old friend. "Not that we were perfect, of course."

"Goodness no."

"I mean, don't you remember—?" I stopped and looked at her. I had almost asked her if she didn't remember the two of us sneaking across campus at night, heading toward faculty Cabin 1, where some of our friends were already waiting for us. But, on second thought, I didn't want to bring it up.

"Remember what?"

"Oh, nothing." I shrugged my shoulders and tried to pass it off with a small laugh.

"Well, anyway," she said, "I'm just so glad you're here."

"I am too. So tell me, how's life?"

"Good. Things are good. The kids are doing great, staying healthy. How about you?"

"I'm fine, I guess. A little nervous about school starting in a couple of days."

Suddenly Natalie's face collapsed into a picture of concern. I was about to assure her that I was always nervous at the start of a school year and that I'd soon get over it, but her mind was on something else.

"What about Nick?" she asked hesitantly.

Nick Watson. The man I had left behind in Maryland when I accepted the position here at Seaton.

"It's over," I said.

"There's no hope at all?"

"No." I tried to smile, but the best I could offer was an uncertain tremor at the corners of my mouth. "I couldn't get him to commit. After three years, when I told him I wanted to move forward or break it off, he dawdled for a while and then just kind of drifted away." I didn't have to go into detail;

Natalie knew most of the story already through e-mails and phone calls.

"I'm sorry, Beth," she said quietly.

I waved a hand nonchalantly. "You know me. Unlucky in love."

When she didn't respond, an uneasy silence fell over the room. I found myself groping for words to fill the void. "Hey, do you keep up with the old gang at all?" I finally asked, trying to sound cheerful.

"Umm, no. Not really. Last I heard, Janie was still up in Rochester working for some sort of chemical company. I don't know if you knew, but her husband left her a couple years back."

I nodded. "Yeah, she told me about it in a Christmas card."

"After almost twenty years together too." She clicked her tongue and sighed at the thought of Janie's failed marriage.

But I didn't want to talk about that. "What about the guys?" I asked.

She frowned in thought. "I've been really bad about keeping up with people. As far as I know, Ken's in Washington doing something or other with the government. I saw a notice in the alumni magazine about him once, saying he was married and had a couple of kids. At the time he was working as a lobbyist, I think—out there trying to persuade politicians to see things his way."

"Sounds like Ken."

"Yeah. And Ray—he's a doctor. I know that much for sure. He's over at Wilmington General, if I'm remembering right. I saw him briefly at the twentieth reunion but haven't seen him since."

"I remember hearing that he'd gone on to med school. I always knew he'd do well."

"Yeah, no question there."

"It's too bad we haven't kept in better touch. After the tenth reunion I never got back here again to visit, not even for homecoming. There didn't seem to be much reason to visit Delaware after Dad retired and the folks moved to North Carolina."

"Come back for homecoming?" Natalie said with a laugh. "I live right here in Hockessin, and I've hardly been to any of the reunions myself. Life just gets busy."

"That it does."

She was quiet a moment, then said, "Oh, and Artie! Apparently he's fallen off the face of the earth. The alumni office is trying to update its records, and no one can find him."

"Maybe he really did go off to the Belgian Congo to become a mercenary. Remember how he used to always talk about that?"

"He was one crazy kid."

"Yeah. But then, weren't we all?"

There were six of us in the old gang that hung out together in upper school. Three boys and three girls. The group congealed early in the eleventh grade when Mr. Fossett, the chemistry teacher, mysteriously failed to show up for class one morning. It was the period right before lunch, so with a couple of hours on our hands, five of us responded when Raymond Schmidt asked, "Anyone want to grab lunch at Burger King?" Ray drove a souped-up Camaro to school, and it was that car the six of us piled into, risking barn duty for the sake of Whoppers and fries. Ray had connections of sorts, since he was the great-nephew of the school's assistant headmaster, John Pettingill. Ray figured if we got caught leaving campus during school hours, we could go to his uncle and talk our way out of trouble. I wasn't so sure. Pettingill was known around campus as Commander because of his stint as a navy flyer during the Second World War. The product of military training in wartime, Commander generally ran a tight ship at Seaton and didn't put up with any nonsense. But I wasn't about to miss out on this midday adventure, even if it meant cleaning out the horse stalls later as punishment. So off we went to the strip of fast-food joints on Kirkwood Highway, returning right before fifth-period class without having piqued the suspicion of any of the staff. We pulled into campus high on sugar and saturated fat, laughing hysterically over the cardboard Burger King crowns we came back wearing. We were easily entertained in those days and found laughter in just about anything.

After that excursion it was understood that those of us who ventured out that day were a clan of sorts, bound to do everything together, as indivisible as a couple going steady, except we were six instead of two. We even gave our group a name, calling ourselves the Barbarians. As I remember, we chose the name after a history lecture in which Mr. Flint quoted someone as saying, "The future belongs to the barbarians." Surely that was us, wasn't it?

In addition, calling ourselves the Barbarians just seemed incredibly funny at the time. Most likely because no epithet could have been further from the truth.

We were a bunch of straight-laced kids, bookish, mostly clean-cut, out for the A, and all headed for college. We never got into any real trouble, never dabbled in drugs, knew nothing of sex beyond an occasional game of spin the bottle. We were the parents' dream in the ongoing nightmare of the sixties and seventies counterculture.

On graduation day, Raymond Schmidt and Jane Kidder shared the stage as class valedictorians. All of us were honored with awards—Ray and Janie for leadership and scholastic achievement, Arthur Sochs for his skills in mathematics, Ken Cunningham for his work on student government, Natalie Primrose for art and design, and me—I won the award I had long coveted, the Frank P. Milne Literary Award.

Oh, the future was ours, wasn't it?

But even on that day, in the midst of our accomplishment, in the midst of celebration, there was for four of us a certain melancholy that overshadowed all else. There was something left undone—no, something left unknown—and it gnawed at us like a cancer nibbling ever so slightly at someone's insides.

Now, all these years later, Natalie and I sat in the living room of Pine Glen, moving from vague memories of the past to talk of the present—her freelance artwork, her children, my new position as English teacher at Seaton Preparatory School. Before we knew it, night had settled in, and at ten o'clock she rose to leave. We stood, and in that moment I felt the old ambivalence come over me again, that distant but very real sense of dread.

As we walked across the room, I asked, as if on sudden impulse, "Do you ever think about Mr. Dutton?"

She gave me an incredulous look, as though I had asked the unthinkable. But then she laughed—actually laughed— and said, "Heavens no. Why on earth would I think about him?"

She hugged me then and dashed to her car, waving. She

left with a toot of her horn and the spinning of tires on the gravel drive.

She must have made her peace with it, then. I never did. I had tried to forget, but I found myself unable to erase the memory. It lessened over the years, of course, becoming a dull and intermittent ache, but still I went on wondering. There seemed to be no clear answer to the mystery that was Theodore Dutton, with all the whys left dangling before me like fruit gone bad on the vine.

CHAPTER 2

I like to tell people I went to school in a barn—which is very nearly a true statement, though of course it must be qualified. What was known on campus as Heath Hall had originally been a barn until it was converted into a three-story classroom building in 1930. They brought in chalkboards and desks and chairs. They carpeted the stairs while leaving the classroom floors a bare hardwood. They slapped some steel fire escapes on either side of the structure to meet the safety codes of the time. Finally, they painted the whole thing white, and after that there was very little about the building that was barnlike, except that the silo had been left intact, and with flooring and plumbing added, it became the bathrooms.

It was a lovely place, really, this school that I attended and from which I graduated in 1977. Seaton Preparatory School was nestled on eighty-one acres of former farmland in Hockessin, Delaware. I'm not sure of all that the farm produced, but I do know there were apple orchards on the land because some of the trees survived, and between classes we would pick the ripest apples and eat them.

The original farmhouse was a large Victorian, and when the Seaton family purchased the farm with the idea of starting a school, the house was redone to suit that purpose. The first floor ultimately housed the school's main offices and cafeteria. Music was taught on the second floor, and for many years Mr. Barrister, the French teacher, lived alone in the small apartment on the third floor. Whenever the cooks grilled onions in the cafeteria, Mr. Barrister complained of his eyes watering.

From these first two original buildings, the school grew and expanded over the years to include numerous classroom buildings, dormitories, gymnasiums, faculty housing, athletic fields, tennis courts, a swimming pool, two stables and a riding ring, and down in the valley beyond the headmistress's house, a chapel named for one of Seaton's students killed in the Second World War.

I suppose you might think it was a school for children from wealthy families, but this wasn't necessarily so. True, I can think of at least one student from upstate New York who arrived on campus every semester in a chauffeured limousine. But once he was there, he was subject to dorm life and campus chores just like every other boarding student. I remember seeing him carrying trash and raking leaves, as part of Seaton's philosophy was not to pamper students but to teach them discipline and cooperation through helping to maintain the school grounds. Oddly enough, most of these chores were carried out on the weekends, making day students exempt and helping to create a schism between those who lived on campus and those who didn't. Not that friendships didn't form across that line, because they did. But it was no secret that boarders looked upon day students with a certain envy, wishing they too could go home at night to a house instead of a dorm, a family instead of a roommate.

Every year the dorms were filled with students from any number of states as well as from around the world. During the years I was there, I knew kids from Europe, Asia, the Caribbean, and the Middle East. In the 1970s we had quite an influx of boys from Iran trying to escape the draft. They had connections to America and enough money in the bank to get there. The student body was a "we are the world" mixture of whites, blacks, Orientals (as we called them then), Jews, Catholics, Protestants. You name it; we had it.

But I'm digressing. The point is that most of us who were students at Seaton came from ordinary middle-class families. Not a few, on scholarship, came straight from the working class. Seaton was not, by a long shot, the most prestigious school in Delaware, and it certainly was not the most expensive. The kids who really reeked of wealth attended Sterns Valley or Mencken Hill, and when we played their teams in field hockey or lacrosse, we knew we were considered inferior. But we didn't care. Especially when we beat them.

I was myself from a middle-class family with a stay-at-home mom, a dad who worked as an engineer for DuPont, and two sisters who stood on either side of me in age. We lived two miles from Seaton, so I was a day student, driven to school by my father in the morning and picked up by my mother in the afternoon—an arrangement that lasted until I was old enough to drive myself my senior year.

Along with my sisters, I attended public school until I was twelve years old, but when I entered eighth grade, I was sent off on a different path and enrolled by my parents at Seaton. I credit this lucky happenstance to an earthworm. That may sound like another of my embellished statements, something along the lines of attending classes in a barn, but again, there is some truth to this.

To say I was a shy and quiet child would be an understatement. A skeletal, freckle-faced, red-haired kid who was afraid to so much as answer "Here" at roll call, I was a born target for class bullies. I attracted ridicule the way a citywide fire might attract a heat-seeking missile. By the time I was in seventh grade, I was crying myself to sleep every night while my parents paced the kitchen floor below, wondering what to do.

And then came the morning when some kid whose name I didn't even know got on the bus and threw an earthworm in my face. When my mother learned of this—because, of course, I told her—she threw up her hands and exclaimed to my dad, "Really, Ed, I think this is the final straw." The next thing I knew, I was touring Seaton as a prospective student while the middle school principal told my folks happily, "We know your daughter will do well here."

Sometimes I wonder how my life might have been different had it not been for that earthworm. Overall, I count my years at Seaton as a blessing, but still, a person can't help but wonder.

CHAPTER 3

The view from the window where I stood in Heath Hall was of the farmhouse—called Anderson Hall—and the Green where the amphitheater is. That's where we sat on the day we graduated, on that shady stage in our long white gowns and dark formal suits, ready to go out and conquer the world.

I went out and stayed out for a long time, but I did not conquer the world. And then I came back.

I was questioning the wisdom of that particular decision as I stood there looking out at the Green. The dread hanging over me was more than the ordinary anxiety of starting a new school year. This dread had more to do with the school, with Seaton itself. It was a feeling that floated upward like gossamer from some deep place, and I knew exactly where that place was. So I was thankful when my thoughts were interrupted by a friendly voice. "How goes it, Elizabeth?" I turned to see Joel Sexton, my fellow English teacher, standing in the doorway to my classroom.

"Just fine," I replied, hoping I sounded upbeat.

He nodded and smiled. "The campus hasn't changed much, has it, since—when did you say you graduated?"

"Seventy-seven."

"Hasn't changed much since then, has it?"

"Very little," I agreed, "except for the barns and the riding program." The stables had been torn down, and the pastureland on the north side of campus, once used for riding, had been sold for development. What sat there now was a neighborhood of cul-de-sacs and pompous houses. The sale had kept Seaton going during a bumpy financial time in the late 1980s and had been necessary for the survival of the school. But that neighborhood was what I saw from my bedroom window in Pine Glen, and I most often kept the shade drawn against the change that time had brought.

"So," I asked, "what do we hang over the kids' heads now that we can't threaten them with barn duty?"

Joel laughed. He obviously remembered the punishment of raking the muck out of the stables and whitewashing the stalls. Joel was once a student at Seaton himself, a half dozen years behind me. He was still in middle school by the time I graduated, so our paths never crossed on campus. But he too was destined to become a veteran of morning assembly when upper school principal, Mildred Bidney, read the announcements for the day. She stood at the podium with a pad of ruled paper and a perfectly sharpened pencil, and as she read, she tapped the podium with first the tip of the pencil and then the eraser, and then the tip and then the eraser. I'd watch the pencil turning pinwheels while Mrs. Bidney droned on, finally reaching the last dreaded announcement of the morning. At that point the pencil was stilled, laid to rest on the ledge of the podium while Mrs. Bidney flipped the page on the ruled pad. The time had come to read the names of the students who had earned themselves barn duty.

Our principal obviously relished the opportunity to make public that list of perpetrators. Slowly she worked her way down the list, pausing for several nerve-wracking seconds after calling out each name. She peered out over the rim of her glasses, her eyes roaming the room. A hush as thick as a London fog settled over the assembly as those same eyes landed, hawklike, upon the unfortunate bearer of the name. Only the most defiant student dared to meet that gaze without dropping his head in shame.

"Oh yeah, good old Mildew," Joel said now, for that was what we called the principal behind her back. Mildew or Old Biddy, which we thought uproariously funny. Joel laughed again as though he had returned briefly to adolescence and then shook his head as the laughter trailed off to a satisfied sigh. "But you don't have to worry," he added. "Jack has his own ways of keeping the kids in line."

Jack Farrell, upper school principal since 1997, had succeeded the principal who had succeeded Mildred Bidney. Mildew had retired sometime in the 1980s, right around the time the barns were torn down. I don't think there was any connection, but I can't be certain about that.

"So, Elizabeth," Joel said, "ready for classes to start?"

"Ready as I'll ever be," I said, resorting to clichés. "By the way, you can call me Beth. It's easier."

"All right then, Beth."

I had invited him to call me Beth a couple times before, but each time he had reverted back to my full name. There was a bit of the absentminded professor about him, but he had a charming smile and was genuinely friendly, and I counted myself fortunate to be teaching with him. Seaton's student body remained small, and Joel and I were the only two English teachers in the upper school. We each had our own classroom on the second floor of Heath Hall, but we shared an office that once belonged to Beatrice Mann and Tom Goss and later Theodore Dutton, the teachers under whom I fell in love with literature and poetry.

The phone rang in that office now, and Joel left to answer

it. I took another look around my classroom and, feeling satisfied with the seating arrangement, joined Joel in the office. He was well settled in, having been there six years, so that his half of the room was a slipshod collection of books, papers, and cardboard boxes of who-knew-what. I didn't bother to ask. My half of the office, including my desk, was neatly arranged, with books and supplies carefully in place. I intended to keep it that way. I always felt better when I was organized.

I sat at my desk while Joel talked to the invisible someone at the other end of the line. As I waited, I thought I could smell the thousand cigarettes once smoked within these walls. Between classes both Mrs. Mann and Mr. Goss would retreat to their desks and light up, so entering the room, one would literally walk into a cloud of tobacco smoke. We thought nothing of it at the time. Now Seaton School was a tobacco-free campus, with no smoking at all, anywhere. That would not have gone over well in the 1970s among faculty and students alike.

When Joel hung up, he looked greatly in need of a cigarette himself, though as far as I knew he didn't smoke. "That was my wife," he said. "She's just been talking with the insurance adjuster. We had another car end up in the living room a couple nights ago."

For a stunned moment I couldn't speak. How could a car end up in their living room? Finally I muttered, "What do you mean?"

He laughed lightly, and it sounded forced. "Now I know why the property was such a steal. We've been in the house only a year, and twice already we've been awakened by cars crashing through the front wall."

"You're kidding."

"I wish I were."

"What happens?"

"We live over by Hoopes Reservoir, on one of those steep winding roads." He looked at me to see if I was tracking. I nodded and he went on. "Our house is right on a curve and set just off the road."

"Oh?"

"You know what Hoopes is famous for."

I did know. Kids drinking. All around the reservoir were secluded areas where kids could park their cars and work their way through a few bottles of anything from Boone's Farm Apple Wine to Mad Dog 20/20. At least that's what they drank back in my day. I knew about it because my older sister had been up there once or twice when she was supposed to be somewhere else.

"So nights can be dangerous in that part of town," Joel went on.

"You mean cars have actually crashed through your front wall?"

He nodded. "First a Mustang and now a Buick. Both came to rest just short of the entertainment center. At least the TV and stereo system were spared. We've had to replace two couches though. Both were pretty much totaled on impact."

I was aghast at the thought. "Has anyone been hurt?"

"Only my wallet. So far."

"My goodness, Joel! Maybe you ought to move."

"I can't afford to move right now. Besides"—one corner of his mouth went up in a playful smile—"my kids kind of enjoy coming downstairs to find the living room rearranged.

Todd calls it the ultimate extreme makeover."

"But just being in that house is dangerous, don't you think?"

"Well, we don't spend a whole lot of time in the living room, especially on Saturday nights. Both times we've had these unexpected guests, it's been on a Saturday night. Or actually, very early Sunday morning."

"And it was young kids out drinking."

He nodded again. "Both times. Well," he paused and looked at his watch, "I'm going to head on home—or back to what's left of it. See you tomorrow morning at the faculty meeting?"

"Yes, I'll be there."

"All right, then. Have a good night and stay out of trouble."

"Yeah, and you—stay out of the living room."

Joel grabbed his briefcase and, laughing, headed for the door.

When he was gone I stayed at my desk for a while going over some paper work. Overhead, the ceiling squeaked and moaned under the weight of someone's footsteps, interrupting my thoughts and pulling my attention to the single window in the office. On the cobbled path below, Jack Farrell moved along at his usual fast clip, apparently headed for Pratt Lodge, longtime residence of the upper school principal. As he walked, he offered a slight bow and a playful salute to an unsmiling Harlan Quinn, headmaster of Seaton School for some half a dozen years now. The cold shell around Harlan Quinn deflected most attempts at the social niceties. Undeterred, Jack went on to wave a friendly hand at Delia Simpkins, who worked as administrative assistant in the office directly below my feet. She was getting into her car, probably heading out for the day. She offered Jack a small ripple of her fingers in return.

I was becoming well acquainted with the life of the school. After several days of faculty meetings and staff socials, I had learned the names of the people who ran the wheels and cogs of Seaton Prep. And now, ready or not, it was time to get this machine going. I only wished I felt a little more ready.

CHAPTER 4

"Good morning, everyone."

I paused to smile. In return, twelve adolescent faces settled into question marks.

"My name is Elizabeth Gunnar." I pointed toward the board where I'd written my name in yellow chalk. "Miss Gunnar," I emphasized. "Welcome to English Composition."

"Whatever," someone said quietly.

I looked around the room. I didn't know who had spoken and wasn't even certain whether it was a boy or a girl. I decided to let it slide.

"As you know, I'm replacing Mrs. Erickson, who welcomed . . . let's see—" I put on my reading glasses and picked up a piece of paper from my desk—"David Jasper Erickson on August eighth, eight pounds two ounces, twenty-one inches long. Mother and baby are doing fine."

This announcement was greeted with nods, smiles, and a number of comments ranging from "That's cool" to "What kind of name is Jasper?" and was finally punctuated with another decidedly disinterested, "Whatever."

"Before we begin the lesson, I'd like to go through the roll so I can start putting names to faces. You guys have it easy. You only have to learn one new name," I said, pointing toward the chalkboard again to indicate that name was mine. "But I have a hundred and sixteen students in upper school that I hope to become acquainted with by the end of the week."

I smiled again. The students stared at me. Their stares were neither malicious nor dull. These kids were merely waiting, watching to see what I would do.

"So let's see." The reading glasses went back on. I looked at the roll book. "Steven Aldridge? Where's Steven?"

A hand flew up. He was a clean-cut, neatly dressed boy, studious looking. "All right, Steven. Thank you. Alexis Cunningham?"

Another hand went up to the accompaniment of jingling bangles and bracelets. "I go by Lexy," she corrected me.

"Okay, Lexy." I made a note of that in the book.

Working my way down the list, I arrived, near the bottom, at the name of Satchel Queen. When I wrote the names in the roll book a few days earlier, I expected Satchel to be an African-American boy, perhaps named after the baseball player Satchel Paige. There were in fact a couple of black students in the class, but neither one of them answered to the name of Satchel Queen.

And that was because Satchel Queen was not a boy at all, but a girl, a pale-skinned girl with straight dark hair, a gold-plated hoop in each ear, and an expression on her face that told me she was the one who muttered "Whatever" at the beginning of class. In response to her name she didn't raise her hand, but rather raised an eyebrow, as though she were calling out a silent bid.

With that, I realized, suddenly, where my challenge lay. There was always one in every class. In this particular section of English Composition, it would be the girl named Satchel.

I finished calling the roll, then turned and picked up a piece of chalk, lifting it to the dark surface of the board. I intended to begin speaking about some basic rules of grammar, but when the chalk tapped against the board, the present disappeared, and I saw distinctly the man who stood on this very spot a lifetime ago writing his name in a tight, left-leaning script. When he finished, he turned and smiled at us and said, "Good morning, class. My name is Theodore Dutton." And with that, every female student there, myself included, was a little bit in love.

The past came rushing back so completely that when the present returned, I didn't recognize the hand as my own, that hand suspended in the air, pressing the chalk against the board.

How old it looks, I thought, the knuckles enlarged, the skin beginning to fold in tiny wrinkles.

I was not old, only middle-aged, and yet I could well imagine how I looked to the fresh and scarcely blooming youths seated at the desks behind me. They saw the strands of gray among the reddish gold in my hair and the reading glasses on a chain around my neck, and they did not know that there was once a time when I sat where they sat now, young and full of hope. Anticipation was the dominant feeling of my adolescence, sometimes trumping even that other constant companion—fear. I expected good things of life; I thought fulfillment was tucked into the years that were yet to unfold. I was at a preparatory school being prepared for life and for success, and I believed that if I worked hard and did everything just right, I would be rewarded not so much with accomplishment but with love. Wasn't love, after all, the important thing, even far above whatever work we chose to do?

When I was twelve years old, I once saw the headmistress, Miss Margaret Seaton, strolling across the Green in her plaid wool coat and her sensible shoes, and because she was a spinster, I thought to myself, *Why, she has never even lived, and now she is old.*

To these children—for they too were still children, not yet eighteen—I was another Margaret Seaton. While I no longer thought that Miss Seaton had wasted her life, I couldn't help but wonder whether I had wasted mine. I felt myself beyond the hope of marriage, and certainly I was beyond all hope of having children, and I knew—I *knew*—that if I turned around I would see it in their faces like neon at midnight, the look that says, *Why, she has never even lived, and now she is old.*

The chalk made a single truncated line on the board. I had lost my train of thought.

Let's talk about words, I said to myself, because that's what Theodore Dutton said on that first day of school in September 1976. "*Let's talk about words and the power of words. . . .*"

CHAPTER 5

From the time I understood that certain shapes on a page were letters, and that letters could be strung together to form words, and words could be strung together to form sentences, and sentences could form paragraphs could form pages could form stories that took you beyond the ink itself into whole other worlds, I have always loved words. I think that was one reason I liked Theodore Dutton so much, because he loved words too. Whenever he read aloud to us from the *Norton Anthology of English Literature*, it was like he was opening his hands toward us and casting pearls at our feet. I sat enraptured, and the sound of his voice went on echoing through my head long after class was over.

But that wasn't the initial reason I liked Theodore Dutton. I was, after all, an adolescent girl, prone to romantic notions. And as I said, on the first day of our senior year when he introduced himself to us, all the girls in the classroom let off a sigh of longing—first, because he was so attractive, and second, because he was so unattainable. He was not married. A quick glance at the ring finger of his left hand settled that question. But we supposed him to be somewhere around thirty years old, which meant him to be nearly twice our age. I myself was only sixteen and would not be seventeen until December.

Natalie sat beside me in that first class on that first morning of our senior year, and not five minutes into the lesson she was drawing hearts all over the otherwise blank pages of her

41

notebook. I rolled my eyes at her, but she responded with a smile and scribbled a little note on the bottom of the page where I could see it: *Thank heavens Silly Goose left.* That was what we'd called Tom Goss, our English teacher the previous three years who had left to take a position at Trenton Academy in New Jersey. Theodore Dutton was hired as his replacement.

You would have had to be around in the seventies, but if you can picture a cross between Paul Michael Glaser of *Starsky and Hutch* and Erik Estrada of *CHiPs*, you'd have a good idea of what Theodore Dutton looked like. He was very tall and well proportioned, and his hair was a thick mesh of brown waves. I can't remember his eyes exactly, but they were probably brown, and they must have been just right, because there didn't seem to be much about him that wasn't perfect, according to the standards of the day. His chin was strong, and his cheeks were dimpled, and his hands were something you followed with your eyes just because they were so beautiful. More than that, he exuded a certain charm, and he seemed to be completely unaware of it, which made him all the more charming. While he commanded respect simply through his own self-confidence and his place of authority over us, we also knew intuitively from the outset that he was on our side, and unlike some teachers, he wanted to be our friend.

He scribbled two words on the chalkboard below his name and asked, "Who can tell me what we mean by reader response?"

A half dozen hands went up, including mine, and after casting a glance about the room, Mr. Dutton pointed at me with the piece of chalk, and I thought, *My goodness, he can see me.*

"Now don't forget," he said, "to begin by telling me your name. Just until I know who you all are."

A small wave of anxiety rolled through me then. I didn't like to speak in class, but I wanted to answer the question. "Um, I'm Beth," I said, willing the telltale crimson flush to rise no higher than my chin. "Reader response is what a reader gets out of a certain text, what a reader thinks a writer is saying, even if the writer didn't mean to say that."

Theodore Dutton stared at me for a brief but unnerving moment. I wished then that he couldn't see me, as I felt the flush rise into my cheeks. At length he said, "Good start, Beth. Does anyone want to add to that?"

I think somebody added to it, but I can't be sure who it was or what he said. I was too busy catching my breath. In the next moment I realized that Ray Schmidt, on the other side of me from Natalie, was casting me a smile and a thumbs-up, and I smiled back at him because, you see, I liked him too.

Heath Hall did not have air-conditioning, so all the windows were thrown wide open and the final breath of summer filled the room. You could hear the birds outside, and I thought about how the skies would soon be filled with those thick black ribbons of birds flying south for the winter. I loved to put my head back and watch, wondering, *Where is the end of the ribbon?* Each one went on and on, a squawking undulating line against the blue. There was so much to wonder about. There was so much to anticipate.

That morning, when Mr. Dutton saw me and Ray Schmidt smiled at me, I thought, *This is going to be a very good year.*

CHAPTER 6

"Who can tell me," I said, "what I mean when I say reader response?"

I turned and found that the adolescent faces behind me had reverted yet again to question marks. But of course. This wasn't Senior Honors English, and the year wasn't 1976. This was Junior Composition, and we had all of us somehow slipped into the twenty-first century. I was now the teacher. What had become of my lesson plan?

Flustered, I glanced at the notes on my desk. "Never mind. We'll get to that later," I apologized, knowing full well we wouldn't get to that later. But I had to somehow pick up the pieces of this class and carry on.

"Let's open to page six of the grammar text. I want to begin by talking about the different types of words."

Surely I was safe with nouns and verbs, adjectives and adverbs. I knew them well, having spent my life among them. They were the last thing, of course, these students wanted to talk about, and frankly, at the moment, it was the last thing I wanted to talk about as well. But I stumbled ahead, my eye on the clock, willing this hour to be through, and then the next and the next.

As the seconds ticked off, I became more and more aware of a certain dissonance rising inside of me like nausea. I should not be standing up here as teacher; I should be there—a student, a child. I should not have come this far and still gotten nowhere.

Is this, I wondered, what they call a midlife crisis?

A warm wind blew in through the open windows and ruffled the papers on my desk. Heath Hall still didn't have air-conditioning, and the day was hot. There was talk of tearing this old building down and putting up a new one. Such a shame. Such a shame that nothing lasted, that we could not come to a moment of satisfaction and push a pause button and stay there. I would have pushed it long ago when I was young and living at home. I wanted to go home now, to the home where I had lived with my mother and my father and my sisters. But that wasn't possible. I could go to the house where I grew up just two miles down the road, but it was not my home. Everything about that life had sunk deeply into the past.

Through the milky haze my mind had become, I saw the minute hand on the clock had at long last reached the six. It was nine thirty, the end of the first class.

"Your homework assignment," I said, "is to finish reading this chapter and to answer the questions at the end."

The scraping of chair legs against wooden floor was a welcome sound as the students rose to go. I leaned against my desk, trying to connect, to offer a "See you tomorrow" or "Have a good day" to the students as they filed out.

Satchel Queen lingered. Or maybe it was simply her nature to move slowly. She dropped her grammar book into her backpack and slung the pack over one shoulder. When she rose from her chair, she lowered her eyes, avoiding my gaze. Her eyelids were painted an earthy shade of yellow, all the way up to her eyebrows. The eye shadow appeared to be the only makeup on her otherwise colorless skin. Her hair, so dark as to be almost black, was parted in the middle and held back with a couple of childish barrettes. Her large hoop earrings knocked against her slender neck as she moved. Narrow-faced and square-nosed, she was not a beautiful child, though I thought she might stand half a chance if she smiled.

She wanted to pass by me unseen, I was sure, yet I felt compelled to say something. "Satchel?"

She looked at me then with unconcealed suspicion. "Yeah?"

"Is this your first year at Seaton?"

She hesitated a moment. "Don't you know?"

"No, I'm afraid I don't."

"Yeah? I thought you guys had files on us, like permanent records or something."

"Well, yes, we do have files, but I can't remember everything I've read about each student."

"Uh-huh."

"So?"

"Yeah?"

"Is this your first year?"

"Yeah. Why?"

"I was just wondering. You're a boarding student?"

"Yeah." She nodded slightly, and shrugged the backpack up higher. She wasn't so much unfriendly as simply remote, like someone at the far end of a tunnel.

"Where are you from?"

"White Plains, I guess."

"You guess?"

"Yeah."

"You aren't sure?"

"Yeah, well, we just moved there this summer."

I offered her a smile. She remained expressionless. "I hope you'll like it here at Seaton."

"Uh, sure. Well, it's not exactly like I'm here because I want to be."

Generations of students had said the same thing, especially the boarders. I'd heard it a thousand times before in the years I was a student at Seaton. But when Satchel said it, I didn't know how to respond.

She must have sensed my predicament because she went on to explain. "See, like, my mom got married this summer and didn't need me around anymore. So she and Roger—that's her new husband—they decided to ship me off here."

"I see." Whether or not she was considered disposable by her mother, I didn't know. But obviously that was what Satchel believed. I frowned at the hurt she undoubtedly felt and the resentment she harbored toward the two people who had sent her here. I knew it would be superficial of me to say, *Oh, but I'm sure you must be wrong. I'm sure your mother loves you* when I wasn't sure of any such thing. So I simply said, "I was a student here once myself, you know. I think you'll find Seaton's not so bad. You may even find you like it here."

She looked at me a long moment, her eyes conveying her skepticism. Then she asked, "Is there anything else, Miss Gunnar? Because I really got to get to chemistry, you know?"

It was a long tunnel, and she was such a tiny figure at the far end. "No. Nothing else," I said. "Well, you have a good day, Satchel."

Her countenance remained amazingly blank. "Yeah, sure. Whatever."

CHAPTER 7

I somehow reached the end of that first day of teaching at Seaton. It was a tiresome journey, one that required all my reserves of energy. I had found myself navigating not only the byways of new faces and botched lesson plans, but also through the tumultuous emotions unearthed by my simply being there. As I walked the short distance from Heath Hall to Pine Glen in the late afternoon, I felt a weariness I had seldom known before.

Yes, I will admit that even in childhood, the first day of school generally had a negative effect on me. Certainly, on the one hand, there was the anticipation of being with old friends, making new friends, meeting new boys. That shiny surface life, that glowing patina of socializing was unquestionably alluring. I looked forward to parties and dances and football games and flirting and laughing and maybe even something like falling in love, because young people are naturally romantic and equipped with seemingly endless resources of hope.

But beneath all that was the ever present sense of dread. It was at times a subtle fear and alternately a gripping panic, and it was rooted in this one belief: School was a testing ground, and it was here that my worth as a person would be determined. If I did not do well at school, I would not do well at life, and then what would become of me?

You see, every time final exams came around and they set up those tables in the gym and had us solemnly file in with our blue books and sharpened pencils, I knew all this wasn't done simply to find out if I could diagram a sentence or work through an algebraic equation. I knew the real question at the heart of the matter was this: Are you good enough?

In my own heart of hearts I was never quite certain that I was. In fact, I was very nearly convinced that I wasn't. Life, I believed, was good, but I wasn't good enough for life.

Never mind the track record; never mind the fact that not once did I end up with a grade lower than a B, not even in chemistry, a subject which left me hopelessly confused. I was not for a moment appeased by the fact that each semester my name appeared on either the first or second honor roll posted outside Mrs. Bidney's door. That, oddly enough, meant little to me. My sights were set only on this: Every test, every class was simply a new opportunity to fail. It could happen yet.

What I remember most about those final exams was the little pool of sweat that gathered on the table beneath my right hand while I waited for the signal to turn the test over and begin. That small collection of liquid fear was large enough that it sometimes moistened the pages of my blue book and caused my pencil lead to smear. It's a wonder I could keep the pencil within my slippery grasp at all.

By the time exam week was over, I was exhausted and numb and prone to dreaming about running away and joining a hippie commune, where all a person had to do was tend a garden and prepare food in the communal kitchen and in the evenings sit around singing folk songs while a couple of bearded, unwashed guys strummed out-of-tune guitars. I could drop out of life and do that if it came down to it. As soon as I started to fail, this option, at least, was open to me.

Of course I never ran away. Somehow, I was able to outwit the world, and no one ever discovered what I really was inside. But it was like being Cinderella at the ball. I was all the time waiting for midnight to expose me as a pauper at a party where I didn't belong. Not knowing when the hour would come and the clock would strike twelve, I danced warily, with the hope that once I was out of school for good, I'd be home free. After that, I'd never have to prove myself again.

How young and naïve and wrong I was! I didn't know school was only the beginning, that the threat of being tested and found wanting would follow me all of my life.

When I reached Pine Glen at the end of that long first day of teaching, I was no different from the child I'd been years ago. I was just as afraid as ever that any second now the clock would strike midnight and flashes of imploding fairy dust would reveal me for what I was: Not good enough to be here, a chambermaid without an invitation to the ball.

CHAPTER 8

That night I turned to the first place I always turned for solace: my books. They were always there and never changing. They were completely dependable. Sometimes all I had to do was stand in front of a bookcase and read the spines all lined up neatly in a row, and I'd begin to feel better. But when I opened the pages—now, that was the real thing. With that, I was out of my own world and into the world I chose, where I could be another person, live another life. What could offer a better balm than that?

I was curled up with Dickens—who always made me smile—and my third cup of chamomile tea when the phone rang. I didn't want to be interrupted, but I reluctantly reached for the cordless on the side table by the couch.

"Hello?"

"So how'd it go?" It was Natalie.

"Well," I confessed, "I've had better days."

"So what happened?"

"Nothing, really. The classes went reasonably well, and there are some really great students here. It's just that . . . I don't know. I'm wrestling the old demons, I guess."

"That's because it was your first day in a new job. That's hard for anyone."

"I don't know, Natalie." I sighed heavily.

"Well, what then? Am I going to have to resume my role as cheerleader? Rah rah, go Beth; you can do it."

"Your enthusiasm overwhelms me."

"So I'm out of practice. Anyway, when are you going to realize you're both bright and competent?"

"At the rate I'm going, about three years after I'm dead."

Natalie laughed loudly. It was a beautiful sound. "Well, at least you've still got your sense of humor."

"Yeah, I guess. So how are you?"

"All right," she responded. "Same old, same old, really. Ron works too much, and the kids fight too much, and I'm drowning under piles of laundry, and I've got an impossible deadline to meet with this latest freelance job, and so, you know, the beat goes on."

"Sounds like a nice life to me."

"You're kidding, right?"

"No. No, I'm not."

"Sure, Beth. So let's switch places, just for a day."

"I would if I could."

"No, you wouldn't."

"Yes, I would."

She sighed. Or snorted. Anyway, it was some sort of sound of amused disgust coming from the other end of the line.

Then she said, "Listen, when's homecoming this year?"

"I'm not sure. First weekend of October, I think."

"Find out for sure. I want to put it on my calendar. We have to be there, just to see who comes back. You want to go, don't you?"

"It'll probably be expected of me. But yes, I want to go."

"Good. Maybe even Artie Sochs will come back from the Belgian Congo."

"Wouldn't that be something?"

"And Ray. He's local. He'll probably show up for some of the activities."

Raymond Schmidt. Natalie had spoken of him before, but tonight, at the mention of his name, I realized I would very much like to see him, to reconnect, to see how his life had turned out so far. He had always been the boy most likely to succeed, and I knew that, on some level at least, he had succeeded, and I wanted to know that he was happy.

"Okay, I'll find out when homecoming is, and we can plan on going together," I told Natalie.

We talked for a while then about comfortable things: a play she and Ron had seen at the Hotel du Pont, the stray dog her kids had brought home from the park, my thoughts about visiting my parents in Asheville over the Christmas break.

Finally, stifling a yawn, I was just about to tell her I needed to call it a night when she said, "Listen, I just have to ask you something because I'm curious."

She paused, seemingly needing my permission to go on. "Okay."

"Why did you ask me the other day if I ever thought about Dutton?"

I should have had a ready answer, but I didn't. "I don't really know," I said. "I've thought about him over the years but, boy, being here really brings it all back in living color."

"Yeah, no doubt. But don't let it bother you. I mean, you tend to dwell on things, you know? That's what you introverts are good at, isn't it—brooding on things."

"I suppose so."

"Take my advice and forget it. It was a terrible thing, but it was a long time ago. The man's been dead for ages—"

"But we really don't know that, do we?"

"Oh, come on, Beth. Don't tell me you think he survived. Ray was there; Ken too. They saw it with their own eyes."

"But why would Commander and the others have lied, then?"

"Who knows? They thought they were sparing us. They thought we were too young to handle the truth."

"I'm not so sure, Natalie."

"So Google him."

"What?"

"Type Theodore Dutton into Google and see what comes up."

I hadn't thought about that. "I guess I could. But I don't know if I'd be able to find out anything that way."

"Well, in this day and age, I should think you could find out just about anything about anyone, certainly about whether he's dead or alive."

Suddenly I wasn't so sure I wanted to know. I shut my eyes and tightened my grip around the receiver.

Natalie seemed to sense my fear. "Beth," she said quietly, "forget I suggested anything and just let it go. The man was crazy."

"No, he wasn't!"

"Well, you know what I mean. Back then we didn't know about things like posttraumatic stress syndrome and—"

"You think that's what caused it all?"

"Of course. He'd been in 'Nam, remember? And you know how he wouldn't talk about it, even when the guys asked him point-blank."

"That doesn't really explain it."

"I think it does. He looked like he had it all together, but he was just one more messed up vet."

We were quiet for a long moment. Then I said, "We should have done something."

"Like what? None of us knew he was ready to self-destruct."

And that was it, I suppose. That was the problem. Why did none of us have a clue? How could we have loved him and yet known so little about him?

"Don't let it eat at you, Beth. Just forget it."

I forced out a small laugh. "Easier said than done."

And then we said good-night and hung up the phone.

CHAPTER 9

Natalie didn't have much compassion left for a man she once called Teddy Bear. What started out as a scribbling of hearts in her notebook turned into a near obsession by the third week of our senior year. Natalie was thoroughly smitten with Theodore Dutton.

Of course, as her best friend, I was the only person who knew. I do imagine now, however, that Ken Cunningham had his suspicions. Ken had a crush on Natalie, but his pursuit of her—which had apparently been going well during our junior year—suddenly hit a snag somewhere early that fall of 1976. He and Natalie continued to date off and on, but Ken knew he had a rival somewhere.

"I want to marry Teddy," Natalie told me once.

"You're an idiot," I shot back.

"Why?" she asked, sounding genuinely pained.

"He's too old for you."

"Things like that don't matter. Older men and younger women get married all the time."

I decided to let her dream.

To tell you the truth, though, if I had been honest with Natalie, I would have admitted that that very thought had crossed my own mind. I just never fleshed it out with words the way Natalie did. Either my practical nature or my self-doubts dismissed the thought of marrying Theodore Dutton as readily as it appeared.

That year Ray Schmidt became a boarding student. His

father had been transferred to Virginia, and rather than switching schools his senior year, Ray decided to board at Seaton and room with Ken. Ken had been a fixture in the dorms since ninth grade, when he came to the school to escape his parents' peripatetic lifestyle. His father was a military man, and by the time Ken was in the eighth grade, he'd been to thirteen schools around the States and overseas. He finally asked his parents to send him to a boarding school so he could stay in one place for more than a year.

Oddly enough, our friendship with Ray and Ken was what led Natalie and me to a more intimate relationship with Theodore Dutton.

It happened this way. I often spent the night at Natalie's house, which was in the West Hill neighborhood right next to Seaton. In fact, Natalie's yard backed up to the school. The two properties were naturally divided by a narrow strip of woods and a shallow rocky creek. Natalie walked to school, but she got there by walking to the end of her street and taking the path into Chapel Valley. That's what we called the valley where Seaton's chapel was. From there she walked the road that included a little arched bridge over the creek, then up the hill to the large circular drive at the center of the school.

This was the route we took that first night we ended up at Mr. Dutton's cabin. It was a Friday night, and we had agreed to meet Ray and Ken on the Green at seven o'clock. We had no particular plans, and when we met the boys, we spent several minutes trying to decide what to do. They asked us what we wanted to do, and we said we didn't care, what did they want to do?

Ray said, "You guys want to go somewhere?" Even though he was a boarder, he still had his Camaro on campus.

I asked him, "Did you get permission?" because boarders were not to leave campus without prior permission.

He said, "No"—not that that really mattered to any of us. We'd gone off campus before without permission, and that was, as I mentioned, how we'd become the Barbarians.

But then Natalie said, "They're holding auditions for the play over in Hawthorne. Anyone want to go watch?" Hawthorne Gymnasium, the smaller of the two gyms on campus, housed the stage where all the productions were held.

"What are they doing this year?" Ray asked.

"I think it's *South Pacific*."

Ken shrugged. "Why not? Should be good for a few laughs."

So Ken put his arm around Natalie's shoulder, and Ray took my hand for the first time, and we headed across campus toward Hawthorne Gymnasium. But we never got there because as we came upon the two faculty cabins behind Cedar Hall, we saw Mr. Dutton standing in the open doorway of Cabin 1, just standing there leaning against the doorframe with his hands tucked deep into the pockets of his jeans.

"Mr. Dutton!" Ray called, and our English teacher raised a hand and beckoned us over.

"Ray, I've got that volume of Byron you wanted if you can hold on just a minute." He disappeared into the cabin.

I looked at Natalie, and she was beaming. When we reached the cabin, she poked her head through the open door, and I heard Mr. Dutton say, "Come on in, everyone. I know the book's here somewhere."

Students were allowed to visit in the faculty homes as long as we went in groups. We had frequented the gatherings at the Buckleys', but I had never been in either of the cabins.

That was exactly what this was too—a rustic log structure of three small rooms with wooden floors and paneled walls. The cabins were generally assigned to the young unmarried male teachers like Theodore Dutton. Another bachelor and a science teacher in the middle school, Clarence Fosset, lived in Cabin 2.

Mr. Dutton waved toward a couple of worn couches and invited us to sit. As he went on searching for the elusive volume of Byron, he apologized for not being able to put his finger right on it. The problem was obvious, though. The room was full of books. Mr. Dutton's collection filled three large bookcases and spilled out onto the coffee table and even onto the floor. Across the room from the couches was an overstuffed chair where Mr. Dutton must have done his reading. Three or four books lay open and facedown on the footstool.

"Aha, here it is!" Mr. Dutton pulled a slim volume from one of the cases and whirled around to present it to Ray. "I think this will help you with your paper."

"Thanks, Mr. Dutton," Ray said as he thumbed through the pages.

"No problem. So what are you kids doing tonight?"

"We're heading over to Hawthorne to watch the auditions," Ken told him.

"But we're not in any hurry," Natalie added.

"Good, because I was just about to cut into a watermelon. Care to join me?"

Our enthusiastic response sent him scurrying to the kitchen. A banging of drawers and a rattle of dishes followed, and after a moment Mr. Dutton returned with a tray of thick slices of melon and a pile of paper plates and napkins. We all sat down on the floor and helped ourselves to one of the seeded half-moons of fruit. As we ate, the juice dripped down our chins and ran in sticky rivers down the insides of our arms, and soon the napkins were moist balls of crumpled paper scattered about the floor.

Mr. Dutton and Ray spoke briefly about the essay Ray was working on. Earlier that week Mr. Dutton had given us the assignment of analyzing a poem from the romantic period. I myself had chosen one by Keats. Natalie was attempting one by Coleridge, but at the moment that was the last thing on her mind.

"Where did you come from, Mr. Dutton?" she asked, and then to clarify she said, "I mean, where did you teach before you came here?"

"I spent a couple years teaching at a public school near Philadelphia. But I didn't like it. I wanted a change. So here I am." He smiled.

"And what about before that?" Ken asked.

"I was at the University of Pennsylvania earning my master's degree in English."

And then, as though it were a game, Ray asked, "And what about before that?"

Mr. Dutton looked at Ray a long time before he said, "Before that, I was drafted and spent a year in 'Nam."

A soldier in uniform! With that knowledge, our awe of the man gained even greater heights. Of course we had all been swayed by the climate of the times and counted ourselves among the war protesters—though, as children, we had never once actually gone out in public waving placards. But to think that Mr. Dutton had *been there* and fought for our country! What could be more romantic than that? I could almost feel the waves of admiration rolling off of Natalie, and even the boys were impressed.

Ray said excitedly, "Cool! Tell us about it."

But Theodore Dutton shook his head and dropped a piece of watermelon rind onto his plate. "No," he said. "I'm not going to tell you, because it's better for you not to know."

For about twenty awful seconds no one said anything at all. Ray looked embarrassed and chastised and as though he should apologize. Natalie and I exchanged a quick glance but otherwise didn't move. During that long silent interval Mr. Dutton didn't look at anyone, just down at the rind and the black seeds floating in the pink pool of juice on his plate.

Finally Natalie saved us all by saying, "Maybe I should try out for the part of Nellie in *South Pacific*. What do you think?"

Ken jumped in and said, "I think you'd be great if only you could sing."

While Natalie poked Ken with her elbow, Mr. Dutton looked up and smiled, and I knew he had rejoined us, coming back from wherever it was he had been.

We never did make it to the auditions that evening. We stayed with Mr. Dutton until long past nightfall, and he seemed to want us there as much as we wanted to be there. I don't remember all that we talked about that first night, but I do remember the way my best friend Natalie looked at Theodore Dutton, and I knew that she was dreaming of marrying him.

And I—because he was handsome and kind and brave and he loved books—I allowed myself to go so far as to dream: *I will marry someone just like him someday.*

I was absolutely certain it was possible, because that's the way adolescent girls think. And that's because they are too young yet to see the world as it is.

CHAPTER 10

My Home
by Satchel Queen

In the middle of my house is a very tall spiral staircase. I climb the stairs, going around and around and around until I reach my room on the top floor. Sometimes I try to count the number of steps as I go, but I always lose track. Once, I got to three hundred and I still wasn't at the top, so I know there are more than that.

You might think it isn't worthwhile to climb so many stairs just to get to my room, and sometimes I almost think so too, but that isn't the case once you get there. When I reach my room and look out one of the twenty-five windows, I know I'd climb those stairs all over again just to see what I can see from there. First there's the harbor and on the other side of that there's this peninsula that's like no other peninsula in the world. If the Native Americans who used to live on that land saw how the place looks now, they'd either drop dead of fright or they'd beat their drums and worship the Great Spirit, or maybe they'd just worship man, who most of the time thinks he's God anyway, because he can do things like build the buildings that make up the skyline of Manhattan.

If you pick out just one of those skyscrapers and you think about the hours of manpower that went into building it, and you think about all the steel and concrete they used and consider the fact that hundreds of people can walk around inside and it doesn't fall over, it's pretty impressive. Now multiply that by the number of buildings in Manhattan, and you can hardly even wrap your mind around it. I can't anyway.

What's even more interesting is the ferry that travels from Manhattan to Staten Island. I can watch it for hours. I like the way it cuts through the water and leaves a V-shaped wake behind it. The wake always makes me think of a peacock's tail. I also like to watch the gulls circling behind the boat, squawking and swooping down for food. Sometimes the people on the ferry toss them popcorn or bread, and the gulls get all tangled up with each other just trying to get at it. All day long the ferry goes back and forth, back and forth, and I wonder who's on it and where they're going and whether they're coming back. And most of all I wonder, are they happy?

At noon, when the sun is highest over the water, there are about a million little lights flashing on the surface of the harbor. It's like the ferry is traveling through pixie dust or a field of diamonds or maybe the Milky Way. And I think, if all those people down there could see the way it looks from up here, if they could see themselves surrounded by all those dancing stars, they might like the trip across the harbor a little better. It might even make them happy—if they're not already. Just for a minute anyway.

I can see a lot from my room in my house. I wouldn't want to live anywhere else. Someday I'm not even going to leave here anymore. People can come up and see me if they want, but I'm going to stay right here, looking over the Manhattan skyline and watching the ferry sailing through the stars.

CHAPTER 11

"Satchel, do you know the difference between fact and fiction?"

The dark-haired girl standing by my desk nodded without changing expression. "Yeah."

When she didn't continue, I prodded, "Would you please tell me what it is?"

"Facts are true and fiction is made up."

"That's right." I picked her essay out of a pile of partly graded papers on my desk. "I asked you to write a brief essay describing your home, and you wrote about the view from the Statue of Liberty."

She looked at me just long enough to make me feel uneasy. I hoped her face would reveal a hint of either sudden understanding or sincere contrition, but neither look materialized.

Finally she muttered, "So?"

I didn't want to have to resort to my tough-teacher tone of voice. For one thing, I wasn't very good at it, and for another, I seriously doubted it would help. But I was beginning to feel annoyed. "Your essay is very creative, Satchel, but this isn't a creative writing class. You were simply to write a brief essay about your real home, the actual house in which you live."

She lifted her chin slightly. "So how can I do that?"

"What do you mean?"

"I mean, I'm homeless. How do you expect me to write about a home I don't have?"

For a moment I had visions of shopping carts and cardboard boxes and campfires for reheating food dug out of garbage cans. But that was hardly Satchel's situation. "Look," I said, "I know you live in the dorm and that makes you feel homeless, but can you work with me here and give me an essay about the house where your folks are—you know, the place you'll be going to for Thanksgiving break?"

"I don't think I can do that."

"Why not?"

"Well, like I told you before, Mom and I just moved to White Plains this summer when she married Roger. Roger already lived there, and we just moved into his house. Well, Mom did, anyway. I never lived there except for just a few weeks before coming here, but that doesn't make the place my home."

"Oh. Okay." I was beginning to see her predicament. "So where did you live before your mom got married and you moved to White Plains?"

"Brooklyn, mostly. But I was born in New Jersey. Hoboken. I don't remember much about it. We moved to Brooklyn when I was three."

"I see." I looked at her paper in my hand, at the grade written in red ink at the top. "You know, when I said your paper was very creative, I meant it. You enjoy writing, don't you?"

She nodded tentatively.

"And I have an idea that you like to read."

"Yeah."

Her eyes narrowed, but in them I saw something like surprise. "I had a feeling you were a fellow bibliophile. Do you know what that is?"

"Someone who likes books?"

"Yes."

We looked at each other as though we had reached some sort of understanding. Then I said, "I gave you an F on this essay, Satchel, because you failed to fulfill the assignment. But I want to give you a chance to pull up your grade. I'm willing to forgive this F if you'd be willing to hand in a new essay by Friday."

"Yeah?"

I nodded.

"So what do you want me to write about?"

"Well . . ." I thought a moment. "Why don't you write about the home you'd *like* to live in?"

Her gaze dropped from my face down to the paper, then slowly moved back up again. "Like, that's what I already did, Miss Gunnar."

Tess Standefer, who'd been lingering in the hall since I called Satchel aside, now stood timidly in the doorway. Tess and Satchel were roommates and apparently had become friends as well.

"Excuse me, Miss Gunnar," Tess said, "but if Satchel and I don't get going, we're going to be late for Mr. Wadino's class again. We already got our second tardy from him yesterday."

They'd been late twice already? After only two weeks of school?

"All right," I said. I looked at Satchel. "We'll talk about this more later."

I expected her to toss out her usual response of "Whatever." But she left without saying anything at all.

CHAPTER 12

I was sitting at the dining room table reading student essays around ten o'clock that night when I heard a knock at the front door. Or I thought I did. The sound was so faint I couldn't be sure.

But when I went to the door and opened it, there was Satchel Queen standing on the wooden stoop, looking small and pale under the dim outside light.

"Satchel, do you know what time it is? What are you doing out of the dorm?"

She shrugged without pulling her hands out of the pockets of her jeans. "I thought you wanted to talk some more about my paper."

"Now?"

She shrugged again.

"Who's your dorm parent?" I asked.

"Miss Wilson."

"Does she know you're here?"

"I don't think so."

"You just walked out of the dorm without telling her?"

"Not exactly. I climbed out the window." The shoulders went up again. "No big deal; my room's on the ground floor."

"But you're not supposed to leave the dorm after nine."

"Listen, Miss Gunnar, if you don't want to talk—" She moved backward one step.

"No, it's all right," I blurted, suddenly wanting her to stay. "Since you're here, why don't you come on in?"

She looked at me a moment as though to determine whether I meant it. When I opened the screen door and stepped aside to let her in, she entered slowly and stood in the front hall. Her eyes moved left then right, taking in the dining room and the living room.

"So this is where you live," she said mildly.

I shut the door. "Yes, this is it."

I flipped on the overhead light in the living room and motioned for Satchel to sit. Before she did, though, she stood in the middle of the room and turned a full circle, taking in a 360-degree view of my bookcases.

"Whoa," she said. "You really are one of those book-lover people, aren't you?"

"Yes, I guess I am. They become kind of like friends, if you know what I mean."

She nodded. Then she looked at me straight on, and her face opened into something like a smile.

"Would you like something to drink?" I asked. "Bottled water? A soda?"

"No thanks."

"I just bought some ice cream. How about a bowl?"

"No," she said. "I don't eat ice cream anymore. But do you have any dried mango?"

"No. I'm afraid I don't."

"That's okay."

"You sure there's nothing else you'd like?"

"I'm sure."

"Well, let's sit down, all right?"

She sat in the wing chair by the fireplace and propped her feet up on the footstool like she owned the place. I settled myself on the couch.

Her eyes continued to scan the room until they came to rest on me. "I don't want to flunk your class, Miss Gunnar," she said.

"I don't think you're going to flunk my class."

"I pretty much have an F average so far, don't I?"

I thought of the F I'd given her on her composition. "Well, like I said, I'm willing to let you rewrite your paper. I know you can get a higher grade."

Her eyes were wandering again. She seemed captivated by my collection of books. I watched her carefully, glad to find a student who enjoyed reading. "I don't like math," she remarked abruptly, her eyes alighting on me once again. "I'm not good at math."

I didn't know why we were suddenly speaking of math, but I said, "All right."

"And I don't like science. It's a bore."

"Okay."

"But I like to read. I even kind of like to write."

I nodded. "That's good. I'm glad you do."

"Not poetry, though. I mean, I know people my age are always spilling their guts writing poetry, but I don't do that. I just like to read it. Like Emily Dickinson, you know? I like Emily Dickinson."

I was beginning to warm to Satchel Queen. "Really?"

"Yeah, because she's real. You read her and you think, this lady knows what time it is. You know what I mean?"

Again I nodded. "I do know what you mean, Satchel. She seemed to understand the human condition, didn't she?" I thought I would take a chance by adding, "She knew what it was to be alone."

This time Satchel nodded, very slightly. "Yeah."

"Do you have brothers and sisters, Satchel?"

"Naw. It's just my mom and me. And now Roger."

"Do you like Roger?"

"He's all right. He's got a lot of money."

"Uh-huh. Enough to send you here to Seaton."

"Yeah."

"I'm sure you'd rather be at home with them."

"Naw. Not really. My mom—" she shook her head—"she was always dating these jerks. It was like she was a magnet for losers. So they'd dump her, and she'd come crying to me, and I had to make everything better, you know—like *I* was the mother and *she* was the kid. I got tired of it."

How sad, I thought. Aloud I said, "Yes, I guess you would."

"So she finally met a decent guy who was willing to marry her, and I don't know, I guess after that she didn't need me anymore."

Once again I didn't know how to respond to Satchel Queen. I was surprised at her willingness to tell me about herself. At the same time I was stunned by her mother's weaknesses and seeming indifference toward her own child.

At length I asked, "Have you ever actually been in the Statue of Liberty?"

She lifted her chin and let it drop. "Yeah. My dad took me up there once, all the way up to the crown. That was when you could still go up there. I was really little, but I remember it. He lifted me up on his shoulders so I could see out the windows. I thought it must be what it's like to fly in an airplane and look down at everything."

I wanted to ask about her dad, but instead I asked, "You've never flown?"

She shook her head. "Naw. I've never been anywhere, really."

"Maybe that's something you can do when you're grown up."

"Uh-huh. I'd like to travel around the world, just to see what it's like. You ever been anywhere?"

"Yes. Europe and parts of Asia and South America."

"Wow, you're lucky."

"Well, I never married and had children, so I've had the freedom to travel."

She nodded knowingly. "Yeah, I'm never going to get married either."

I gave a little laugh. "Well, you're only—what? Sixteen?"

"Seventeen."

"You're too young to say you'll never get married."

"It never works out, even if you do."

"You don't think so?"

"Naw. It's a huge crock. It's no use thinking someone will love you all your life."

She is too young yet to know that, I thought, and the instinct to protect her rose in my chest. "I know some people who are happily married," I replied.

"Yeah? Well I don't."

"Not even your mother and Roger?"

"I guess they're happy right now, since they're still practically on their honeymoon. But who knows how long it'll last."

"You shouldn't be so negative, Satchel."

"Why not?"

Why not indeed? What had she seen all her life but her mother's failed relationships?

"Just a minute, all right?" I rose from the couch and went to the dining room to find her essay among the piles on the table. Satchel stared at me quizzically when I returned. "Here's what I'm going to do, Satchel," I said. "I'm going to raise your grade on this paper to a B. Now, say the Statue of Liberty was your house. The assignment still was to write about your house, not the view from the window. If you'd written more about the statue itself, I'd have given you an A."

Satchel stood and took the paper I was offering her. Once she saw for herself that I had crossed out the F and changed the grade to a B, she smiled briefly. "Thanks, Miss Gunnar."

"But next time be sure to stick to the subject."

"What's it going to be? I mean, what are you going to ask us to write about? Maybe I can start thinking about it now."

"I'm going to ask you to write about a particular event that's been significant to you. It can be something you've lived through personally, or it can be something that happened in history. It doesn't matter, so long as you describe the event accurately."

"Okay."

I offered what I hoped was a smile of encouragement. "I'm glad you came tonight, Satchel."

"Yeah."

"But you'd better get back before Miss Wilson does room check at eleven. If you're not there, we're both in trouble."

"Don't worry, Miss Gunnar. She'd never notice if I weren't there."

"Oh yeah?" I laughed. "What makes you think that? You're not invisible, you know."

She looked at me askance, as though she couldn't understand what I had said. And then we headed for the door. I turned the knob and pulled back the barrier to the warm darkness and the night songs of the cicadas.

"You're not, you know," I pressed.

"Not what?"

"Invisible."

She hesitated, her intense eyes searching my face. And then she said, almost in a whisper, "I guess not."

Then she stepped onto the stoop and disappeared into the night.

CHAPTER 13

The child thought of herself as invisible, which I understood only too well. That was how I myself had felt for much of my own childhood. I really don't know whether that was because I tried so hard not to be seen, or because I actually believed my insignificance rendered me unseeable.

I was twelve years old and new to Seaton when I first came to think of myself as invisible. Our class was practicing for a Reader's Theatre performance of "The Highwayman" for middle school assembly when our teacher made the unfortunate decision to give me a solo part.

The tragic poem by Alfred Noyes, when read aloud, has a galloping cadence, echoing the horse's hooves pounding the road toward a lonesome inn. In that faraway place somewhere in old England, "the wind was a torrent of darkness among the gusty trees, the moon was a ghostly galleon tossed upon cloudy seas," and "the road was a ribbon of moonlight over the purple moor" when "the highwayman came riding, riding, riding up to the old inn door." When "he whistled a tune to the window, who should be waiting there, but the landlord's black-eyed daughter, Bess, the landlord's daughter, plaiting a dark red love-knot into her long black hair."

On the night of the poem's events, though, Bess was not at the window braiding her hair as she had been a hundred times before. On this night the inn had been overtaken by Red Coats, and the landlord's daughter was dragged to her room and tied up with a musket beneath her breast. From the window she could see the road her lover would ride to the inn, and she knew when he arrived, King George's soldiers would kill him. She knew she must warn him. She struggled against the rope that bound her hands until one finger touched the trigger. And then . . . "her finger moved in the moonlight, her musket shattered the moonlight, shattered her breast in the moonlight and warned him—with her death."

The poem was hauntingly beautiful, and as our class read it in unison, I found myself lost in it. But then Mr. Echols said, "Okay, when we get to the part where she shoots herself, I want everyone to be quiet while one person announces her death."

That one person was me, and those final three words were my solo part. It shouldn't have been difficult. It should have, in fact, been rather dramatic. The class fell into the rhythm of the poem, galloping toward the fatal shot, building up to the crescendo of the young lover's sacrificial act, then suddenly falling silent for the announcement that I had been chosen to deliver.

I said the words. I really did. I felt those three words—"with her death"—pass through my throat and out my mouth. But they were greeted with a stunned silence. Then a snicker. And then the question, "Did someone say something?" followed finally by outright laughter.

Mr. Echols didn't give up on me right away. I think it wasn't until the next rehearsal that he gave the part to someone else.

Still, that was when I knew I wasn't able to do something because, in a very real sense, I simply wasn't there.

CHAPTER 14

Several days after Satchel came to see me at Pine Glen, my phone rang early in the morning. I reached for the extension in my bedroom.

"Hello?" I was leery. I didn't like early morning phone calls.

"Beth, it's me."

"Oh, hi, Natalie."

"You awake?"

"I'm getting dressed for class. Why? What's up?"

"There's been an accident."

"What—"

"It's on the local news right now. A bunch of kids went off the road over by Hoopes."

"Who?"

"I don't know. They haven't released names."

"Then what—"

"They're Seaton kids, Beth. Boarding students."

"How do you know?"

"One of the kids in the car told the police. But that's all the info the media has released."

"Was anyone hurt?"

"All of them."

"How badly?"

"At least one is critical."

A wave of anxiety slammed against my ribs. "I've got to go, Nat."

I hung up and dialed Joel Sexton's home phone number.

"Sexton."

"Joel, it's Beth. Listen, did a car crash into your living room last night?"

He breathed out what sounded like a laugh. "Yeah, and good morning to you too, Beth."

"No, I mean it, Joel. There's been an accident."

"Where?"

"Out your way. Somewhere over by Hoopes."

"Well, it wasn't here. I'm sitting in my living room right now drinking a cup of coffee."

"It was Seaton kids."

He responded with an oath, and I heard a crashing sound, like a coffee mug coming down hard on a table.

"Who?" he asked.

"I don't know. Names haven't been released."

"Oh my—"

"I've got to go, Joel."

In another minute I was down the stairs and out the front door. I scarcely knew what I was doing as I climbed the grassy hill to Leeds Hall, the girls' dorm. I knew only that I had to see for myself whether Satchel was there.

The front door was unlocked at six thirty each morning so the kids could start going to breakfast. Just inside the door and to the left was Miss Wilson's apartment. I knocked rapidly, hoping she wasn't showering or otherwise couldn't hear me.

In the next moment the door flew open, and Miss Wilson started to say something less than welcoming. But she stopped abruptly when she saw that the person pounding on her door was an adult.

"Good morning, Miss—"

"Which room is Satchel Queen's?"

"What?"

"Satchel. Which room is hers?"

She cocked her head and frowned. "Room 106—last one on the right at the end of the hall. Why? Is she in—"

I didn't wait for her to finish. I rushed down the hall in long strides and, without knocking, flung open the door to room 106. The shades were drawn, and the room was dark, but I could see a slumbering figure in one of the beds. The other bed was empty. I didn't know which bed belonged to Satchel and which belonged to Tess.

I found myself calling out her name. "Satchel!"

The shadowy figure sat up in bed and rubbed her eyes. She turned on the lamp on the nightstand next to her bed.

"Miss Gunnar? What are you doing here?" It was Satchel, and she was frowning at me.

I was so relieved I wanted to go to the bed and throw my arms around the young girl. Instead, I asked, "Where's Tess?"

Satchel shrugged. "I heard her get up a few minutes ago. She must have gone to the bathroom. Why?"

I couldn't respond. I couldn't get the words unstuck from my throat.

"Miss Gunnar?"

I nodded.

"What happened to your shoes?"

I looked down at my bare feet, wet with morning dew and crisscrossed with blades of freshly mown grass. I wanted to laugh. But even in the midst of my relief, I realized someone had been hurt, students from Seaton, and I didn't know who.

"There's been an accident, Satchel."

"What happened?"

I thought a moment. "I'm sure Mr. Farrell will tell us what he knows during morning assembly."

She was quiet a minute before saying, "Okay."

Tess entered the room then, yawning. "Oh, hi, Miss Gunnar."

"Good morning, Tess."

She padded over to her closet and pulled out a shirt and a pair of jeans. "Come on, Satchel," she said. "Let's go get breakfast. I'm starving."

It didn't seem to surprise her that I was there, and I thought that might be the best moment to make my exit.

"See you girls in assembly."

"Yeah." Tess lifted a hand sleepily and waved me off.

Satchel said nothing. She continued to stare at me through perplexed and narrowed eyes, as though my unexpected appearance in her room was the strangest event imaginable.

Maybe to her it was.

By the end of the day everyone knew the names of the students whose night out in a beer-laden Mitsubishi had ended abruptly after an encounter with a tree. While all four of them—two boys and two girls—remained hospitalized, chances of recovery looked good. The driver, who had at first been critical, was upgraded to serious.

I was in the office talking with Joel shortly before five o'clock when Satchel appeared in the doorway.

"Miss Gunnar?"

I smiled. "Yes, Satchel?"

She must have gone out of her way to find me. The day students had long before headed home, and the boarding students were beginning to meander to the cafeteria for supper.

Satchel pulled back a corner of her mouth as her eyes moved to Joel. He took the cue.

"Well," he said, "I'm going to drop these papers off at the front office and then go home. See you tomorrow, Beth. Take it easy, Satchel."

"Sure, Mr. Sexton."

She took a step farther into the room but didn't sit down. "Are the kids who were in the accident going to be all right?" she asked.

"Yes, I think so."

"What's going to happen to them?"

"What do you mean?"

"Like, is Seaton going to kick them out?"

I sighed. "First, they'll simply be allowed to recover. After that they'll probably be suspended for a week or two. I'm not sure, but that's my best guess."

Satchel nodded. She was wearing her backpack, and yet she clutched a pile of books tightly against her chest. I had a feeling those books were a breastplate in a suit of armor.

"Miss Gunnar?" she said again.

"Yes, Satchel?"

"You thought it was me, didn't you? I mean, you thought I'd gone out drinking and got in that accident."

I pressed my lips together in thought. "I'm sorry, Satchel. Yes, I was afraid it was you. I should never have assumed you'd go out drinking like that. I'm sorry," I said again.

"No," she said quickly. Then she stopped and frowned. "I mean, you came up the hill in your bare feet and all just to see if I was okay."

For a moment neither of us said anything more. We simply looked at each other. Then I said, "Yes, of course. I had to know whether you were all right."

The perplexed gaze remained, but she nodded slightly. As she did, she took one step backward. Her lips were a thin line. She turned halfway toward the door. "I'll see you tomorrow, Miss Gunnar."

"Okay, Satchel."

"And, um, thanks, Miss Gunnar."

I smiled, though I'm not sure she saw, because even as she spoke the final word she was disappearing out the door.

CHAPTER 15

I wanted to do for Satchel Queen what Theodore Dutton did for me. At least what he did for me before the tragedy happened.

Those months that he was with us, Theodore Dutton didn't let me be invisible. He simply wouldn't allow it. He'd call on me in class even when I didn't raise my hand. He'd read portions of my essays aloud if he thought they were particularly good. He asked me to be his senior assistant for his two freshman English classes, which meant helping him grade grammar tests and giving feedback on student writing assignments.

I was honored beyond all words that he would put such faith in me, and for the first time I felt something at the core of my being that I understood to be confidence. Theodore Dutton believed I was capable, and I could only accept his faith in me as a gift. Each time I went to the English office to sit at his desk and work on the pile of papers he had left for me, I was deeply satisfied in a way I'd never been before.

"I've decided I'm going to be an English teacher," I announced to him one day.

"But of course you are," he responded simply, and my future was sealed.

Natalie was understandably jealous of the attention Mr. Dutton gave me. It almost brought us to blows, until I finally convinced her that the extra time I spent with him had nothing at all to do with the man and everything to do with

English. I was a lover of literature the way she was a lover of art.

And while we both loved Theodore Dutton, I would scarcely admit it even to myself, much less to her.

The best times were those when we gathered at Mr. Dutton's cabin, Ray and Ken and Natalie and me. Sometimes Janie and Artie joined us, but since they both lived more than ten miles from school, it was hard for them to get back to campus in the evening. They had to plan ahead to finagle the car keys from their parents, which the other four of us didn't have to do. I just had to spend the night at Natalie's, and from there the two of us met the boys outside the cabin at the designated time.

We got in the habit of going there every Friday night and sometimes during the week as well. There were only a few times Mr. Dutton wasn't there and our knock on the door went unanswered. Once or twice we suspected he was inside, but he didn't come to the door. We thought perhaps he was napping, and we didn't want to wake him.

It never occurred to us that he might have a life outside of Seaton, that there might be other people he wanted to see, other things he wanted to do. We were the center of our own world, and we thought we were the center of his.

I suppose that was because when we were with him, he engaged us so completely. He listened, he laughed, he led us on amazing adventures through stories and poems and ideas until we felt we had traveled the world, though we'd never even left the cabin. If Ken brought along his guitar and played a piece he'd been working on, Mr. Dutton would rest his hands behind his head and stare up at the ceiling, listening with as much enjoyment as if he were at Carnegie Hall.

"Hey," he said one night, "my nephew is coming next weekend, and he's a really good guitarist. Why don't you guys come on over, and he and Ken can do some jamming?"

So we did. The rest of us sat around eating popcorn and drinking Cokes while Ken and this kid named Lennon Dutton strummed songs by Dan Fogelberg and Cat Stevens and Lynyrd Skynyrd. We nodded our heads and tapped our feet, and sometimes we sang along, and when the two of them played "Free Bird," I thought I'd just about died and gone to heaven.

Mr. Dutton's nephew was a shy skinny kid with bangs that fell over his eyes and a complexion marred by acne. But he had an attractive smile that made dimples in his cheeks and a laugh that was like a shot of adrenaline straight to your spine. In between songs we laughed until our sides ached, and most of the time I don't think we even knew what we were laughing about.

It was just that good to be alive.

Before we left that night, I asked Lennon Dutton if his parents had been Beatles fans.

"No," he said. "Why?"

"I thought maybe they'd named you after John Lennon."

"Nope," he answered. "I don't think so."

"If I know my brother," Mr. Dutton interjected, "they probably named Len after the Lennon sisters."

I thought of the buxom girls who shot to fame on *The Lawrence Welk Show*, and Lennon Dutton must have been picturing them too because he rolled his eyes and laughed his infectious laugh. "Yeah, over Mom's dead body," he said.

After that night we saw Lennon Dutton a few more times when he came from Pennsylvania to visit his uncle. But mostly we spent our time at the cabin just talking among ourselves or listening to Mr. Dutton read aloud.

I was never invisible at those times. I was fully there and fully seen. And like I said, it was so good to be alive you could feel the ache of it in your bones. That little cabin was my corner of Eden, the place where life was first breathed into my soul.

CHAPTER 16

"Miss Gunnar?"

"Yes, Satchel?"

"Do you think you're either a saint or a poet?"

"Excuse me?"

"A saint or a poet. Do you think you're one of those?"

I was getting used to Satchel showing up at my house in the evenings, sometimes early, sometimes late. She often came with questions about the essay she was working on for my class or the latest book she had checked out of the library. She sometimes came and looked over my bookshelves, then sat silently reading while I worked at the dining room table grading papers. She seemed simply to want to be there, even if there was no particular reason. I liked having her there.

We sat in the living room now on a chilly September night. She pulled a copy of Thornton Wilder's *Our Town* out of her backpack. It was the play the upper school was producing this year; auditions had already been held, and rehearsals were under way. Satchel, a self-described behind-the-scenes person, had joined the stage crew.

"You know this play, right?" She held the book up for me to see.

"Of course. It's one of my favorites."

"So you know how Emily comes back from the dead and she's allowed to relive one day of her life, and so she lives an ordinary day from her childhood, right?"

I nodded, indicating she should go on.

"It's when she comes back from the dead that she realizes life is really wonderful. And it isn't the big things—it's the small things that she thinks are, like, so incredibly beautiful." Satchel opened to a page marked with a Post-it note. "So she's heading back to the grave, but then she breaks down crying and she has to stop a few minutes and look at everything again and say good-bye. And she starts saying good-bye to all the things she realizes she loved in life, like her home and her family, but also the little things like, like—" Satchel paused and looked down at the book—"like clocks ticking and sun-flowers and new ironed dresses and hot baths. And she turns to the stage manager, and she asks, 'Do any human beings ever realize life while they live it?—every, every minute?' And the stage manager says, 'No.' But then after a minute he says, 'The saints and poets, maybe—they do some.'"

Satchel let the book fall to her lap as she raised her eyes to me. She seemed to think I had an answer for her, but I didn't, because I wasn't quite sure what she was asking.

Finally, I said, "And that's how you want to live?"

"I don't know if I can," she answered. "I don't know if anybody can, really."

"Why not?"

Instead of answering my question, she asked another. "Do you have to believe in God to be a poet or a saint?"

"I'm not sure Emily did, beyond the conventions of the time."

"Do you?"

"Believe in God?" I asked.

She nodded.

"Yes," I said.

She thought about my response, then said, "I don't know.

I mean, how can anybody know something like that?"

The question disturbed me so that I stood and walked to the front window. A dark and starless night pressed up against the pane, and briefly I thought of the poet Sylvia Plath's image of a fatherless heaven. It made me shiver, and I hugged my sweater more tightly around me. From the time I first read Sylvia's poems, that image had nettled me, and I wanted to grab the poet and argue, *You cannot have a heaven without a Father*. But I couldn't argue with her because she was dead. Like Virginia Woolf, she had killed herself, laying her head upon an oven door and turning on the gas.

I turned from the window and looked at Satchel. "I think we can know that God is there."

"Yeah?"

"Yeah, I do."

"So, like . . ." She looked pensive a moment. "Where do you have to go to find Him? Tibet or something?"

"No," I offered tentatively. "No, I don't think we have to go anywhere, not even to church."

Her largely expressionless eyes, which had been making the rounds of the room, came to rest on me. I thought I saw in them a flicker of something like curiosity, or maybe it was simply doubt.

"Really. I don't think we have to go anywhere," I repeated. "I think He comes to us."

CHAPTER 17

I told Satchel then of the day I heard the bells in the basilica. I had heard them many times before, but this time it was different.

For about a year I lived and worked in Minneapolis, teaching remedial reading at a community college on the edge of downtown. During breaks between classes, when the weather allowed, I walked around the lake in the public park next to the college. Also nearby—just across the street—was a large Catholic basilica whose bells called out the hour with deep echoing rings.

On this particular autumn day I walked through the park with my eyes downcast, looking at the crisp colored leaves on the path at my feet. I was terribly unhappy, wanting desperately to be visible but instead was lost, like the wind-grieved ghost of which Thomas Wolfe spoke. I felt the warmth of the sun and heard the rustle of the wind-tossed leaves, but they were far less real to me than my own inner emptiness. "Which one of us is not forever a stranger and alone?" Wolfe asked. And in anguish and in isolation I knew that he was right. "O waste of loss, in the hot mazes, lost, among bright stars on this most weary unbright cinder, lost! Remembering speechlessly we seek the great forgotten language, the lost lane-end into heaven, a stone, a leaf, an unfound door . . ."

I could not find the way out of the aloneness. And I thought that it would consume me before I ever found the way.

Following the path around the lake, I heard the bells in the basilica strike three o'clock. And that was when it happened. When those notes rang out and drifted down from the sky soft and rich as scattered rose petals, I heard the forgotten language, and in that instant, I understood.

It was a voice, unmistakable, saying, *I'm here, and I love you.*

The language is sometimes forgotten but not lost, because I had heard and understood it before. The first time it came, I was walking beneath the tall pines on the road leading into Seaton. There, amid the pine needles and the resinous scent of the trees, I heard it saying, *I'm here, and it's all right. Everything will be all right.*

Just as God had come to me on the road into Seaton, it was God who broke in when, walking through the park, I could find no slit in the veil, no hint of light in the dark and wordless isolation.

But that wasn't the end of the story. As lovely as the bells were that rang three times, I wanted to hear them chime the hour at noon. I wanted to hear not just three times but twelve times that He loved me.

The next day I returned to the park and sat on a bench across from the basilica. It was shortly before twelve. In another moment the bells began to chime. Slowly and heavily they tolled, calling out the hour. I counted along. One, two, three, four . . . I was satisfied at twelve, but the bells didn't stop there. They rang once more, and then again, and on and on. For a full three minutes they rang like laughter over the park, over the city, over me.

I knew then what I hadn't known before: How great is the love of the One who made us.

What I didn't tell Satchel was that I had long forgotten about the bells until that night when she asked me about God. I hadn't thought about the bells in the basilica for years. I didn't tell Satchel that a person can go on believing in God without giving so much as a passing thought to His love, which in the end completely misses the point of believing and leaves one as helpless as a cloud in a fatherless heaven.

CHAPTER 18

"So maybe they were just working on the bells," Satchel suggested. "Testing them or something. Or maybe they got stuck."

"Probably," I agreed. Then I added, "But it's the timing that's interesting, don't you think? It happened when I needed it to happen."

"I guess so." She sounded unconvinced.

I drew in a deep breath, buying some time to try to read her thoughts. Then I said, "But I didn't answer your question about the poets and the saints, did I?"

She shrugged. "That's all right. It doesn't really matter. I'm not a poet, and I'll sure never be a saint." She offered me a small dry laugh.

"But you *are* a poet, Satchel."

"Naw." She shook her head. "Remember? I don't write poetry."

"No, but I mean, you have the eye of a poet anyway. I think you notice things, the way Emily did when she came back from the dead."

She was quiet a long time then. I let her think.

Finally she said, "You know what I really like, Miss Gunnar?"

"What, Satchel?"

"The smell of dead fish and gasoline."

I thought she might be joking and that perhaps I was supposed to laugh. But I took my cue from her expressionless face and only cocked my head to ask her to explain.

"Really," she said. "I can't smell fish and gasoline without thinking of the best summers of my life. Okay, so see, when I was little, my grandma—my dad's mom—owned a cottage on Lake Conesus in upstate New York. We used to go up there for a week or two in the summer—my mom, my dad, and me. And my dad, he'd always rent a motorboat so we could go out on the lake. He'd wake me up early, and we'd go out on the water just as the sun was coming up. Well, the shore of the lake usually had dead fish on it, you know? Like, they'd die and wash up there on the rocks and start to rot. So there'd be that fishy smell, and then Dad and I would walk out on the dock and get into the boat and tie our life jackets on. And then when he started the motor, there was the smell of gasoline, and then we'd push off from the dock, and we'd be flying over the water. . . ." She paused and shut her eyes. "And I'd sit there in the front of the boat holding my arms out, and I'd feel like I was flying. That's the only time I've really felt like I was—I don't know—alive, I guess." She opened her eyes and looked at me.

"It sounds wonderful, Satchel," I said.

"It was. There were so many things, like—well, sometimes we'd build a fire on the shore at night and roast marshmallows. Or Dad and I, we'd walk along the edge of the water and collect rocks and put them in a bucket. And sometimes"—her eyes grew brighter—"sometimes Grandma watered her grass with a sprinkler, the kind that looks like a huge fan waving back and forth. You know what I mean?"

I nodded.

"And if you looked at the sprinkler from just the right angle, you'd see rainbows in the water because of the way the sun was shining on it. I remember running through the sprinkler even with my clothes on and jumping around saying, 'Look at me, Daddy! I'm jumping through rainbows!'"

She stopped then, her smile lingering while her eyes misted over. But she didn't cry. She pulled the tears back into herself and said, "I wish I could do it again. But my grandma died and the cottage got sold, so we never went there again."

I asked, tentatively, "Where is your father now?"

Her lips became a taut line at the center of her face. She dropped the copy of *Our Town* into her backpack and pushed herself up from the wing chair. "I gotta go, Miss Gunnar," she said. "I promised Tess I'd study for the French test with her."

As I watched her turn to go, I understood that I wasn't going to hear about her father tonight. "Is the test tomorrow?" I asked.

"Yeah. But I'm not worried. Mrs. Connelly's tests are pretty easy because, to tell you the truth, I don't think she's fluent in French herself."

"Oh!" I frowned. "Well, that's not good."

Satchel shrugged. "So who needs to speak French when anywhere you go in the world, they speak English?"

We had made our way to the door, where Satchel stood with her hand on the doorknob. "Well, thanks for telling me about the bells and all that, Miss Gunnar. Maybe there's something to it."

For the first time I dared to touch Satchel by putting my hand on her shoulder. She didn't flinch, but instead seemed to lean into my touch. "And thank you for telling me about the rainbows, Satchel. I think Emily in *Our Town* would have put jumping through rainbows right up there with clocks ticking and new ironed dresses."

"You think so?"

"Yeah, I do."

She smiled. "Well, good night, Miss Gunnar."

"Good night, Satchel."

CHAPTER 19

Sometime in the fall of 1976 we started reading Virginia Woolf for Theodore Dutton's class. I neither enjoyed nor fully understood her novels, and why Mr. Dutton required us to read three of them in as many weeks was beyond me, except—as I supposed at the time—that was simply what one did in Honors English. We spent more time on Woolf than any other writer, and I think now it was because Mr. Dutton favored her works. I think she spoke to him.

To me, her only intelligible utterances were of sorrow and doom. Think of poor Mrs. Ramsey in *To the Lighthouse*, annoyed with herself for having said, "We are in the hands of the Lord."

"How could any Lord have made this world? she asked. With her mind she had always seized the fact that there is no reason, order, justice: but suffering, death, the poor. There was no treachery too base for the world to commit; she knew that. No happiness lasted; she knew that."

Virginia Woolf was not a cheery person. I pictured her as Mrs. Ramsey sailing toward the lighthouse, proclaiming stoically, "We perished, each alone."

Yet, when at last we read her essay "A Sketch of the Past," it was then I became intrigued by her. She wrote about what she called her moments of being. These moments, she explained, were embedded in the many more moments of life's nonbeing. She described the moments of being as a sudden shock, a welcome shock, in which she sensed something beyond the visible, or, as she wrote, the shock "is or will become a revelation of some order; it is a token of some real thing behind appearances."

When I read that, my sixteen-year-old self whispered, "It's God, of course." But Virginia Woolf was a brilliant woman, and she did not believe in God. "Certainly and emphatically there is no God," she wrote, so how to explain the moments of being?

Because Mr. Dutton mentioned Woolf's published diaries in class, I went on to read parts of them on my own. The copy I read was from the public library, but even so I underlined these words in pencil: "I have some restless searcher in me. Why is there not a discovery in life? I have questioned. Something one can lay hands on and say 'This is it'? I'm looking: but that's not it, that's not it. What is it? And shall I die before I find it?"

I was haunted by that question. "Shall I die before I find it?" I wanted to tell her, "It's so simple, don't you see. . . ?" But I knew that Virginia Woolf had filled her pockets with stones and drowned herself in the River Ouse in 1941.

I wrote an essay for Mr. Dutton's class explaining my theory that Virginia Woolf's moments of being were actually those instances in which God was revealing himself to her.

It was no secret at Seaton that I was a churchgoing believer. I suppose it wasn't so much the way I acted—a person could be a good kid making good grades without being a Christian. No, I think the real giveaway was the bumper sticker on my car that said in two-inch, no-nonsense type: _Jesus is Lord_. By my senior year I finally had my license, and because I was able to drive myself to school, my father bought a new car for my mother and gave me the red and white 1960

Pontiac station wagon Mom had been driving since I was born. With my classmates behind the wheels of Camaros, Mustangs, and Falcons, I wanted neither that rattletrap with fins nor the bumper sticker that came with it. It was either that, though, or walk to school, my parents being understandably reluctant to haul me around any longer. I considered at least scraping off the bumper sticker, but in the end decided that was tantamount to Peter's betrayal in the garden, and I simply couldn't do it. So every morning I drove to campus in an antiquated evangelistic station wagon and parked it amid the jacked-up newer models sporting various rock group decals and racing strips. My strategy was to act as though there was nothing at all different about my car, that it was something that any high school senior would be proud to drive. Apparently my strategy worked, as very little was ever said about that old Pontiac. Now I have to wonder whether it was simply expected of someone like me to drive something like that, making it all a nonissue in the first place.

Anyway, there I was, the campus Jesus Freak writing this English paper about divine revelation and turning it in to be graded by a man who, I assumed, believed in God.

But I was wrong. Theodore Dutton was like Virginia Woolf in that regard. In both their worlds, certainly and emphatically there was no God.

I found that out on one of the nights that the gang went to visit him at his cabin. We were all there, all six of the Barbarians, including Janie and Artie. We were lounging about the room drinking a watery hot chocolate and talking about the Bloomsbury Group of which Virginia Woolf was a member. I was feeling rather smug and proud of myself for writing what I thought was an exceptionally good essay, and I hoped

Mr. Dutton might mention it during the course of the evening.

I sat on one of the couches beside Ray that night, leaning against him with my cheek on his shoulder. I was just about to say something about Woolf's diaries when Artie spoke up and the conversation turned toward agnosticism, one of his favorite subjects, right up there with his fascination for the French Foreign Legion.

Artie Sochs was, like the members of the Bloomsbury Group, a skeptic. According to Artie, the basic principles of empiricism didn't allow for belief in something that couldn't be experienced. Artie was heavy into math and science; he liked the conclusive experiments and irrefutable answers these disciplines offered. He had no patience with philosophical speculation.

"Stephen was right," he said, speaking of Virginia Woolf's father. "When he gave up the faith, he said it was like giving up a huge burden. That's all it is, you know. Belief in God just slows down human progress."

I heard Ray sigh. "Yeah, sure, Artie. We know the drill. You can't see God, so he isn't there. But that's not necessarily so. There are lots of things we can't see, but that doesn't mean they don't exist."

"Like what?"

Ray thought a moment. "Well, like anger, for one. I mean, think about it. Put a little bit of the pure stuff of anger right here in my hand, will you?"

He held his hand out toward Artie. Artie shrugged it off. "Yeah, well, we know anger's there because we see the effects of it. That's obvious."

"And we don't see the effects of God?"

The room fell silent. Artie cast me a look that was a direct challenge to my bumper sticker. He and I had discussed all this before and had reached an impasse, neither of us willing to budge. I looked helplessly at Mr. Dutton.

Our teacher sat backward in a ladder-back chair brought in from the kitchen, his forearms resting on the top rail. He frowned while scratching absently at one sleeve. "We're all entitled to our individual beliefs," he said, "whatever they may be."

"Yeah, so," said Ken Cunningham, lying on the floor with his hands beneath his head, "what do you believe, Mr. Dutton? Do you think God exists?"

Mr. Dutton seemed to hesitate ever so slightly. Then he said, "No, I don't. But I would never try to convince another person to believe—or not believe—the way I do."

"Still, you'd call yourself an atheist. Right?" Artie asked.

"I don't like labels, but if I have to have one, I guess that'd be it."

Artie looked triumphant. My own cheeks burned, and I was glad the lighting in the room was dim.

We went on then to speak of other things as though this one issue had been settled and we were reluctant to bring it up again. The sage had spoken; the students were silenced. I had let myself be silenced, melting into my cloak of invisibility.

Mr. Dutton handed back our papers later that week. He gave me an A, along with the comment, "Well written. Interesting premise."

But I didn't want the A. I wasn't interested in premises. I

wanted what I had written to be true, not just for me but for Theodore Dutton. That it wasn't true for him rattled me more than I cared to admit, and it cast a shadow into my personal corner of Eden.

CHAPTER 20

"So this is where you grew up, huh?" Satchel asked.

"This is it."

We stood in front of a two-story fieldstone house on Heritage Drive in a neighborhood called Westminster. I had told Satchel I grew up right here in Wilmington, and she asked to see the house. We drove out from Seaton on a Sunday afternoon and parked on the street where my family and I once lived.

"Who lives in the house now?" she asked.

I shrugged. "I have no idea."

"Want to ring the doorbell and find out?"

"No, I don't think so. I wouldn't want to bother them."

"You could tell them you used to live here."

I felt as though I should live there still, as though I should be able to walk in through the front door and find my mother and my father and my sisters at home. Dad should be reading the paper in his easy chair, his feet propped up on the footstool, our dog curled up on the floor beside him. My sisters should be upstairs listening to the Top 40 Countdown while curling their hair in front of the bathroom mirror, and Mom should be in the kitchen cooking a pot roast and kneading dough for homemade bread. That's how it should be and would be if time hadn't changed all that, wiped it away like chalk off a blackboard. That was probably why I hadn't come to see the house since returning to Delaware. This place that still housed so much of my heart—how could it not belong to me?

"See the upstairs middle window?" I asked, pointing.

"Uh-huh."

"That was my bedroom."

She looked up, squinting against the sun. "Well," she said finally, "it looks like it was a pretty nice place to grow up."

"It was," I said, nodding, "though I didn't know it at the time."

"What do you mean?"

"Well—" I stopped and thought about her question. "I just took everything for granted. And I thought Delaware was boring. My friend Natalie and I called it Dullaware, as in D-u-l-l."

She didn't respond for a while. Then she said, "You mean, you went to school, and you came home and your mom was there, and then your dad came home from work, and you all sat around the kitchen table eating supper?"

I laughed lightly. "Yes, that's how it was. Every day."

She looked at me, then looked away, but not before I saw the way her eyes narrowed and two lines formed between her brows.

"So, do you want to walk around the neighborhood?" I asked.

"Sure."

The center of the neighborhood was a lopsided circle of intersecting streets, exactly one mile around, with other streets like tendrils leading off the main loop. I knew every foot of it by heart.

"Are your parents still alive?" Satchel asked as we started out.

"Yes, they are."

"You're lucky."

I nodded.

"Where do they live now?"

"Asheville, North Carolina. They retired there. My dad always wanted to live in the mountains."

"That's cool."

We walked to where Heritage Drive meets up with Ambleside Drive. Turning right, we came upon the covered bridge that passed over the little creek running through the neighborhood.

"This is where I waited for the bus when I went to public school."

"Yeah? Under a covered bridge? That's cool," she said again. "So how come you ended up going to Seaton?"

"Well, I was a quiet kid, very shy. My parents thought I'd do better in a smaller classroom."

"I get it. You were one of the kids all the other kids ragged on."

I smiled. "I guess you could put it that way."

"But it was better at Seaton?"

"Oh yes. For the most part. As I've mentioned before, I made some good friends. I was happy there."

It was a long gradual climb up Ambleside, then down again toward Cheltenham. We took a right turn and went up again toward the crest of Cheltenham, the best hill in the neighborhood to sail down on a bike or a sled. All these years later I could still feel the wind in my face, the sensation of weightlessness, of flying without wings.

"I think I would have liked living here," Satchel said. "And if I'd had your life, I think I would have known I was lucky."

"I suspect you might have, Satchel."

"I don't think your childhood was boring. I think it was more, like, innocent. I mean, the way a childhood is supposed to be, you know?"

"Um-hmm." I nodded. We started the trek down Cheltenham. "That reminds me of something Edna St. Vincent Millay once said."

"Yeah? No offense, Miss Gunnar, but everything reminds you of something some writer once said."

I laughed. "I suppose you're right."

We kept walking, our feet slapping against the pavement as we descended the steep grade.

"So what'd she say?" Satchel asked.

I stole a moment to catch my breath. The hill I ran up as a child now left me winded going down. "She said that childhood is the kingdom where nobody dies." Then I added, as Millay had, "Nobody that matters, that is."

We walked the length of Cheltenham, over the concrete bridge arching the creek on this side of the neighborhood, then turned back onto Heritage Drive. "She was right, you know," I went on. "When you're a kid, you're so full of life, you don't have time to think about anything else."

We reached my car, parked along the curb in front of my former home. Satchel began to open the passenger side door when she stopped and looked up at the house.

"Well," she said, lifting her shoulders in a small dispirited shrug, "I guess by that definition, I never even *had* a childhood, not even a boring one."

On the two-mile drive back to Seaton, Satchel turned on the radio and fiddled with the dial, finding just the right music to fill the void where otherwise words might have been.

CHAPTER 21

September receded and October rolled in, and still I knew nothing about Satchel's father. I suspected he was no longer living, but I didn't ask, and she didn't tell. I would simply have to wait until the time was right for me to know.

Natalie reminded me that I'd promised to go to homecoming with her that first weekend of the month. I wanted to go to the Saturday night reception, but starting early in the morning I had a pounding headache that wouldn't let go, and by early afternoon I called Natalie to tell her I might not make it. She retorted that if I didn't come of my own accord, she'd show up at Pine Glen and drag me there herself, as she had no intention of going without me. I took a couple more aspirin and slept the afternoon away and was feeling well enough by evening to get dressed and head over to the larger of the two gymnasiums, Kennemac Gym.

"You're late," Natalie said when I found her holding a plate of hors d'oeuvres just inside the main doors. "People have been mingling for an hour."

"You're lucky I'm here," I said groggily, "and I just hope you appreciate the sacrifice I'm making for you."

"Yeah, right. You know you wouldn't miss this night for anything."

We both laughed, friends long enough to engage in some harmless bantering.

"You'll never guess who else is here," she said.

"Who? Artie Sochs, home from the Belgian Congo?"

"Better than that. It's Ray."

"Ray Schmidt?"

"Who else?"

Of course Ray Schmidt. I'd been wondering whether he'd show up. In fact, I'd been thinking about him that morning when the headache settled in. "Did you talk with him?" I asked.

"Not yet. He's only just arrived. Must have come in while I was in the ladies' room. See, he's over there."

"Where?"

"There."

I tried to follow the nod of her head, but the gym was large and the crowd was thick, and I couldn't see anyone who looked like the Ray I remembered.

"He's got his back to us."

"Oh." I pretended I didn't care. Turning back to Natalie, I asked, "So did the hubby come with you?"

"No." She bit into a cheese-laden cracker and shook her head. "Jason had a game, so Ron took him to that. Believe me, he'd rather watch softball than come to a high school reunion with me."

"Yeah, I suppose so. Well, anyone else here we know?"

"Ken Cunningham's around here somewhere. I haven't spoken with him yet, but I saw him."

"Really? It's practically a Barbarian reunion."

Natalie laughed. "Yeah, except for Janie and Artie. Other than that, there are a few here from our class but not many."

I nodded. "Well, I'm going to get something to eat."

"Don't you want to see Ray?"

I did. And I didn't.

"Let me get something to drink first."

"The punch isn't spiked, if that's what you mean."

"That wasn't what I meant." Though if I'd been a drinking woman, that's exactly what I'd have meant.

We moved together to the serving tables piled high with various finger foods, chocolates, and cakes. Someone was dipping out cups of punch and offered me one. I took it and clutched the cup nervously.

"Hey, listen." Natalie cocked an ear and pointed off toward nothing in particular. "Remember how we used to call the radio station and request this song?"

Listening, I recognized the tune as one that was popular when we were in school. It drifted over from a far corner of the gym where a three-piece band sat nestled under a dubious spotlight. The space in front of them served as a dance floor where a few brave souls were trying to revive their long-forgotten disco moves.

"Yeah," I said, "and now it's a golden oldie."

For the next half hour or so Natalie and I mingled within the swirling mix of music and conversation and laughter. I sought out familiar faces with an increasing sense of disappointment, resorting finally to looking at name tags and realizing that many of the alumni were far younger than I. No wonder so few people were attempting to dance. Seventies music wouldn't mean much to a nineties audience. The anachronistic band played on, though, trying valiantly to coax down memory lane a crowd of people who simply couldn't go back that far.

At some point Ken Cunningham approached us, greeting us each with an awkward hug we could only half return without spilling punch down his back. He had thickened, becoming chinless and jowled, and his hair was prematurely gray, an unflattering crown that aged him beyond his years. He introduced us to his wife, a rather nondescript woman who looked so unhappy to be there that I considered yelling "Fire!" so we could all clear the gym and go home.

"You girls look great," Ken gushed, looking from Natalie to me and back to Natalie again. "You both look more beautiful today than you did in high school."

His obvious flattery only served to shrink his wife even further. He sounded tipsy and unctuous, and I wondered what had happened to him in the years since we'd been in school. He'd spent too much time among politicians, I thought, and I suddenly had no real desire to speak to him. But I asked him anyway, "So how've you been, Ken?"

"Great!" he responded loudly. "Doing great. How about the two of you?"

"Good, Ken. Good," Natalie answered. "You still in D.C.?"

"Oh sure. I mean, where can you go from there? It's addictive, you know?"

"I bet." That was me, growing more despondent by the second.

"Yeah, I'm thinking of running for office."

"Oh yeah?" Natalie asked. "What, specifically?"

"President," he said.

Natalie's brows flew up. "President of the United States?"

"What else?" He finished off his punch in one long gulp. "On the Democratic ticket, of course. I want to out-Clinton Clinton, especially when it comes to the interns, you know?" He gave a raucous laugh, fueled with alcohol.

I looked at his wife. She was studying the floor and didn't meet my gaze.

Turning to Natalie, I said, "I thought you said the punch wasn't spiked."

"What's that?" Ken asked.

"Nothing," Natalie said, casting me a sideways glance meant to shut me up.

Ken's wife looked up from the floor. "Will you excuse me a moment?"

"Sure, hon'," Ken said. "It's through those doors and down the stairs."

He waved her off to the ladies' room, not noticing that she headed toward the front door of the gym instead. He didn't notice because he was too busy paying attention to Natalie. "Hey listen, Nat, they're playing our song. Wanna dance?"

To my surprise, she did. Natalie was thoroughly committed to her husband, I knew, but I was less certain of Ken's commitment to his wife. Obviously I didn't know who Ken was anymore.

Left alone, I decided it was time to seek out Raymond Schmidt. I'd get it over with and then go home.

Until that moment I'd put off seeing Ray out of fear. It was the memory of who we'd been to each other our senior year: steady dates, confidants, the one with whom we'd shared goals and fears and dreams. I was afraid to see the person I'd considered my first love.

Too, I was afraid simply because he had been there. He had lived through senior year with us, including the final dreadful months.

But when Natalie and Ken moved off toward the dance floor, I turned and scanned the room, then tentatively wandered through the crowd until I found him. He was by himself too, looking at some photographs taped to the far wall, a history of Seaton in a series of black-and-white moments. I touched his elbow. When he turned to see who it was and I could look at him straight on, I saw that the years had been kind to him. He appeared older and more mature, but at the same time more refined. He looked strong and self-assured, and he looked pleased to see me.

"Beth," he said, and my name sounded like delighted laughter in his mouth.

We hugged, not awkwardly, but as though we were used to falling into each other's embrace. "Hello, Ray. Or I guess it's Dr. Schmidt now, right?"

He smiled. "It's been Dr. Schmidt for a long time—almost too long," he said with a laugh. "You look great, Beth, really great."

Coming from him, the words sounded sincere.

He added, "I was hoping you'd be here."

"You were?" I asked, but he didn't hear me, and he went on to ask me how I was. "Good. I've been good," I replied. "And you?"

"Not bad. Hey, I hear you're teaching here now."

"That's right. I'm part of Seaton's faculty, if you can imagine that."

"You like it?"

"I do. It's strange being here as a teacher instead of a student."

"Yeah, I guess it would be. You'll have to—whoa!" A small child with tousled hair sideswiped him. "Slow down, buddy. Wait a minute." Ray laid a hand on top of the child's head to stop him. "Let me introduce you to my old friend, Mrs.—"

He stopped then and looked at me.

"Gunnar," I said. "It hasn't changed."

For a moment Ray looked unsure. Then he said to the boy, "Ben, this is an old friend of mine, Miss Gunnar. Can you say hello?"

The boy looked up at me with his father's eyes. Obediently, he said, "Hello."

"This is my youngest," Ray explained. "Ben."

"I'm happy to meet you, Ben."

Ray's hand remained settled on top of the boy's blond curls. His wedding band glinted in the artificial light of the gym's fluorescent lamps.

In the next moment a woman was there beside us, a very young woman, blonde like Ben and beautiful. She was far younger than Ray and I, and I thought, *She must be his second wife.* But that was speculation. She and I exchanged a tentative smile, and Ray started to say something when suddenly he stopped and, reaching into his breast pocket, pulled out a cell phone.

"Excuse me a minute," he said. "I've got a call." He moved to an open door and stepped outside.

The child ran off then, and the woman smiled apologetically at me as if to say, *You know what children are like,* and then she took off after him, and I was once again alone. But only for a moment.

When Ray came back, his whole face a frown, he said, "I'm sorry, Beth. There's an emergency. I have to go."

"Oh! I understand—" I began.

He cut me off by saying once more, "I'm sorry. We'll have to talk another time." And then he looked about the room to find his wife and son and, spying them, gave my shoulder a quick squeeze and then was gone.

I was disappointed. I would have liked to ask him about his life, his family, his work. But I decided that in those few moments I had learned as much as I needed to know. He was a busy doctor with a beautiful wife and an adorable young son and presumably one or more older children too. He looked trim and successful and happy. What more did I need to know? He had done well for himself, and above all else, I was happy for my old friend.

Left with that impression, I found it rather odd when a few days later Raymond Schmidt called Pine Glen and invited me to dinner.

CHAPTER 22

"Do you mean," I asked, "have dinner with you and your family?"

"Well, no," he said. Then he rushed to add, "Of course I'd like you to meet the kids sometime, but for now I was thinking just the two of us could grab something to eat over at the Lincolnshire. You remember the place, don't you?"

I did, and it was no fast-food restaurant where people grabbed something to eat. It was a place where patrons dined leisurely at tables arrayed with silverware and crystal and delicate china on stiff white tablecloths.

It was startlingly inappropriate for a married man and a single woman, even those simply sharing a meal as old friends.

"Yes, I know the Lincolnshire, but I'm afraid, well, I'm afraid I can't do that, Ray."

"If you're busy this Saturday, we could make it the following week."

"No, it's not that. It's—" I stopped. I couldn't believe the conversation we were having. I felt silly saying what should have been perfectly obvious to Ray, *would* have been obvious to the Ray I'd known in high school. I tried to laugh, but that only made me sound nervous, which I was. Finally I blurted, "What on earth would your wife think?"

"My wife? What's she—" Ray stopped. Then he said, "Oh, wait a minute, you think—"

"I know we're old friends but—"

"No, no, no. Hold on a minute. I was just assuming you knew."

"Knew what?"

"Well, that I'm not married."

Not married? The towheaded boy? The dazzling blonde? The wedding ring?

Once more I fumbled for words. "But, the woman at homecoming—"

"Oh, now I understand! That was Ingrid. I forgot I didn't—I had to leave before I could introduce you to her. Ingrid is my au pair. From Sweden. She helps take care of Ben and Lisa. Not that Lisa's incapable of taking care of herself, since she's a senior this year. But I need someone around the house. . . ."

And on he went about the child care, the housework, all that he couldn't do because of the hours he spent at the hospital. When he finished, I wanted to ask again about the wedding ring, which he hadn't explained, but I decided by that point I would be going beyond what I needed to know and risking an attitude of peevishness. After all, if he wanted to wear a wedding ring even though he wasn't married, what was that to me?

I made a mental note to ask him about it later.

"So would you like to have dinner with me Saturday night?"

What could I say? There was nothing in the world to keep me from saying yes.

CHAPTER 23

My Dad
by Satchel Queen

People say you can't remember anything from when you were a baby, but I think they might be wrong. I have a memory in my head, and I must have been a baby or maybe a toddler because I'm lying in my crib looking up at my dad's face. He's smiling and making funny noises that might have been words, but I don't know because I didn't know yet what words are. But I knew my dad was happy, and it seemed to have something to do with me.

When I was born my father was twenty years old and my mother was nineteen and I was what people call a surprise. My mom and dad weren't married and even though I came along they never got married. The three of us lived together, though—mostly.

For Dad, I was something good, like a surprise party. I was something to celebrate. For Mom, I guess it wasn't what you'd call a party having me. It was one of those unexpected things that catches you off guard and you wish life wouldn't bring you.

Dad was a good-looking man and very big. At least he seemed really big to me because I was a baby. Even when I got bigger, he was still big. If I shut my eyes today I can feel what it was like when he picked me up and carried me against his shoulder. It was warm and safe and it smelled good there because of the aftershave he wore. It was a cheap aftershave because we never had much money, but I didn't know that at the time.

Dad was an artist, but he worked for the sanitation department in Brooklyn. He said that artists are meant to create beauty, and that by collecting garbage and getting rid of it, he was helping the world to be more beautiful.

Mom didn't like Dad being a garbage man. I know because I used to hear them fight about it late at night when they thought I was asleep. I was asleep, until their yelling woke me up. Sometimes our neighbor in the next apartment woke up too because I could hear him banging on the wall, telling Mom and Dad to pipe down. Well, he didn't put it that way but I won't write what our neighbor really said.

Dad was always happy anyway. Except for our neighbor and maybe my mom sometimes, everybody liked him. He had about a thousand friends, I guess, because everybody wanted to be around Daniel Queen. He'd take me to the corner bar on Friday nights—the owner was Dad's friend and let me in even though I was a kid—and everybody said, "Danny Queen, tell us a story!" And he would. Dad could tell a story like no one else. When he got done the place was so full of laughter I could feel the floor shaking.

When he wasn't working, Dad took me all over the city. We went to the Statue of Liberty and Central Park and Grand Central Station and Lincoln Center, when it was all decorated for Christmas. He took me to the top of the Empire State Building and up to the top of the World Trade Center too, back when the towers were still there. If you've ever seen the city from the top of buildings like that, you never forget it.

One summer day when I was eight years old, Dad took me to the beach at Coney Island. Like most times when we went somewhere, it was just the two of us. We went to Coney Island pretty often because we both liked the ocean. We liked to walk along the shore right at the spot where the waves come in and go back out. I was always fascinated by the little shells and pebbles that did somersaults over the wet sand as the water went back out. Dad and I would collect some and put them in our pockets.

Anyway, this one summer day was different than the others. We bought ice cream cones, and we sat on a bench on the boardwalk to eat them. Dad got butter pecan and I got plain chocolate. The wind kept blowing my hair into the ice cream until Dad took off his baseball cap and stuck it on my head backward.

"That better?" he asked.

I nodded. He always took care of everything.

We kept on licking our ice cream and watching the seagulls flying around and listening to the waves coming in. There were lots of people walking on the boardwalk and lying on the beach. I loved to be there because it made me feel like I was part of something good.

I heard people laughing and there was music coming from somewhere, and I asked Dad if he had enough money for me to ride the merry-go-round. He said he did and we'd go there as soon as we finished our cones.

And then he said, "Satchel, you'll never forget your old dad, will you?"

I didn't know what he meant but I thought maybe it had to do with Father's Day that was coming up, so I said, "Don't worry, Dad, I won't forget," because I had already made him a card with hearts all over it.

He said, "That's good, Satchel," and he put his arm around me and squeezed my shoulder and said, "I'll always love you."

I said, "I'll always love you too, Dad."

Then I rode the merry-go-round, and every time I passed Dad he raised his hand and waved at me, and I had no idea he was waving good-bye.

The first time I read the poem called "Richard Cory" by Edwin Arlington Robinson when I was about fourteen, I had the creepy feeling that this Robinson guy knew Daniel Queen. My dad wasn't rich, but everyone admired him and watched for him to come and were happy if he so much as said, "Good morning."

And then, like Richard Cory, one calm summer night Daniel Queen went home and put a bullet through his head.

He didn't need to worry. Even if I live to be a hundred years old, I will never forget my dad.

CHAPTER 24

Just as I reached the final paragraph of her essay, Satchel appeared on the hillside sloping down from the dorm. It was almost as though she knew I was reading her story and she was coming to weigh my reaction. Hurriedly I pushed back from the table and stepped to the bathroom, where I dried my eyes and tried to steady my breath.

Then I met Satchel at the door.

"Can I come in a minute, Miss Gunnar?"

"Of course."

The chill of autumn had settled in, and Satchel wore a denim jacket and a pair of jeans. Both were tattered and faded and right in style. She sat down in the wing chair, kicked off her shoes, and tucked her legs beneath her.

"So what are you doing?" she asked.

"I've just been grading essays."

"Don't you ever do anything, you know, just for fun?"

I thought a moment. "Well, I'm going out to dinner tonight, if that counts."

"With a man?"

"Yes."

"So it's a date?"

"No. He's an old friend. We were classmates here at Seaton. We thought we'd get together and just catch up."

She gave me a look that said she didn't believe me. "So what's this guy do?"

"He's a doctor."

"Oh yeah? Mr. Moneybags, huh?"

I laughed. "I don't know. I suppose he does all right."

Satchel nodded. "Yeah, so if you marry him, maybe you can stop teaching and spending all your time reading boring essays."

"Good grief, Satchel, I don't intend to marry the guy, and I don't want to stop teaching. I happen to like what I do. Besides, I don't think the essays are boring at all. In fact . . ." I paused a moment, then said, "I just finished reading yours."

She fidgeted in the chair. "Yeah?"

"Yes. And I want you to know that I'm sorry."

"For what?"

"About your father. I didn't know."

She shrugged. "How could you know? It's probably not part of my permanent record or anything, is it?"

I looked at her until she dropped her eyes. I said, "The suicide of a parent is a terrible thing for a child to live through. It's something you never get over. I know you must miss your father terribly."

Keeping her gaze on her lap, she nodded. "You want to know what's really rotten, Miss Gunnar?"

"What's that, Satchel?"

"When he died, I think my mom was just relieved. I mean, I never saw her cry. Not once."

I struggled to find something to say. "Well, maybe she did cry, when she was alone. Maybe she didn't want you to see her cry."

"Why not? I saw her cry plenty of times later when this boyfriend dumped her or that boyfriend cheated on her."

I shook my head and sighed heavily. "I don't know,

Satchel. Some people are hard to understand. I'm sure your mother's not a bad person—"

"Yeah, right. You can say that because you don't know her."

I flinched, then ceded the argument to her. "You've got a point. I don't know her."

This child was an orphan, with an indifferent mother and a father who had loved her, although not enough to stay alive for her.

"I'm glad you shared your story with me, Satchel," I said. "Thank you for that."

"Yeah sure. Like, I just thought you ought to know."

"I appreciate that." Then I added, "After . . . this happened, did you ever talk with anyone?"

Satchel's eyes narrowed. "You mean, like a head doctor or something?"

I nodded in reply.

"Naw," she said. "Why should I? Talking isn't going to bring my dad back."

"No. But sometimes it helps."

"Helps with what?"

"Well, with the grief. It can help you find closure."

"No offense, Miss Gunnar," she said with a roll of her eyes, "but I hate that word *closure*. It's a stupid word."

"Yeah," I agreed. "You're right."

"I don't want anything closed, and I don't want any help. I just wanted you to know what happened."

"All right."

She leaned against the arm of the chair, her chin in one hand, staring absently at the empty fireplace. Finally she said, "So tell me something good, Miss Gunnar."

With those words Satchel declared her father's suicide a mute topic. She had said all she wanted to say, and now we were done. I would honor that and follow her lead in this conversation. "Something good?" I repeated.

"A story. Like the story of the bells."

"Oh. Well . . ."

The room was quiet while my mind tossed about anxiously, trying to find something to say, something appropriate. What, I wondered, would Satchel consider good?

Thankfully she helped me out by asking, "This guy you're having dinner with tonight—what's his name?"

"Raymond Schmidt. Ray."

"So tell me what it was like when you and Ray were kids."

I smiled then. "We had fun. We were part of this group—there were six of us, three guys and three girls. We called ourselves the Barbarians."

Satchel looked at me doubtfully. "No offense, Miss Gunnar, but I don't think the name works. I mean, I don't really see you as a barbarian, you know?"

I laughed. "No. The truth is, we were anything but barbaric. I guess that's why we thought it was funny."

She shrugged. "Okay. Whatever works."

"The six of us hung out together and did—I don't know—lots of crazy things."

"Like what?"

"Well, things that would probably sound pretty tame to kids today."

"So tell me."

"We'd sneak off campus to go to Burger King, or we'd climb up the fire escape on Heath Hall after dark and sit around telling stories and drinking sodas."

She sat motionless for a moment as though waiting for more. When I didn't go on, she said, "That's not only tame, Miss Gunnar. That's pretty lame."

I couldn't help laughing. "I guess so. But being part of that group is one of the best memories I have."

She nodded as if she understood, but I was fairly sure she didn't.

Then she said, "I bet you and Ray had a thing going, didn't you?"

"We dated for a while," I confessed. "Nothing serious."

"And now you're having dinner tonight?"

"Yes."

"He never married?"

"He's divorced."

"Everyone is. Except you."

"Well, not quite everyone."

She turned her gaze back to the fireplace. "So you liked it here when you were a student?"

"For the most part, yes."

"What'd you like about it?"

"Lots of things."

"So name one."

"My friends."

"And?"

"You said one."

"So name another."

I thought a moment. "I liked the campus. I liked the valley where the chapel is. We called it Chapel Valley. Have you been there?"

She nodded.

"In the spring the valley is filled with daisies. It's really beautiful."

"Yeah?" She sounded unconvinced.

"Sometimes we had picnics there on the weekends—the six of us. We'd grab some fast food and take a couple of blankets out there and eat lunch in the shade of the chapel."

"Sounds like a crowd. You should have gone with just Ray."

"I did once."

"Yeah? What happened?"

"Nothing, really. Though I do remember picking a daisy and pulling off the petals and asking it if Ray loved me. You know the old custom, 'He loves me, he loves me not. . . .'"

"Yeah, well, that's rigged. It always ends up with 'he loves me.'"

"This time it didn't. When I pulled off the last petal, it was 'he loves me not.'"

"Really? So what did Ray say?"

"Nothing. At least nothing I remember."

"He didn't say he loved you?"

"No. I'm sure he didn't say that."

"The creep."

I shrugged. "By then it didn't matter. We were only days away from graduation, and we knew we were going our separate ways. Different colleges and all that."

"You didn't love him?"

I shook my head. "We were kids."

"Kids can love each other."

"Well . . ."

"So what *didn't* you like about Seaton?"

132

I didn't have to think long to find an answer. "I didn't like being afraid all the time."

"Afraid of what?"

"Of failure, mostly."

Her face grew small as she frowned. "You'd never fail, Miss Gunnar. You're too smart."

"Maybe. But I always thought I might."

"That's crazy."

"That's exactly what my friend Natalie used to say."

"Yeah? And she was right."

But I didn't want to talk about that, so I asked, "And what about you? What do you like about Seaton?"

"I like your class."

I smiled. "And what else?"

She shrugged. "Not much."

"Really?"

She shook her head.

"That's too bad, Satchel. I wish you were happy here."

"I'm not exactly *un*happy."

"No?"

"No. Anyway, there's one good thing."

"What's that?"

"I'd rather be here than with Mom and Roger."

How does one respond to something like that? We simply looked at each other because there were no appropriate words to fill the gap.

She rose then, wiggled her feet back into her shoes, and stuck her hands in the pockets of her jacket. "I guess I better go get lunch before the cafeteria closes. Grilled cheese sandwiches today. Lucky me, huh?"

I stood too, but neither of us made a move for the door. I sensed she had more to say.

After a moment she said, "It's okay, isn't it? Me writing about my dad and all? I mean, that was the topic, wasn't it, to write about someone we know?"

"Of course it's okay. You did a wonderful job. The essay is excellent."

"I just didn't want to mess up like I did on the first one."

"No, you didn't mess up. All of your essays have been very good."

"Okay. Thanks."

Still she stood there, unwilling to leave. "Miss Gunnar?"

"Yes?"

"Have you ever known anyone who killed himself?"

I thought of Theodore Dutton. "I don't know, Satchel."

"You don't know?"

"No. I knew a man once who—" I stopped and shook my head. "I think—"

"Well, you'd know if he killed himself," she interrupted, "because like you said, it's something you never get over, you know? Like, you live with it every day of your life after something like that happens."

"Yes, Satchel. I know you do."

After she left, I went back to the pile of essays in the dining room and reread Satchel's story. And then I put my head down on the table, my forehead pressed against her words, and took up where I had left off earlier, with nothing now to stop the tears.

CHAPTER 25

The daisy had told me that Raymond Schmidt loved me not. Then we went our separate ways.

Now two middle-aged people sat across from each other over white linen and candlelight, one of them feeling giddy as a schoolgirl.

How I hated that feeling. Despised it. To be giddy was to be high on hope, and hope was a bumpy ride, no matter where it took you in the end. Only too often I'd crashed. The night I went with Ray to the Lincolnshire Restaurant, I was well aware of the risk. How many calamitous journeys in my life had started at a table for two just like this one?

Ray's left hand was bare, the wedding ring left behind on a dresser or bathroom counter somewhere. Of course I noticed that. I noticed it while his hands were still on the steering wheel of the car; I noted it with silent satisfaction as the two of us moved down the road on the wings of small talk. I assumed it was a purposeful decision on his part to take off the wedding ring. Best not to accompany a woman to dinner while wearing the trappings of a former relationship.

Now, as we waited for our food to arrive, Ray folded those same bare hands on the table, leaned forward slightly, and said, "So . . ."

Upon such a small word, such a slim foundation, relationships have been built, people have been born, deals have been closed, corporations have merged, empires have been built, treaties have been signed, wars have ceased, dreams have come true, and hearts have been irretrievably broken.

"So, Beth, tell me how you've been all these years."

I inhaled deeply. "Good, Ray. I've been good," I said, which was almost as good as saying nothing at all. "And you?" I asked.

He nodded, as though he were agreeing instead of answering a question. "Fair to middling," he quipped, offering me the same boyish smile he had offered me a thousand times in high school. "It's strange to think you're teaching at Seaton. You say you like it?"

"Yes. I really do. I'm glad I came back."

"I am too, Beth. That is, I'm glad you have work you enjoy."

"Don't you?" I asked. "Don't you enjoy your work?"

"Sometimes. And sometimes I'd rather be almost anywhere than at the hospital."

"Well, that's an honest answer."

He smiled, lifted his shoulders. "When I was in med school, I studied diseases. I learned the names, the causes, the symptoms. I was so busy learning about diseases I almost forgot medicine had anything to do with people. But when you start to practice, that's when you hear the stories. No, that's not it. The thing is, you become part of the stories. You're the one who delivers the bad news. You're the one who can't cure the disease, can't save the life, can't keep families together." He looked down at his hands and shrugged again. "After a while there are just too many stories."

I absorbed his words, trying to understand. "But surely you see a lot of stories with happy endings. I mean, people do get better; you help them get better."

"Yes," he agreed. "And that's what I try to dwell on. It's just hard to forget the others."

"I'm sure it is, Ray," I offered quietly.

The waiter arrived then, bearing a tray with two large platters of seafood fettuccini, a basket of warm bread, a side dish scooped full of real butter. I hadn't had food prepared like this in ages.

"It smells delicious."

Ray picked up a fork. "Well, dig in."

A certain sadness clung to him the way the scent of tobacco settles into the woven fabric of a smoking jacket. I could see that now. He didn't want me to see it, I'm sure, because he smiled valiantly, the practiced smile of one with a polished bedside manner. But I knew Ray, knew who he had been, saw who he was now, and detected the subtle nuances between the carefree boy and the careworn man.

We began to eat, and after a bite or two, Ray said, "You never married, Beth?"

The bread I was swallowing became a lump in my throat. I washed it down with water and shook my head.

"May I ask why not?" His voice was gentle, as though he were probing a wound with gloved hands.

"I simply never met the right one."

"Well . . ." He paused and broke another piece off the loaf of bread. "Maybe that's better than thinking you've found the right one, only to discover years later that you were wrong."

I was about to spear a scallop with the prongs of my fork, but I stopped and lifted my eyes to Ray's face. "Is that what happened to you, Ray?"

For a long moment neither of us moved. We both seemed

to be waiting for something, though I couldn't imagine what it was.

At last Ray said, "To tell you the truth, Beth, I'm still not really sure what happened."

"What do you mean?"

He shook his head. "Well, it's just that one day Brenda—my wife—was there, and quite literally the next, she was gone. Ben was a newborn, not two weeks old, when she woke up one morning and said she'd had enough. She left and didn't come back."

"You never heard from her again?"

"Only from her lawyer."

I sucked in air, held it in my lungs. I wanted to say, *That's terrible, terrible. . . . What kind of woman would leave her baby, her family, just walk out and never come back?*

Instead, I only murmured, "I'm so sorry."

He shook his head again, as though to say I shouldn't be sorry. Then he added, "Actually, that's not quite true. I've spoken with her a few times on the phone when she's called to talk with the kids. Or she tries to talk with them. They're not real interested. But anyway, she took off a long time ago, and I eventually got over it. Ben's six now. Best little guy in the world." He smiled; this time it was genuine.

"He's adorable," I agreed, remembering the little blond boy at homecoming. "And you have other children as well?"

"Yes. Josh is nineteen, in his second year at Penn State—"

"Premed?"

"No. Business, thank heavens. Maybe he'll be able to work reasonable hours, unlike his old man. Or, unlike his old man before he sold his practice and became a hospitalist a couple of years ago."

"A hospitalist?"

"I had my own practice as an internist for years, but I sold it. Now I work at the hospital and pretty much choose my own hours. Pretty nice. Plus, it helps when it comes to parenting. Which brings me to Lisa, my daughter. She's seventeen and a senior in high school this year. Smart as a whip. Seems to be interested in international marketing. I think she wants a job that will allow her to see the world."

"Nothing wrong with that."

"Not a thing. I predict she'll do well and have fun doing it."

I thought of this young girl with her whole life ahead of her. The clean slate appeared enviable, and I wished her well. I hoped all the lines would fall to her in pleasant places. *That happens sometimes, doesn't it?* I wondered.

"And then of course there's Ben," Ray went on. "A bit of a surprise but the apple of my eye."

And quite possibly the reason for Ray's divorce, though of course I'd never say as much. "You're a lucky man, with children like yours."

"Yes, I am. They're three great kids. You'll have to meet my older two someday."

"I'd like that."

We smiled at each other.

Then, as we ate, we spoke of other things—of old times, old friends, memories unearthed by this sudden intersecting of our lives. I wondered whether after this night I would ever see Ray again, let alone meet his children. People get busy and forget. Sometimes people think twice and choose to stay away. One candlelight dinner does not necessarily lead to a second. White linen is not necessarily an open door.

This may be my only chance, I thought. I wanted to know everything there was to know about Raymond Schmidt. And when that topic was exhausted, I wanted to ask him one more thing. What did he see that April night in 1977? What did he see the final time he was in the cabin where Theodore Dutton lived? He had told me before, but I wanted him to tell me again. I wanted to know if he could shed any light at all on that vague dark image that had haunted me for too many years.

But, in the end, I didn't ask. Because if I was to have just this one night with Ray, it simply seemed like too sad a place to go.

CHAPTER 26

We had made plans to meet at Theodore Dutton's cabin at midnight on that Friday in April 1977. Mr. Dutton didn't know we were coming. It was the first of the month, April Fool's day, and Ray and Ken came up with the idea of pulling a sort of practical joke on our teacher.

Earlier in the week a convict serving a life sentence for murder had escaped from the men's prison in Smyrna, about thirty-five miles south of us in central Delaware. This provided the boys fodder for their joke. Exactly what they intended to do, Natalie and I didn't know. We were simply to show up at the appointed time.

We were late. I was spending the night at Natalie's, and we wanted to exit the house no later than 11:45, but Mr. and Mrs. Primrose chose that night to stay up drinking bottomless cups of decaf in the kitchen. Their voices reached us in low murmurs, like mourners at a wake.

"They're probably talking about Tony." Natalie sounded irritated at the thought of her younger brother. "He and Brian were caught smoking pot by Brian's dad earlier this week. They lit up right in the basement, the idiots. What'd they expect?"

"I didn't know Tony smoked pot."

"I didn't either, till now."

"What are your mom and dad going to do?"

Natalie shrugged. "I don't know, but I wish they'd hurry up and decide so we can get out of here."

She wanted nothing to stand in her way when she was ready to visit Theodore Dutton.

Moments later we heard muted footsteps on the carpeted stairs, husband and wife ascending in soft-soled slippers. Natalie and I scrambled into bed fully clothed, pulling the covers up to our chins. Sure enough, the silhouette of Mrs. Primrose stopped briefly in the doorway before moving on. It was exactly what my own mother would have done, in spite of my age. And I liked it, in spite of my age. I always felt warm in such moments of maternal care.

We heard a door close, a toilet flush, a light switch swatted. We lay still, breathing in measured breaths, waiting for the slow descending of sleep, not upon ourselves but upon Natalie's parents. Outside we heard the night songs rising up from the grass and then, shrilly, a siren slicing the night somewhere in the distance.

"Oh great," Natalie whispered. "Rotten timing."

It came closer, alarmingly close, then stopped. Whatever it was—ambulance, fire truck, police—it must have turned down one of the country roads just beyond Seaton and disappeared.

The quiet settled over us again. Finally, after what seemed a very long time—in reality it was only a few minutes—Mr. Primrose's snores signaled the all clear.

"Do you think your mom's asleep too?" I asked.

"Yeah. She's always out cold as soon as her head hits the pillow."

"What if she's not, and she catches us?"

Natalie threw back the covers and sat up. "Don't worry. Let's just go," she said.

I followed her. Down the stairs, out the side door, along

the street to the valley where the daisies would soon be in bloom. As yet, though by the calendar it was spring, we were still riding the coattail of winter, and the chill in the air was enough to turn our breath to fog. We zipped up the jackets we had grabbed on the way out and thrust our hands deep into the pockets as we hurried through the valley and up to the center of campus.

The night was lighted by a dazzling array of stars and a thick slice of moon. I hung my head back as I walked and drank in the beauty of it. And I shivered, not so much against the cold as with the thrill of being somewhere I wasn't supposed to be, seeing something I wasn't supposed to see, which made it all the more enchanting.

I must have stopped a moment because the next thing I realized Natalie was pulling on my sleeve and pointing toward a twirling light coming from the parking lot beyond Cedar Hall.

"What in the world—" she began, and then the light moved down the drive, a siren jolted our flesh, and the ambulance we thought had disappeared somewhere in rural Delaware was right there ahead of us. Its taillights cut a blurry red line through campus, then finally disappeared at the curve in front of Pine Glen. We heard the ambulance turn out onto the highway, becoming nothing but a siren tearing down Route 41 toward Wilmington.

Natalie and I looked at each other and started to run. We didn't know why we were running or what we would come to at the end, but we ran toward Mr. Dutton's cabin because we knew the boys would be there. And they were. We spotted them outside on the strip of grass between the cabin and the path, fidgeting amidst a murmuring crowd of cops and faculty members. Someone must have summoned Mildred Bidney, who lived across campus in Pratt Lodge, because she stood there with a scarf on her head that scarcely concealed the sponge rollers underneath. She wore a long wool coat that wasn't quite as long as the nightgown it covered and a pair of rubber-soled house shoes. Stan Buckley was there also, presumably awakened when the ambulance passed Pine Glen on its way into campus. He and Clarence Fosset of Cabin 2 both stood shivering in slacks and V-necked undershirts; Mr. Fosset lit a cigarette and, holding it between his lips, momentarily curled his palms around the burning tip for warmth.

Cabin 1 was dimly lighted, but we could see people moving around inside. Every once in a while there was a small burst of light, like the flash of a camera. As Natalie and I approached the scene, the grown-ups greeted us with expressions of shock and surprise. The thought of being punished might have crossed our minds, but our fear and curiosity overrode it.

"Girls, what are you doing here?" Mrs. Bidney asked angrily.

Natalie responded with another question. "What happened?" The panic in her voice was palpable.

No one answered. Mrs. Bidney and the cops exchanged glances.

Ken's face was ashen; I could see that, even in the dim glow cast from the policemen's flashlights. He clutched his stomach as though he were ill. Ray, to my astonishment, was crying. Not huge sobs, just quiet tears that he brushed away with the back of one hand. My heart stopped in my chest, and I couldn't get my lungs to take in air. I didn't yet know what had happened, but I knew it had to do with Theodore

Dutton, and that it was something terrible.

At long last Stan Buckley broke the silence. "Mr. Dutton has been taken to the hospital, girls."

"But why?" Natalie's voice was shrill now and demanding. She turned to Ken. "Tell me what happened."

"Girls, you'll have to step aside." The policeman who spoke had a deep and lilting voice, full of authority. "We're taking the boys to the station for questioning."

"Are they under arrest?"

I thought of their practical joke, of the escaped murderer, of their intent to scare Mr. Dutton, and I wondered, *What on earth have they done?*

Mrs. Bidney looked at us with wild eyes. She was obviously afraid of what was unfolding here. "Natalie, Beth, do your parents know where you are?"

"She's staying with me," Natalie answered dumbly.

"You shouldn't be out here. We'll need to contact your parents—"

"I'll take care of the girls," Mr. Buckley interrupted. "Let's just let these officers finish their business."

Mrs. Bidney looked sharply at Mr. Buckley, then back at Natalie and me. She took a step toward us, peering at us through her glasses. "Mr. Dutton is ill. He's been taken to the hospital. Do you understand?"

Not understanding at all, we both nodded. I gazed at Ray then, my face surely rife with terror and questions, but he only shook his head as if to say, *Don't ask.*

Ken, though, sent a hand signal to Natalie which I easily intercepted. He made a knife of one index finger and sliced it back and forth over the opposite wrist.

Natalie gasped loudly. I wanted to reach out and grab Ken

by the collar and demand, *What are you saying? What do you mean?* but I discovered that my bones were locked and my muscles frozen. More than that, I sensed that if I did move, it would be into a world that I wanted desperately not to enter. In the next moment I became aware that the policemen and the boys were walking away toward a tangle of squad cars parked pell-mell in the lot, Mildred Bidney was stepping across campus with Mr. Fosset, and Mr. Buckley was still there with Natalie and me, saying something absurd, something like, "Don't worry, girls. He's going to be all right. I suggest you run on home now." But I couldn't hear him anymore because Natalie was screaming, and then her knees buckled and she slumped to the damp ground. She rolled up into a tight ball with her forehead pressed to the grass, and when I knelt and put my arms around her, I could feel each relentless shiver as she wept.

That was the instant when life as I knew it came to an end. The stars seemed to tumble right out of the sky and my childhood shattered like glass, and something inside of me crept off on wounded feet to a small dark place, a crevice sealed over like a tomb.

CHAPTER 27

Commander Pettingill got up at Monday morning assembly and told us Mr. Dutton had suffered a heart attack. "But he's receiving the best possible care at Wilmington General, and we're sure he'll recuperate in due time," Commander said. "We plan to keep you updated as we receive more news ourselves."

Until that moment I would never have believed that adults might actually lie to you. As Commander stood at the podium smiling down his assurances upon us, Raymond Schmidt, Ken Cunningham, Natalie Primrose, and I sat with lips pressed firmly into taut lines. We had been expecting this announcement, but I'd been hoping against hope that we'd be told the truth. Now I knew that wasn't going to happen.

The fact was that Theodore Dutton was a suicide.

I knew that because the people who knew the truth had told me so. The previous afternoon, on Sunday, Natalie and I met Ray and Ken in the valley.

"Dutton killed himself," Ken said flatly, his hands hanging over his knees like deflated balloons. A chilly breeze blew over the steps of the chapel where we'd agreed to meet, and where we now sat.

"Are you sure he's dead?" I asked. "I mean, completely sure?"

Ray nodded. "No one can lose that much blood and not be dead."

Natalie started to weep, and Ken put an arm around her

shoulder. I sat motionless a moment, trying to take it in. I'd been trying to take it in for the better part of two days, but it was too big to fit into my heart all at once, so I was taking it in piece by little piece. Theodore Dutton had sliced his wrist open. Theodore Dutton was dead. Theodore Dutton was not coming back.

I began to cry silently, tears spilling over and running down my cheeks. Ray took my hand in his, squeezing it firmly. I asked in a near whisper, "What happened Friday night before we got there?"

They had snuck up quietly on the cabin, Ray told us. It was dark inside. They peered in all the windows but couldn't see much. It looked like maybe Dutton was under a pile of blankets on the bed, but he didn't wake up when they tapped on the window. "Let's try the front door," Ken had said. So they did. It was unlocked. This was going to be good. They were going to scare the pants off Mr. Dutton.

They entered the cabin smiling, trying not to laugh out loud. Served him right not to lock his door when there was a murderer on the loose. It took them only a moment to find him. But he wasn't where they thought he was. He wasn't in the bed. He was on the bathroom floor, curled up in a circle of blood. His left wrist was sliced open like a piece of fruit. His right hand still clung loosely to a razor blade. There was more blood on the floor than would fill the empty Jack Daniels bottle at Mr. Dutton's feet.

"No way he could have survived that," Ray concluded.

"Did you feel for a pulse?" I asked.

Ray shook his head. "We didn't touch him. We just called the police."

"Could you tell if he was breathing?"

He looked down at the ground. "I didn't wait long enough to notice. I ran for the phone. After that, I didn't go back into the bathroom."

I turned to Ken.

"Did you, Ken?"

"Did I what?"

"Did you go back in and notice if he was breathing?"

He shook his head, dropped his eyes just as Ray had done. "Naw, I couldn't. I—"

Ken tightened his grip on Natalie, who was crying into the sleeves of her jacket.

No one spoke for a long time.

Then Ray said, "Listen, we can never tell anybody any of this."

"Not even our parents?" I asked.

"No."

Natalie lifted her head, wiped her eyes on her sleeve. "What about Janie and Artie?"

"Not even them."

"Why not?"

Ray looked at me, then away. Referring to his great uncle, Commander Pettingill, he said, "Uncle John is going to tell everyone on Monday that Mr. Dutton had a heart attack."

"How do you know that?" I demanded.

"Just a minute. There's more," Ray said. "They're going to tell everyone he's still alive."

"What?" I was dumbstruck.

Ray and Ken exchanged a glance then. Ken nodded. Ray sighed.

"Uncle John picked us up at the police station Friday night," he explained. "Well, by then it was pretty much

Saturday morning. Apparently Bidney called him and told him what was going on. So he picked us up and drove us back to campus. We'd already spent half the night telling a bunch of cops what we saw in Dutton's cabin. We had to keep telling the same story over and over till we felt like we were about to go crazy. So then Uncle John comes and gets us, and he takes us back to the dorm and tells us to get a few hours' sleep because at ten o'clock he wanted us to meet him in his office. So by ten o'clock we were up, and we went to his office. Bidney was there and some other people—Buckley and Fosset and some bigwigs on the board of directors for the school. The first thing they told us was that if we hadn't stumbled across Dutton when we did, he'd be dead."

"But he is dead!" I interrupted.

Ken said, "Yeah, but they don't want anybody to know that."

"Why not?"

"Well, obviously, Beth," Ray answered, "they don't want anyone to know Dutton committed suicide."

"But why not?" I asked again.

Ray shook his head and took a deep breath. "I don't know. I don't know." The words were almost a moan. "Maybe they want to protect his family—"

"Come on, Ray," Ken said, "you know the real reason. They don't want a suicide on campus becoming public news. I mean, think of how it would make the school look. Right? If parents learn a teacher killed himself, they're going to start getting bad feelings about Seaton. They might start pulling their kids out—"

"I can't believe that," I interrupted.

"Think about it, Beth," Ken went on. "Seaton's always

been holding on by a shoestring. We don't get to dip into public funds, remember? The school is at the mercy of parents willing to shell out tuition money. Something like a suicide might make parents panic. . . ." He seemed to want to say more, but he stopped and shook his head.

I felt my jaw tighten. "So how are they going to hide it? How are they going to keep it out of the papers?"

Ray said, "Think of who's on the board of directors for the school, Beth. Do you think they don't have all sorts of connections?"

I knew who he was talking about. Members of wealthy Delaware families who had practically built the state's economy with their own hands. People with clout. People who could pull strings and watch other people dance.

No one was ever going to know that Theodore Dutton had committed suicide on the campus of Seaton Preparatory School.

Both Natalie and I had stopped crying. We were angry now and mystified. Natalie asked, "Doesn't Bidney know— doesn't anyone know that Beth and I know what happened?"

Ray shook his head. "They think you don't know. Even though you were there—well, Mr. Dutton was already gone by then. You didn't see him yourself, and nobody told you. And . . ." Ray paused. His mouth became a small tight line.

"What, Ray?" I asked.

"The second thing they told us Saturday morning is that we were never to tell anyone that Dutton slit his wrist. They let us know it would be in our own best interest to stay quiet."

"And you agreed?"

Ray dropped his eyes to the ground and nodded. "If they

knew we were talking to you right now, we'd be expelled for sure."

"I can't believe it," I whispered.

Ken looked at me with resentment in his eyes. "Believe it," he said.

"So Monday morning Uncle John is going to tell everyone Mr. Dutton had a heart attack and that he's okay. And the four of us, we have to keep our mouths shut."

"You think we should never tell anyone the truth?" I asked warily.

"From this point on," Ray said, "I think we should just stay out of it."

"It doesn't seem right."

"You've got to promise, Beth."

"Maybe Commander will change his mind. Maybe tomorrow he'll decide to tell what really happened."

But he didn't. As the upper school students filed out of assembly on Monday morning, we listened to the murmurs of the other kids talking about the heart attack. Several girls cried. Someone cracked a joke, saying working in a prison camp like Seaton had done Mr. Dutton in.

Ray grabbed my arm and pulled me down the side hall. Ken and Natalie followed. We were awkwardly quiet as a kid pushed passed us on his way to the bathroom in the silo. When the bathroom door eased shut, Ray looked at the three of us.

He opened his mouth, shut it again. He looked at the floor then back at us. Finally he said, "Another couple months and we're out of here. We just have to keep our mouths shut for a couple of months, and then we never have to think about any of this again."

He was right about one thing. We'd be graduating in a couple of months. But as for the part about never having to think about Theodore Dutton again, he was dead wrong.

CHAPTER 28

At the end of that school day I drove myself home in my 1960 Pontiac station wagon with the fins and the *Jesus is Lord* bumper sticker, just like always. And just like always, Mom was there in the kitchen already peeling potatoes for supper.

"Hi, honey," she called when I came in the door. "How was your day?"

I dropped my books in the den and stopped to pet Shadow, our rat terrier who went nuts with joy whenever anybody came home. Then I met Mom at the kitchen sink, where I kissed her cheek.

"What's for supper?" I asked, ignoring the question she had asked of me.

"Hash and eggs. Want to use the grinder for me?"

"Sure."

She made her own hash by dropping cubes of cooked beef and chunks of raw potato into the meat grinder. Turning the handle of that grinder had always been one of the coveted chores among my sisters and me, ever since we were small kids. We liked to watch the meat and potatoes come out the other end a blended mess.

I stood at the kitchen table, where the grinder was screwed temporarily onto the edge, and began dropping the ingredients in as I cranked the handle.

Mom washed her hands and wiped them dry on her apron. Then she started unloading clean dishes from the dishwasher. "Don't forget, you and Carrie have Youth Club at

155

church tonight," she remarked absently.

"I know."

"You'll want to get your homework done before you go."

"All right."

She started to hum as she lifted the dishes from the washer and into the cupboards. I recognized the song as a hymn.

"Oh, hey," she said suddenly, interrupting herself. "We got a letter from Marla today."

Marla was my older sister, in her sophomore year at Gettysburg College. "Yeah? How's she doing?"

"She got a date for the spring banquet, so I guess you could say she's doing pretty well!" Mom said cheerfully.

"Anyone we know?"

She shook her head. "A Dave Something-or-other. She says she's known him awhile, but this is the first time he's asked her out."

"That's good." I went on turning the crank.

Just then the public school bus squealed to a stop at the corner, and I knew it was dropping off my younger sister. After a moment we heard the front door open.

"Mom?"

"In the kitchen, honey."

Shadow yelped and ran to meet Carrie, then, leaping and wagging her tail, she walked with my sister down the hall to the kitchen. When Carrie saw me cranking the grinder, she said "Hey, can I finish doing that?"

I stepped away from the table. "Go ahead if you want."

In another hour Dad came home. Shadow went wild again, doing her special Daddy's Home dance on the footstool in the den. Still clutching his briefcase, Dad paused long enough to scratch Shadow's head and tell her she was a good dog. He came into the kitchen and gave Mom a kiss and patted my shoulder as I sat at the table doing homework. Then he changed his clothes and read the paper for an hour while eating a snack of crackers and cheese.

At five thirty, just like always, we sat down to dinner. Dad said grace. Mom dished out the hash and the fried eggs. Dad asked what was new, and Carrie piped up about cutting two seconds off her time at track practice, and Mom said she was probably going to break some school records before she graduated.

I didn't say anything. Shadow nudged my leg under the table, and I slipped her a little hash on the end of my finger.

"Beth's feeding Shadow again!" Carrie squealed.

Mom frowned. "Not at the table, Beth."

Dad asked for the pepper, and Mom picked up the shaker to pass it to him. Suddenly that hand-painted porcelain shaker stopped in midair, almost directly in front of my face. Mom turned to me and said, "Oh dear, Beth, how could I have forgotten?" Dad reached for the pepper, and Mom let her empty hand fall back to the table. "Darla Primrose called today and told me your English teacher had a heart attack over the weekend. She said he's over at Wilmington General. He's an awfully young fellow to have a heart attack, isn't he?"

The room fell silent. Of course I knew they would hear the news eventually. Soon everyone would know the story about Mr. Dutton. I just wasn't ready to talk about it. I stared at my plate, at the hash and eggs with the red ketchup poured out over it in neat red stripes, and I began to feel the tears press heavily against the back of my eyes. Slowly I lifted my gaze to my mother's face.

When she saw my tears, she smiled kindly and laid her

hand across my forearm. "Oh, honey," she said, "don't cry. I know how you like your English teacher so well, but—don't worry. Mrs. Primrose said he's going to be fine. She said she called Commander Pettingill as soon as she heard, and Commander told her he'd just hung up from talking with Mr. Dutton himself. Apparently he was doing much better and resting comfortably."

Liar, I thought. *He's lying.*

The tears escaped and slid down my face. I glanced at Carrie, who rolled her eyes at me.

"Good grief, Beth, you'd cry if a leaf fell off the willow tree in the backyard."

"That's enough, Carrie," Dad said. "Your sister is understandably upset."

Oh no, I thought. *No, you don't understand at all.*

I looked at Dad, then back at Mom. How I loved those two people, trusted them, needed them. "But Mr. Dutton . . ." I started, "it was . . . he . . ."

It was all there, the whole story right at the back of my tongue, but I swallowed it. I had always told my parents everything, but not this time.

"Can I be excused?" I whispered.

Mom glanced over at Dad. He nodded. "You go on, honey. And you don't have to go to church tonight if you don't feel up to it. But listen, Beth, a lot of people recover from heart attacks and do just fine. Try not to worry too much."

They had always treated me gently because I was the "sensitive one." I took things harder than most people, they said. I was born with "a thin skin over deep feelings" was how they put it. My sisters had another name for it. They said I was a crybaby. My sisters' assessment may have been more accurate, but this time I felt I had a right to my tears. I just didn't have the right to explain.

I left the table and went to my room. For the first time in my life, I wished my heart was made of stone.

CHAPTER 29

"Mr. Dutton was kind of young to have a heart attack, wasn't he, Commander?"

"Yes." Commander Pettingill cleared his throat. "It's unusual, but these things happen."

I sat in a stiff wooden chair in Commander's office on the first floor of Heath Hall. Three days had passed since his announcement about Theodore Dutton. The previous night I'd worked up the courage to call Wilmington General to see if they had a patient by that name. The person who answered the phone sounded rushed and harried and hung up directly after telling me they didn't.

So I worked up my courage again to confront Commander. I'd asked Natalie to come with me, but she refused, saying Mr. Dutton was dead and the school wasn't going to change its story, so what was the use of talking with Commander?

For whatever reason, I thought I might be able to back him into a corner, catch him in his lie, make him confess—if only to me. But after I made the comment about Mr. Dutton being too young to have a heart attack, I had no idea what else to say. Commander agreed with me, putting that topic to rest, and after that there was really nowhere else to go. I could hardly come right out and tell him I knew he was lying. He was, after all, the assistant headmaster of Seaton Preparatory School, and I, only a student. I felt weak with fear and gripped the arms of the chair to steady myself.

Commander Pettingill must have mistaken my fear for concern because he leaned forward with his hands on his desk and smiled at me kindly. "Don't worry, Beth," he said. "We're staying in touch with the doctors. Mr. Dutton is coming along nicely."

Commander had no idea at all that I was there to confront him. He thought I had come to him seeking reassurance! How to back him into that corner?

"Do you think," I began, but the words were so small I had to start over. "Do you think I could visit him in the hospital then?"

"Oh no, no." He leaned back in the large leather chair that rocked against his weight. "I'm afraid that's not possible. You see, he's been moved. He's been taken to a hospital in Pennsylvania, closer to his family."

"Oh?" What a tangled web we weave. "Do you know the name of it? The hospital?"

"Let's see." He formed a tent with his hands and laid them against his lips. He did an admirable job of frowning, as though deep in thought. "St. John's? No, that's not it. It's on the tip of my tongue but . . . hmm. Goodness, what's become of my memory?"

I waited. His memory refused to cooperate.

After a moment, the old man shrugged. "Well, it'll come to me. Is there anything else, dear?"

I managed to hold his gaze momentarily before shaking my head and rising from the chair. "No. I guess that's it."

"Well," he said, rising as well, "I know this unfortunate event has come as a shock to you, but try not to let it interfere with your schoolwork." He gave me a small obsequious smile.

I had always liked Commander Pettingill, had always had

the greatest respect for him. Until now.

I didn't say good-bye. I walked toward the door, stone-faced.

When I had almost reached the threshold, Commander said, "Oh, Beth?"

Turning back, I lifted my chin slightly, defiantly.

"Perhaps you'd like to send Mr. Dutton a card at his parents' address? You know, a little get-well card or something?"

What was he saying? I waited, trying to comprehend as he went on. "I have the address here somewhere. What did I do with it?" Shuffling some papers on his desk, he came up at last with a small scrap bearing an address. "Yes, here it is. Let me copy it for you." He did and handed me the paper. "I'm sure he'd enjoy hearing from you."

I felt my eyes narrow almost to slits. "This is his parents' address?"

"Yes. I'm sure they'll get your letter to him if you'd care to write. At any rate, he should be out of the hospital soon and recuperating at his parents' home."

I looked at the address scribbled on the paper, and for one brief instant wondered whether it was a real place or a spontaneous fabrication on the part of Commander Pettingill. By now I wouldn't put it past him.

I moved my gaze to Commander's face again. "Okay," I said, feeling as though I was accepting some sort of challenge. "I'll write to him. Thanks."

That afternoon I drove to Eckerd's drugstore and picked out a get-well card. I told Mr. Dutton we all missed him and hoped he'd be better soon. I asked him to please write and let us know how he was, and I put my address inside the card as well as on the outside of the envelope.

The card went out in the next day's mail.

For a week or so I actually entertained the idea that I might hear back from Theodore Dutton. But I suppose that was only a morbid sort of wishful thinking, and in the end I wasn't too surprised that I never got a response.

CHAPTER 30

And so we moved forward with our lives, simply because there was nothing else to be done. I left Delaware, went to college, immersed myself in my career, and sometimes, for long stretches, I was able to forget. But never completely. It always came back, often as sorrow, other times as guilt or regret or anger. The ghost that haunted me took many forms, but I always knew where it came from.

When Jack Farrell called me in the spring of 2003 and offered me the teaching job at Seaton, I thanked him and asked him for a few days to think it over. But I knew right away I would accept it. I was ready for a change, ready to leave Maryland, and perhaps most of all, ready to make a clean break with my unwilling-to-commit boyfriend, Nick Watson. Returning to my hometown, my own alma mater, to teach was an opportunity that came out of nowhere just when I needed to go somewhere other than where I was.

By mid-October I was certain I had made the right decision. If not completely happy, I was at least content. I enjoyed the students, loved living in Pine Glen, was glad to have rekindled my friendship with Natalie after so many years apart. She and I talked on the phone, exchanged e-mails, and sometimes she'd come over to sit and chat or walk around the campus.

On the Sunday after I had dinner with Ray, Natalie and I found ourselves strolling over the hills of Seaton and through the patches of apple trees, past Heath Hall and Anderson Hall and the headmaster's house and Webb Hall, where the lower school met, down and around the chapel in the valley and back again. The day was warm with sunshine and autumn colors both, one of those Indian summer days that never fails to call you outdoors.

As we circled around the chapel and back toward the footbridge, Natalie got around to asking what I knew was on her mind. "So Ray took you to the Lincolnshire last night, huh?"

"Yes, believe it or not."

"Pretty fancy."

"Yeah, and he drives a Lexus too."

She looked at me sideways. "I don't mean wealthy fancy. I mean romantic fancy."

"Oh." I shrugged. "Well, it wasn't like that. I mean, it wasn't a date really."

"Oh? Then what would you call it?"

"Just a couple of old friends catching up on their lives."

"Right, Beth. And I'm Secretary of State Condoleezza Rice."

"Come on, Natalie. You know it's not like that."

"Are you kidding? It's perfect. You come back, run into your old high school sweetheart at homecoming, he happens to be divorced, you get back together, and live happily ever after."

I laughed out loud, hoping it sounded sincere. "I don't think so, Natalie."

"Why not? Don't you want to get married?"

"Well, yes, I suppose—"

"So there you go. Who better than Ray?"

"Ray?"

"Of course! He wouldn't have asked you out if he weren't interested."

"I don't know—"

"Listen. You two have known each other all your lives, you were crazy about each other in high school, he needs a wife, and you want a husband. It's a fairy tale in the making."

"You always were a dreamer, Nat."

She stopped and looked at me. "You never dreamed enough, Beth. Why don't you try to think a little positively here, like maybe it *could* happen? Or what? Don't you like him?"

"Sure, I like him." I shrugged nonchalantly as we walked together up the hill toward the circular drive at the center of campus. "He's a great guy. But that doesn't mean we're meant to be together."

Natalie sighed. "Honestly, Beth. If I didn't know better, I'd say you're still single because you never really wanted to get married."

"That's not true," I countered, but even as I said it, something flinched inside of me. "I've always wanted to get married. I just never found the right one."

"Uh-huh."

Her tone told me she wasn't convinced.

"So if he asks you out again, will you go?"

"Sure. Why not?"

"Why do you try so hard to pretend like you're not thrilled?"

"I'm not a kid anymore, Nat. As the saying goes, I've been around the block a few times."

"Yeah, and now you're back here where you belong, so maybe things will finally work out for you."

"Maybe."

"Oh, Beth." Another huge sigh.

We walked past Cedar Hall, and I followed Natalie's lead when she turned up the path toward the spot where the faculty cabins had been. I was surprised when she stopped in front of Cabin 1. No longer used for faculty housing, it was now a storage shed for the middle school's gardening tools. Cabin 2 had been demolished somewhere along the way, the land turned into a vegetable garden that the students planted and tended each spring as part of the middle school curriculum.

I hadn't been this close to Cabin 1 since returning to Seaton two months earlier. I had purposely avoided it. Now Natalie said, "You know, I've been thinking about Theodore Dutton since you mentioned him."

"You have?"

She nodded.

"I thought you told me to just forget about him."

"I did. But then I became curious. Did you ever Google him?"

"No."

"Well, I did."

I froze. "What'd you find out?"

She was looking at the cabin rather than at me. She frowned when she said, "Not much. Nothing, really. There are some Duttons out there, but nobody that matches our Theodore."

No. Of course not. Because he wasn't out there to be found, was he? I said, "Well, I guess it doesn't really matter."

"No, it really doesn't. He's been dead a long time. What else is there to know?"

My gaze followed Natalie's toward the cabin. I almost shivered in spite of the sun. "I've sometimes wondered whether he might have survived the suicide attempt. I mean, Commander and the others were so adamant that he was alive."

"Of course they were. To protect the school. Ray and Ken saw the man, and he was dead." She lifted her shoulders, let them drop. "Hard to discount the testimony of eyewitnesses."

I nodded. "But it was dark, you know. And they never touched him to see if he was breathing or had a pulse."

"They said no one could survive after losing as much blood as he did."

"I know. I remember."

"But—" she turned to me and offered a sad smile—"what would you do, anyway, if you found out he was alive?"

I didn't have to think about that for long. "I'd ask him why he did it."

"As if he would tell you," she said. "And anyway, I can't see you asking him. It'd take a lot of nerve, you know, asking somebody a question like that."

"But haven't you ever wondered why?"

"Sure. I wondered for a long time."

"How did you stop?"

She took a breath, thinking. "It wasn't any conscious thing. I got married, had kids. I ran out of time for pondering mysteries like some guy we once knew who tried to kill himself. Who *did* kill himself."

"Yeah, I suppose." I paused a moment. "You know, he didn't care what it might do to us."

"No." She looked at me sharply then and shook her head. "No, he didn't. And maybe that was part of it too, for me. He

169

didn't care about us, so I stopped caring about him."

We started to walk away then, back down the path running beside Cedar Hall. "Did you ever tell anyone? That it was actually suicide, I mean?"

"No. Did you?"

"No."

She shook her head again. "I can still remember Commander getting up at assembly that morning and telling everyone it was a heart attack."

"I'll never forget it."

"It was a rotten thing to do to a bunch of kids, all the way around."

"Yes, it really was."

"But you know what?"

"What?" I asked.

"Welcome to the world, baby Jane."

I nodded, letting out a small laugh. "Yeah. And you wonder why I'm not more of a dreamer."

We exchanged a rueful smile, then walked in silence back to Pine Glen.

CHAPTER 31

"Ray, there's something I've been meaning to ask you."

Ray lifted his eyes at me over the rim of the Starbucks cup. He drank slowly before lowering the mocha latte.

Though we had talked on the phone several times, I hadn't seen Ray since we'd gone to the Lincolnshire almost two weeks earlier. So when he called me from the hospital that evening and asked me to meet him for coffee at the Starbucks on Kirkwood Highway, I willingly left my students' essays behind and hopped in the car.

The thought of spilling what was on my mind was somewhat unnerving. For one thing, it felt as though I was entering territory I had no right to enter. For another thing, Ray looked tired and didn't appear as though he would want to go there either. But it had been gnawing on me for these last couple of weeks, and it was gnawing on me right now. And so, whether the hour was right or wrong, I blurted it out.

"I'm just wondering why you wear a wedding ring if you're not married."

Ray looked at the ring with eyebrows raised, as though he was surprised to find it circling his finger. Then he smiled. "I mostly wear it at work. I don't want to appear to my patients to be the eligible doctor, if you know what I mean. It just makes life easier."

Oh. So that was all. The ring wasn't pasted to his finger with sentimental attachment.

Then Ray added. "The staff knows, of course, that I'm

divorced. But wearing a ring around the hospital isn't all that uncommon. I'm not the only single doctor who wears one."

As I nodded, I found I had another question, which I couldn't help asking. "Do you miss her, Ray?"

"Brenda?"

I nodded again.

"For a long time I did. But I don't anymore."

"Do you know where she is?"

"Richmond, I think. She moves around a lot."

"She's remarried?"

"Not that I know of. Last I heard she wasn't."

"Does she ever see the kids?"

A pained expression settled over Ray's face. "No. I think I mentioned before that she calls them sometimes. On their birthdays. Occasionally at Christmas. They don't really want to talk to her. Ben, of course, doesn't even know who she is. It just confuses him when she calls." He took a sip of coffee and waved a hand. "But enough about her. What about you? How's life at Seaton?"

"Good," I said. "We have a bunch of smart kids there; they keep me on my toes."

He smiled. "No troublemakers sneaking off campus to eat at Burger King, are there?"

I chuckled. "Not that I know of." Then I remembered, somberly, the foursome who had left campus shortly after the start of the school year. "Last month, though, we had four students go out drinking and driving over by Hoopes. They ended up going off the road and running into a tree."

"Anyone killed?" Ray asked.

"No, thankfully. They were all injured, the driver pretty badly, but they're on the mend now. They were expelled from

Seaton even though one of the boys had been a student there since first grade. I thought they might just be suspended, but the principal is being tough about it. I think he wants to let the students know the school isn't going to tolerate drinking."

Ray shook his head slowly from side to side. "He's doing the right thing. I've seen too many times what drinking and driving can do."

"I'm sure you have."

"Kids think they're immortal."

"Yes, they do. Unfortunately."

"When we were kids, at least I knew better than to get behind the wheel when I'd been drinking."

I tried to laugh, but it came out sounding like a gasp. "What are you talking about, Ray? We never drank when we were kids."

He hid behind the coffee cup a moment, then lowered it and looked up at me. "Well, *you* never did."

I frowned and shook my head. Maybe I shouldn't have been surprised, but I was. Never once had I seen Ray Schmidt take a drink of anything stronger than Dr. Pepper.

"You mean in college, right?"

"No, I mean in high school."

"Ray, I had no idea you ever drank in high school."

"I didn't very often. Never until senior year, in fact, when I lived in the dorm."

The boarding students had always had a reputation for dabbling in anything off-limits. Pot, beer, even acid wasn't hard to find in the dorms. But Ray?

"Well," I conceded, "I guess it's kind of hard to avoid it when it's going on all around you. I know the dorms could be pretty wild."

Ray shook his head. "It wasn't the guys in the dorms I drank with, Beth. No—" he laughed lightly—"it wasn't them."

"Well, who then, Ray?"

"You really can't guess?"

"No."

"It was Dutton. Remember him?"

"Dutton?"

"Yeah. The guy was crazy."

"Mr. Dutton? Our English teacher?"

Ray laughed again, a small derisive laugh. "Yeah. Good role model, huh? It's pretty unbelievable, when you think about it now. First this guy has Ken and me drinking with him in his cabin, and then, two months before school's out, he kills himself right there on campus. Here we all thought he was such a great guy, and it turns out he was nothing but some crazy jerk."

I didn't know how to respond. Not only could I scarcely believe we were talking about Theodore Dutton, but I certainly couldn't imagine Ray throwing back beers in Cabin 1. I must have been sitting there slack-jawed because Ray looked at me and said, "Well, you don't have to look quite so surprised."

"I *am* surprised," I confessed. "I never saw you drinking with Mr. Dutton."

"That's because we never drank in front of you. I—well, face it, Beth, you were about as straitlaced as they come. Not that there was anything wrong with that. I mean, I liked that about you. And I did like you, Beth. I was crazy about you. You know that."

He looked at me long and hard. I dropped my eyes, suddenly uneasy.

"I knew you wouldn't approve of my drinking," he went on. "So Dutton, Ken, and I—we passed the beer around only when you girls weren't there."

"He gave you beer?"

"Sure, unless he had already moved on to something stronger by the time we got to the cabin. Jim Beam. Jack Daniels. Whatever. Listen, at first I almost took a pass, but—" he stopped and shrugged his shoulders—"I thought, why not join them? I liked Dutton and I wanted him to like me. You know how it is when you're a kid. And Ken—he could already drink like a fish."

My mind flashed back to homecoming. Natalie had fled the dance floor after only a couple of dances because Ken, she said, was DUI—Dancing Under the Influence. *It was not a pretty sight*" was how she put it. But I wasn't interested in talking about Ken right now.

"So did you go to Dutton's cabin often?" I asked. "I mean, without Natalie and me?"

"I guess. Ken and I were right there on campus, you know, living in the dorm. When study hall was over at nine o'clock, we'd just mosey on over there, and Dutton would be glad to see us. He wasn't a man who liked to drink alone. But listen, Beth, it's not as bad as you think. We primarily went there to visit with the guy. I mean, we liked him. We liked talking with him. We didn't always end up drinking. And if we did have something to drink, it was one or two beers, and that was it. Only a couple of times did Ken and I get really plastered."

"And what about Dutton?"

"Well, of course he could drink us under the table. I'm talking sometimes hand over fist. Yeah, he was probably already an alcoholic."

"I had no idea."

"No, probably not. But don't you remember him coming to class with a hangover?"

"No. I don't remember anything like that at all."

"You know, his eyes all bloodshot and his face unshaved and a look that told you he had a pounding headache."

"I don't remember," I said again.

Ray laughed. How he could think any of this was funny, I couldn't imagine. "Yeah, well, you and Natalie were so infatuated with the guy, he could do no wrong in your eyes."

"I wasn't infatuated with Mr. Dutton."

"No?" He looked amused.

"No."

"Listen, Beth. I could tell. . . . I always knew. With Dutton there, I couldn't compete. None of us guys had a chance."

"Ray, that isn't true!"

He raised his coffee to his lips, took a long drink, lowered the cup. He said nothing.

I looked at the drink in my hands. It was only half gone, but my stomach was turning. I asked quietly, "So he was an alcoholic?"

"That's my best guess now, though I never thought about it at the time."

"Maybe he was dealing with something like posttraumatic stress syndrome, since he'd been in Vietnam."

"Yeah, probably that too."

"Well, then, don't you think maybe you should have told somebody? About his drinking?"

"What? Get Dutton fired while at the same time getting Ken and myself in deep trouble?"

"But didn't it seem to you like Dutton needed help?"

Ray shrugged. "I was seventeen, eighteen years old. I sure didn't know then what I know now. I figured he was pretty much like any other guy who liked to drink, which was most every guy I knew. He occasionally came to class with a hangover—so what? You remember Mr. Keaton and his wife, the dorm parents? Where do you think the guys in my dorm got their booze?"

"From the Keatons?"

Ray nodded. "Just the same way they got their pot from the Buckleys, who grew their own stuff."

"I knew that about the Buckleys, but I had no idea about the Keatons. I can't believe it, Ray."

"Believe it. It was a whole different world when you were living in the dorms. As a day student, you missed all that stuff. At least it was a whole lot easier for you to steer clear of it. I won't say you wore rose-colored glasses, but you lived in . . . well, you lived in such a pretty world, Beth."

I felt suddenly defensive. "Was that my fault?"

"Your fault?" He smiled kindly, shook his head. "Not at all. You were lucky."

"But if it wasn't real . . ."

"Your world? Oh no. It was real. You were just sheltered from some of the uglier things."

"You're saying I was naïve."

He shrugged. "We were all naïve to one extent or another. And that's exactly how it should be. Listen, I wish my kids were growing up the way you and I did, in a good home with both a father and a mother. I mean, I do the best I can, and I think they have a good home, but a series of au pairs can't substitute for a mother. I know it's affected my kids. So there's nothing wrong with being sheltered at first, having a taste of what's really good before life starts dishing out the bad. That'll come soon enough."

"Yes." I sighed heavily. "And you know, Ray, I think Dutton's suicide was the first really bad thing ever to happen to me."

He nodded. "We were blindsided. Believe me, if I'd suspected the guy was suicidal, I'd have done something. But how could I have known? Ken and I—we were his drinking buddies, not his confidants. And drinking made Dutton happy, not maudlin. We did it for the laughs. I never thought he'd try to do himself in. Never."

We sat in silence for a time while the coffee shop bustled with people coming and going. My nausea increased, and I longed for fresh air, but I didn't move. At length I said, "Well, I don't know what to say."

"What's to say?" Ray shrugged. "It's all water under the bridge. I don't even know why I started talking about all that. I sure didn't ask you to meet me here so we could talk about some loser we once knew. Actually, I wanted to ask you if you might come with me to a fund-raiser at the hospital Saturday night. These events are a real bore, but it'd be nice to have you there. Think you can come?"

Still stunned by Ray's revelation, I nevertheless managed to smile and nod my acceptance of Ray's invitation.

CHAPTER 32

There was that time in mid-October of 1976 when Theodore Dutton said it was simply too glorious a day to be inside, so he led us like the Pied Piper from Heath Hall to Chapel Valley where we found a bit of shade and laid ourselves down in the grass. Mr. Dutton gave no lecture, asked no questions, expected no response. He simply tucked his hands beneath his head and allowed one poem and then another to roll easily off his tongue until I felt that this unimaginable moment was itself a poem, a snatch of living verse. The images were those of blue sky, warm sun, birdsong, the earthy smell of dirt and clover, and our teacher's strong and reassuring voice.

"Now, I want you to consider this, friends," he said at length. "I want you to consider the improbability of your being here. I mean, think of the centuries of accidents and coincidences that led to your being born. Just the right people had to meet and mate and give rise to other people who gave rise to you. Go back just one generation and consider what would have happened if your parents hadn't met, if they'd married someone else or hadn't married at all. Just one misstep in centuries of generations, and everything would be different. That's enough to make you realize you're lucky to be alive. You made it into the world, every one of you, and that means you're a winner. I hope you savor every minute of your lives while you're here. Now breathe in. Do you feel the air in your lungs? Do you feel that? You're alive, and the world is beautiful, and it all belongs to you."

After dazzling us with his philosophizing, Mr. Dutton fell silent, and no one dared to move. There we were, all of us lying in the field, simply feeling what it was to be alive upon the earth. We didn't have to prove ourselves good enough to be there; we simply had to *be,* and that in itself was enough. To my adolescent soul, it was almost achingly beautiful.

I thought that if Virginia Woolf could have somehow been there with us, she would have exclaimed, *Oh,* this *is it! This is what I have been looking for,* because I felt myself to be held not by the world at all but by God. I was resting in the palm of God's hand, and Theodore Dutton was the priest who brought me there.

I think that's why I loved him. He was the first person to understand and share my appreciation for beauty. He was himself aware of the sacredness of everyday life. Even though he didn't believe in God, I still thought of him as one who could lead us to the altar of truth.

I was a child and unaware of the danger of lesser gods.

When Ray told me who Theodore Dutton really was, even then it was hard to let go of the image of the man lying in the valley, his hands beneath his head, his face to the sun. He was the one who made us believe that life was good, that *we ourselves* were good. He was the one who made me feel unafraid and satisfied in who I was. He seemed at the time to be the one with all the answers. Whoever would have thought he would leave me with so many questions?

CHAPTER 33

The last evening of October 2003 I wasn't really expecting any trick-or-treaters to stop by Pine Glen, but I had a bowl of Hershey miniatures ready just in case. Halloween happened to fall on a Friday this year, and the upper school students were enjoying a costume party in Hawthorne Gymnasium. Pizza and punch, dancing and games, plenty of chaperones. It was scheduled to go on no later than eleven o'clock, at which time day students would have to clear off campus and boarders would be required to return to their dorms.

When my doorbell rang at five minutes after nine, I figured a few stray students had come around looking for a handout. I carried the candy bowl to the door, ready to treat whoever was there. But standing on the stoop was one lone student, dressed in her signature denim jacket and jeans.

"So who are you supposed to be?" I asked.

"Satchel Queen."

"Well, that's creative."

She shrugged. "Once I dressed up like Marilyn Monroe for Halloween. I figured someday some kid might dress up like me. I just beat her to it."

"You've got a point. Want some chocolate?" I held out the bowl to her.

"No, thanks," Satchel said. "You don't have any dried mango, do you?"

"Sorry, I don't." I knew Satchel liked dried mango, but I kept forgetting to buy some when I went to the store.

"Can I come in for a while?"

"Sure. But wouldn't you rather be at the party?"

"Not really."

"Well, come on in then."

We went to the living room and took our usual places. She leaned back into the cushions of the wing chair and propped her feet up on the footstool. I sat across from her on the couch and settled the candy bowl on the side table.

"So you weren't having a good time at the party?" I asked.

"It was lame."

Satchel was a girl who didn't enjoy socializing, I'd begun to realize. She was a loner, though I wasn't sure whether her reclusive tendency was an inborn need for solitude or a learned survival mechanism. Her only real pleasure seemed to come from books and, oddly enough, from visiting me.

"That's too bad," I said. "It sounded like it'd be fun."

"Well, the pizza was a nice change of pace from cafeteria food. But the band . . ." She smirked and shook her head. "And the only person who would talk to me was Tess, and that was only in between dances. Then again, I'm not exactly Miss Popularity, you know."

"Hmm . . . So where's Tess now?"

"Still dancing with Marty, probably."

"Marty?"

"Marty Higgins. They've got a thing going, you know?"

"They're dating?"

"Yeah, I guess you could put it that way."

"Oh, I didn't know."

"Yeah, well, it just happened tonight. He came as Elvis and she came as Dolly Parton, and bingo—next thing you know they're singing the blues together."

I laughed out loud.

Satchel didn't join me.

After a moment she said sullenly, "It seems to be going around, doesn't it?"

"What do you mean?"

"I mean, this pairing up thing."

"Oh?"

"Yeah, I saw you leave campus last Saturday with that dude in the Lexus."

I nodded. "That was Ray," I said. "I told you about him. Remember?"

"Yeah, I remember."

Silence.

"So?" I asked.

"So are you dating him?"

"It seems you asked me that before."

"Yeah, and you said you weren't. You said you were just going out to catch up on the news. But then you went out again. So what? You didn't have enough time to catch up the first time?"

It was an odd question, and I didn't know how to respond. On top of that I suddenly felt as though I were being inter- rogated, and I wasn't sure why Satchel thought I owed her an explanation for something I had done.

"Is this something you've been brooding about all week?" I asked.

"Sort of."

"Why didn't you ask me earlier?"

"I don't know."

"Because if you had," I said, "I would have told you that I went with Ray to a fund-raiser at the hospital where he works." I shrugged nonchalantly, then added, "He warned me it would be a bore, and it was. He had to spend most of the evening talking up the hospital to the men with the wallets. I don't suppose he and I exchanged a dozen words. There was a great buffet line, though. And half a dozen desserts to die for." I smiled and waited, hoping for some sort of positive response from Satchel. But there was none. She sat staring into the fireplace.

After an awkward moment I asked, "Is something bothering you, Satchel?"

"Yeah." She glanced at me, then looked away again. "I guess you could say that."

"Anything I can help with?"

"I don't think so."

I had to steal a moment to think, to figure out where she was coming from. I looked beyond Satchel to the front windows. In the glow of the porch light the pine trees waved their long boughs in the wind. It would be a blustery night for trick-or-treating, I thought, much like the nights my sisters and I tramped around our neighborhood in costume.

"Did you ever go trick-or-treating, Satchel?"

"Sure. My dad used to take me out when I was a kid. But I stopped doing that kind of stuff after he died. My mom never had time to take me."

I nodded, but she didn't notice. "You know, Satchel," I said, "I'll always have time for you. You don't need to worry about that."

She narrowed her eyes and looked directly at me. "That's not what I'm worried about."

"Then what is it?"

"I'm worried about you."

"Me?"

"Yeah. You know, I don't want you to fall in love or anything."

I was taken aback and momentarily speechless. Then I muttered, "But why not?"

"Because you do, then you got something to lose."

She looked angry when she said it, angry and sad and afraid. I knew exactly how she felt, and I knew that she was right, but I didn't want to tell her so. Leaning forward, I laced my fingers together over my knees. "But that's the risk we take, isn't it, Satchel?"

"It's not worth it, Miss Gunnar."

"No?"

"No."

It was Daniel Queen who taught her that, the father's final lesson, given to his daughter in the moment of his death. Actions speak louder than words; the self-inflicted deathblow outshouts life every time. In one irredeemable moment you negate every positive word you ever said.

"Do you think, then, that it's better to always be alone?" I asked.

She fidgeted, then looked at me squarely again. "Tell you the truth, Miss Gunnar, most of the time I don't know what to think."

"Well—" I took a deep breath and leaned back again. "I appreciate your concern, but you really don't need to waste any time worrying about me. I like my life the way it is right now. I'm not planning on falling in love with Ray, or anyone else, for that matter."

She gave me as skeptical a look as she had ever given me. "Yeah," she said, "well, we really don't have any say about that, do we? When you fall in love, it just happens. So let me just give you one thing to think about."

I blinked. I lifted my shoulders in baffled acquiescence. "Well, okay."

"If you don't want to get burned, don't play with fire."

As her English teacher, I almost told her that was a cliché, but then I thought better of it. There was a reason those words had become ingrained in American culture, and that was because they were good advice.

CHAPTER 34

"Beth?"

"Oh—hi, Mom!" I settled on the couch and pulled the afghan over my legs.

"For a minute it didn't sound like you."

"Sorry about that. I'm a little hoarse—just a bit of a cold. How are you?"

"I'm fine, dear. Am I interrupting anything?"

"Yes. I was cleaning the kitchen, so I'm glad you called." I heard her laugh.

"Well, I was just sitting here thinking about you, and I thought I'd get you on the phone."

"Thanks, Mom. I'm glad you did."

"Are you doing all right, other than the cold?"

"I'm doing just fine. I had lunch with Natalie yesterday."

"Oh? And how is she?"

"Fine. She's fine."

"Do her folks still live over in West Hill?"

"Oh no. They moved ages ago. I told you. Remember? They're in Florida now."

"That's right. I don't know why I forgot about that."

"Anything new with Marla and Carrie? I really owe them both a phone call. I don't know where the time goes."

"They're busy too, dear. When you're raising kids and working like they're both doing, you don't have time for much else."

"I suppose not."

We were quiet a moment, and then she got to the real reason for her call.

"How's Ray?" she asked. "Have you seen him lately?"

I sighed quietly. "Well, you know, we talk on the phone and get together for a cup of coffee occasionally."

"He's such a nice boy, Beth."

"He's hardly a boy anymore, Mom. He grew up just like I did. Remember?" I laughed, but it fell flat.

"Well, do you think the two of you might get serious?"

"You were never one to mince words, were you, Mom?"

"I just want you to be happy, Beth."

"I know, Mom. I *am* happy."

"You know what I mean."

"I know."

"I'm not trying to be pushy, dear."

"I know, Mom. You just want me to be happily married."

When she didn't respond, I said, "Tell you the truth, I don't think it's entirely out of the question. I mean, that Ray and I should end up together. I would be interested—"

"Really, dear?"

"Well, we're not serious *yet*, of course. We don't have any kind of understanding. I guess I don't really know how Ray feels—"

"Oh, I'm sure he's interested, dear."

I sighed again. "Well, time will tell, won't it?"

"I do think it's about time you settled down, sweetheart. Why you've never accepted a man's proposal when you've had so many—"

"I haven't had so many proposals, Mom!"

"There've been plenty of men who wanted to marry you. Certainly Nick did—"

"Wait a minute, Mom. Nick was the one who wouldn't commit."

"That's not what he said."

"You talked to Nick?"

"Well, it's been some time ago now—"

"Mom!"

In the background I heard my father say, "Joan, are you getting on Beth's case again?"

"No, we're just talking about—"

"I heard what you said, Joan. Listen, give me the phone a minute. Let me talk to Beth. Beth, you still there?"

"Hi, Dad. Yes, I'm here."

"Listen, how are you, honey?"

"I'm fine, Dad."

"I know you are. And I know we don't have to worry about you. You've made a good life for yourself. I'm proud of you. You know that, don't you, honey?"

"Thanks, Dad."

"Don't let your mother bother you with talk about getting married. She just wants what's best for you, like I do."

"I know, Dad. And I appreciate that."

"Listen, you're coming to see us over Christmas, aren't you? Your sisters and their families are all coming, and we sure would like for you to join us."

"I'm planning to be there."

"Well, that's good, then. I'll be looking forward to seeing you, honey."

"I can't wait to see you too, Dad."

"Hey, is work going all right? Is everyone there treating you all right?"

"It's great, Dad. I'm really happy here."

"That's my girl. Listen, I'll put your mother back on, but tell her I said you can only talk about the weather and the price of gasoline; that's all."

I laughed. "I love you, Dad."

"I love you too, sweetheart."

"And Dad?"

"Yes, sweetie?"

"Thanks for understanding."

I sensed him smiling as he handed the phone back to Mom.

CHAPTER 35

Dusk came early on those leaden and leafless autumn afternoons, making for long chilly evenings. I sometimes stayed in the office till well past six o'clock talking with Joel Sexton, who had lately been looking for any excuse to linger at work a little longer. It seems his wife was after him to sell the house and move, and Joel's reluctance brought a certain tension into the marriage.

"Yeah," he said by way of explanation, "she says she wants to get out while the house is back in one piece. She told me in no uncertain terms that if she wakes up to one more car in our living room, she's packing up, taking the kids, and going back to her folks. And she doesn't want me following her there either."

"But it's not your fault cars drive off the road and into the house."

"No. But Glenda says we should have known the house was susceptible to drunks before we ever bought it."

"How on earth could you have known that?"

Joel shrugged. "You got me. And now I'm supposed to pawn the house off on some other poor Joe without telling him the place is a death trap. I just can't do that with a clear conscience."

"No, I suppose not." I thought a moment. "It seems like there ought to be some sort of guardrail at the curve to keep cars from going over."

"You'd think so, wouldn't you? I contacted the state about

that possibility and ended up being gagged by a mile of bureaucratic red tape."

"Our tax dollars at work, huh?"

"Exactly." He scratched at his jaw before adding, "I think what I ought to do is burn the place down, make it look like an accident and collect on the insurance."

I feigned shock and dismay. "And that you can do with a clear conscience?"

We looked at each other and burst out laughing, true belly laughter that petered out to sighs.

"You know, Joel," I suggested, "maybe you should apply for faculty housing next year. Then you could rent out your house. That way you'd actually make a little income from it."

"Hey, that's not a bad idea. You're not looking to rent, are you?"

"No, afraid not."

"I didn't think so. Besides, you already know about the house's little drawback. You wouldn't want to be rear-ended while watching late night television."

"I'd rather not."

"Well, back to the old drawing board."

"I don't know, Joel. Seriously, think about campus housing for a year or two. At least it will get you out of the death trap and back onto good terms with your wife."

Joel nodded while giving me a crooked smile. "You were smart to never marry," he mumbled.

"Well, that's two against."

"Two against what?"

"Two votes I've gotten against marriage recently."

"Yeah? Anybody for it?"

I nodded. "My mother and my best friend."

"Wow, two people who are supposed to love you."

I laughed again and shook my head. "Yeah, can you believe it? I—" Before I could finish my thought, Satchel appeared in the doorway of our office and gave me a look of distress.

"Miss Gunnar, I'm glad I found you. Can I talk to you?"

"Sure." I glanced over at Joel. I knew he had an exam he wanted to finish composing before heading home, so I said to Satchel, "I'm just about to walk home. Want to walk with me?"

She nodded tearfully and stepped back into the hall to wait. A moment later we were out the door and moving against a brisk wind that slapped at our cheeks and made pinwheels of our hair. "What's the matter, Satchel?" I asked.

"I just talked to my mom."

She stopped, so I asked, "What'd she say?"

"She and Roger are leaving tomorrow for Europe, and they won't be back till close to Christmas. I told her I couldn't stay here over Thanksgiving break because they close down the dorm, and she said I can't stay in her and Roger's house alone. So I said, so what am I supposed to do? And she said I have to talk to the headmaster and see if he can find me someplace to stay. But I don't want to talk to Quinn. Tell you the truth, I'd rather spend Thanksgiving under a bridge or in a culvert or something rather than talk to that old creep. So I don't know. I guess I could talk to Farrell about it, but—"

I finally interrupted Satchel with a wave of my hand. "You don't have to talk to anyone," I said. "You can stay with me over the holiday."

"You're not going out of town?"

"Not for Thanksgiving."

"You mean I can stay at Pine Glen with you?"

"Of course. I'd be happy to have your company. We can even cook a turkey and make a pumpkin pie and enjoy a regular Thanksgiving meal together."

"Wow! Thanks, Miss Gunnar!" She looked happy and relieved and excited, and she went on looking that way until about an hour later. Satchel was still at Pine Glen when Ray called and invited me to have Thanksgiving dinner with him and his family.

"That would be wonderful, Ray! But, I wonder, well . . . one of my students will be staying with me over the break," I explained. "It's Satchel. I think I've mentioned her."

"So bring her along. The more the merrier."

And yet Satchel looked anything but merry when I told her our plans had changed, and we'd now be having turkey with the Schmidts.

CHAPTER 36

It seemed Satchel began to change her mind, though, when we arrived at the Schmidts' spacious home and were greeted at the door by Ray's nineteen-year-old son, Josh. By the time we sat down to eat, I believe she was thoroughly in favor of being there.

"More turkey, Miss Gunnar?" Josh smiled at me and passed the platter piled high with meat. He was a cordial, good-natured young man who looked startlingly like the Ray I'd known in high school. Home from Penn State for the holiday, he had prepared the entire Thanksgiving meal almost single-handedly.

I smiled in return and took the platter. "Thank you, Josh. You're a wonderful cook! Everything's delicious."

"Thanks, Miss Gunnar. I kind of enjoy it."

Josh glanced at Satchel then, and unlike the guarded teen I was used to, she dropped her eyes demurely.

"We'd have starved to death if Josh hadn't taken over in the kitchen after Mom left," Lisa said. "Dad's hopeless when it comes to cooking."

I glanced at Ray to see how he'd react to the mention of the children's mother, but he only gave Lisa an apologetic smile. "So I have one drawback as a parent. You can't be perfect at everything, you know."

"Daddy's like Mary Poppins!" Ben exclaimed. "Practically perfect in every way!"

Ray winked at Ben. "Thanks, son."

"Yeah, you got him trained just right, Dad," Lisa said.

Lisa was the same age as Satchel but a year ahead of her in school. She was as fair as Satchel was dark, as soft as Satchel was hard, yet the girls had taken easily to each other while setting the table for dinner. I hoped they might forge a friendship that would last beyond the day.

"So, like, who cooks when Josh isn't here?" Satchel asked.

"Ingrid. She's the au pair." Lisa glanced at Satchel as she ladled some gravy over a mound of potatoes. "She's here to take care of Ben, not me. But I like that she does the cooking."

Satchel looked around. "So where is she now?"

"New York," Ray said. "She's visiting with a friend over the holiday. Seems someone she knows from Sweden has a job as an au pair in Brooklyn."

"Yeah? That's where I'm from."

"Really?" Lisa asked excitedly. "What's it like? I always thought it'd be so cool to live in New York City."

"Yeah? It's all right, I guess. I don't live in Brooklyn anymore, though. Mom and Roger—that's my stepdad—they live in White Plains. They're in Europe right now, though. That's how come I'm staying with Miss Gunnar over the Thanksgiving break."

"Wow, Europe! I always wanted to go to Europe."

"You always wanted to go anywhere, Lisa," Josh chided. "Anywhere that isn't Delaware."

"Yeah." Lisa sighed. "Someday I'm going to travel around the world. What about you, Satchel? Do you want to travel?"

"Maybe." Satchel shrugged. "I guess I'd like to see some other places. But then I'm going to find a home and just stay put." She looked around the table, then picked up a bowl that was close to her right hand. "Hey, doesn't anyone want any mango?"

Her personal contribution to the dinner had been a bag of dried mango. She passed the bowl around the table, and everyone accepted an obligatory piece. Eating dried mango was an acquired taste, but it was growing on me, now that we had a supply of it in the kitchen at Pine Glen.

"So, Josh, you think Penn State is a good place to study business?" Satchel asked.

Josh had a mouthful of food, but he talked around it. "Sure. It's all right. I like it." He washed the food down with a long drink of water. "You thinking about going into business?"

"Yeah, I think I might."

"Business?" I asked.

Satchel looked at me and nodded. "Sure, why not?"

"I didn't know you were interested in business. How long have you been thinking about that?"

"About an hour now."

She and Josh exchanged a smile while Ray and I swapped a quizzical look. Your son and my . . . my what? I realized I felt possessive of Satchel in a way I had never felt with any other student. We had spent the morning at Pine Glen baking pies and preparing a cranberry salad, and for the first time I could remember, Satchel Queen and genuine laughter occupied the same space. Not that anything was funny; I think she was simply happy. And so was I. Happy to be in a warm kitchen on a chilly morning making pies. While we rolled out the dough and prepared the pumpkin filling, my mind kept drifting back to when my own mother and I kneaded bread dough side by side on the kitchen counter.

Ben piped up then, snapping me out of my reverie. "I'm going to be a doctor like Dad," he said proudly.

"You have plenty of time to think about that," his father responded.

"Yeah, and you have plenty of time to talk him out of it," Josh said. "Just like you did with me."

"I never talked you out of medicine, Josh," Ray countered. "You were never interested in it."

"Not after the hours he saw you working," Lisa agreed. "Who'd want a job that never let you come home?"

For a moment Ray looked uncomfortable. But then he smiled. "Well, that's all changed now, isn't it? I've finally got a schedule that allows me to be home at a reasonable hour."

"Fat lot of good it did me," Josh said.

I looked at him to gauge the emotions behind the words. Where he might have been angry, he was smiling.

"Dad sells his practice just in time for me to fly the coop," he went on. "But at least it's good for Ben." He looked at Ben and winked. "Right, squirt?"

Ben nodded enthusiastically. Then he added, "But I wish you didn't have to work tomorrow, Dad."

"Me too, Ben. It's just for a few hours, though. I'll be home earlier than usual, I promise."

I began to imagine what life must have been like for this family when Brenda left. Too, what it must have been like for them before Brenda left. It seems it had become motherless after years of being as good as fatherless. But I didn't want to think about that right now. It had nothing to do with now, which was far removed from all that. Now was good and worth enjoying without dredging up the past.

We finished the meal with fat slivers of pie and declared

ourselves full. Lisa, Satchel, and I then cleaned the kitchen while Ray built a fire in the fireplace. Josh set up a card table in front of the hearth where the kids later played Monopoly. Ray and I watched the game from a nearby couch, sipping hot chocolate and listening to the chatter and laughter of the kids. Ray's arm was draped casually around the back of the couch, and occasionally his hand touched my shoulder.

I felt as though I had come to rest after a long struggle. Something in my head kept telling me that this was where I was supposed to be, that I had finally made it. At midnight Ray picked up a slumbering Ben from the floor in front of the fireplace. I walked with Ray to Ben's room, where I turned down the covers on the bed. Together we tucked him in. Through it all, he didn't stir.

I thought, *I am completely satisfied. I don't have to look backward or forward anymore. I can just be.*

It was a feeling that didn't last very long.

Early the next afternoon, Satchel and I were watching a video at Pine Glen when Ray called.

"Beth, are you sitting down?"

"Yes. Why?" Had something happened to one of his children?

"Well, I'm not really sure, but . . . ." His voice trailed off. In the background I heard traffic, the sound of horns honking, someone hollering.

"Ray, where are you?"

"I'm outside the hospital. I stepped outside to call you. Listen, it could mean my job if anyone knew I was doing this."

"Doing what?"

My question was met with silence. Then, "It's about a patient, Beth."

"All right. So please just tell me what it is."

"I'm not sure," he said again, "but—you know Dutton? Our English teacher?"

In spite of Ray's warning to sit down, I jumped up abruptly from the couch. I felt something dreadful shiver through me. "Yes. Why? What is it?"

"We have a Theodore Dutton here at the hospital. I think it might be him."

CHAPTER 37

The reason for Ray's uncertainty was apparent. The ailing man in the hospital bed was hardly the robust Theodore Dutton we had known.

This man was heavyset, with a full face and thinning gray hair. His bulbous nose and cheeks were webbed with tiny red veins, and his jawline settled into a double chin. I could find little physical connection between this man and our high school teacher other than an overall vague and questionable resemblance.

"I suppose," I said, "there could be any number of people named Theodore Dutton."

Ray continued to look intently at the patient's face. "I think it's him."

"Why?"

"The age is right. And—"

"And what?"

Ray answered by gently lifting the man's left arm high enough for me to see the protruding pink scar along the wrist. Then Ray settled his eyes on me.

I nodded. So here he was, all these years later. I didn't even have to go looking for him. Life had caught him and spit him out on shore like the lost cargo of some sunken ship, washing him right up to where I'd stumble over him in the sand.

"So what's wrong with him?" I asked.

"He's in a diabetic coma. His wife discovered him unresponsive when she went to bed around midnight last night.

He'd gone to bed earlier, not feeling well. She called an ambulance, and here he is. He obviously hasn't taken care of himself, and yesterday being Thanksgiving—well . . ." He stopped and shrugged.

"Will he come out of it?"

"I don't know."

"You mean he could die?"

"There's always that chance."

We fell silent a moment. A familiar angry squall started brewing somewhere deep inside of me. "Well, that would be pretty ironic, wouldn't it?"

"What do you mean?"

"To find him now, only to have him die like this."

Ray looked at the IV machine that dripped something into Dutton's arm. Before he could turn back to me, we heard Ray's name paged over the PA system, calling him to another room.

"I've got to go."

"I know."

But he didn't move. "There's a cardinal rule around here about patient confidentiality, you know."

I nodded, pressing my lips into a tight line.

Ray went on, "I probably shouldn't have called you, but I thought you'd want to know about this, Beth."

"Of course I do." Then I added, "I appreciate your letting me know, Ray."

He nodded. "I'll call you after I get off work, all right?"

"Yes. I'll be home."

He started to head toward the door but stopped and turned back. "Listen, I'll come by tonight. I'll bring the kids and something to eat. Maybe we'll find a little time to talk."

"All right, Ray. That would be good."

He nodded and smiled briefly, and then he left me alone with Theodore Dutton.

I shivered in the presence of this stranger. The storm inside of me kicked up a myriad of feelings and blew them into a strange whirling mix of wonder, anger, amazement, and fear. I was left reeling, both light-headed and befuddled. The ghost had put on flesh, and here he was, resurrected in the form of an aging and ailing man, someone who both was and wasn't the teacher I had loved.

I don't know how long I went on standing there before a woman entered the room. When she saw me, she looked surprised, almost taken aback. "Can I help you?" she asked.

"No. I mean, I'm just . . . visiting."

"Do I know you?"

"No, I don't think so. Are you—are you family of Mr. Dutton?"

"I'm his wife."

"Oh. I'm—I was his student once. At Seaton. When Mr. Dutton taught at Seaton school."

"Oh?" She seemed to be trying to place the name. "In Hockessin, right?"

"Yes, that's right."

"I see." She hesitantly extended a hand. "I'm Isabel Dutton. And you are. . . ?"

"Beth." I took her hand. Her clasp was firm and warm. "Beth Gunnar."

"Well, it's nice to meet you, Beth." She offered me a flustered smile. "Won't you. . . ?" She let go of my hand and waved toward a black vinyl chair. "Won't you have a seat?"

"Thank you. I'll only stay a minute."

She was a plain woman with short white hair and keen blue eyes. She had an intelligent yet affable face, untouched by makeup. Even her clothes were simple—jeans and a sweater, a pair of loafers. Her only jewelry was her wedding ring. She stood shorter than I by several inches, yet she seemed taller, larger somehow, because of an almost palpable inner strength.

She settled herself on the foot of her husband's bed and leaned her weight against one locked arm. "How did you know Ted was here?"

"Oh!" How to explain without getting Ray in serious trouble? For a moment, I felt the urge to lie, to make up a story about walking down the hall and seeing Theodore Dutton's name outside the door, as though by chance. But I wasn't good at lying, not even to protect someone.

"Somebody on staff here was also a student of your husband's," I began, resolving to take the brunt of the fallout should this woman explode over the breach of confidentiality. I would never reveal the name of the staff member, even if this woman carried a complaint to the hospital administration. "I hope you can understand. He knew I would be concerned and so he called me . . . ."

My words trailed off as I noted the woman's bewildered gaze. Why would someone call me about a man we hadn't seen in decades? I rushed to explain, "You see, your husband was a great inspiration to me. I decided I wanted to teach English too, just like he did. So I am—I mean, I've been an English teacher for many years, thanks to your husband. I teach at Seaton now."

The woman didn't move as she seemingly allowed my words to sink in. Then she smiled. "I see. I'm happy to hear that. I think Ted has been a great inspiration to many young people."

I took a deep breath, and the anxiety that had been ballooning in my chest deflated as I exhaled. Apparently Mrs. Dutton didn't intend to make an issue out of the illicit phone call. Maybe she didn't even realize it went against hospital protocol. "Oh yes," I quickly agreed. "He was wonderful—a wonderful teacher."

Isabel Dutton gazed at her husband and smiled sadly. "He never was good about taking care of himself, though. Whenever I reminded him about diet or medication, he waved me off. He said I was only interfering."

"Oh? I'm sorry. I hope he'll be all right."

"So do I." She sighed then and turned her gaze to me. She waited. Apparently, it was my turn to say something.

"Does Mr. Dutton still teach?" I asked.

"No, not any longer. Actually, we've owned a secondhand bookstore for four—no, five years now. Bel's Book Nook?"

She said the name of the store in such a way that I knew she was asking if I'd heard of it. I had to shake my head no.

"Well, it hasn't made us rich," she went on, offering up this fact with a laugh. "But we both love books; we love what we do."

"Where is your store?"

"Here in Wilmington. On Lancaster Pike."

"You're kidding."

"No. Why?"

"You live right here in Wilmington?"

"Yes. Since buying the store. Though actually we spent most of our married life in New York. Ted has a nephew who attended Cornell and then afterward got a job teaching at a small liberal arts college not far from Ithaca. We went there to be near him. Ted ended up teaching in a private high school there."

When she mentioned the nephew, a vague memory rose in my mind of a boy with a guitar and an infectious laugh whom we occasionally found visiting at Cabin 1. "His nephew," I said. "Would that be—what was his name? Lennon, right? Was that Lennon who went to Cornell?"

She looked surprised. "Do you know him?"

"Not really." I shook my head. "I met him a couple of times when Mr. Dutton was teaching at Seaton."

She nodded. "Len is more like a son to Ted than a nephew, especially since Ted and I never had children. It was hard to leave him, but we finally decided we needed to get away from the harsh New York winters. And Delaware is my home. I missed it. I wanted to come back. So we bought the store and moved down here. It was a good move, I think." She smiled again, then asked, "What about you? Have you always taught at Seaton?"

"Oh no. This is my first year there. I left Delaware right after graduating in 1977. I've lived all over the place, mostly in the Midwest; although before I moved here this past summer, I was living in Maryland on the Eastern Shore."

I wasn't sure she was listening. Her gaze was on her husband; she seemed to be watching intently as his chest rose and fell, then rose and fell again. I thought perhaps it was a strain to talk with a stranger while your husband lay suspended somewhere between life and death.

I stood to go. "Well, I won't keep you any longer."

She didn't try to dissuade me. She held out her hand

again. "Thank you for stopping by. I'll tell Ted you came to see him."

"Please do," I said. "I hope he remembers me."

"Oh, he will. He's got an amazing memory. So far, it's still intact." Another small smile.

"And I hope that he's better soon."

"Thank you."

I started to go but stopped and turned back. "If there's anything I can do, please let me know. Really, I—well, just a minute."

I reached into my purse for pen and paper and scribbled my phone number for her. She accepted it uncertainly, without glancing at it. "Thank you."

"Don't hesitate to call."

"All right. Thank you," she said again.

She was unfailingly polite, and I was sure that under different circumstances, she and I might have been friends. I was sorry to leave her to her solitary vigil, especially since I was just as anxious as she was for Theodore Dutton to wake up.

CHAPTER 38

Ray showed up around seven o'clock that evening with Josh, Lisa, and Ben, as well as three large pizzas and four one-liter bottles of soda. After we ate, the kids, including Satchel, bundled up in winter garb and headed out for a walk around the largely deserted campus.

Ray and I watched them from the front windows, four swaddled figures moving from lamplight to lamplight through a shimmering Milky Way of falling snow. Satchel held on to little Ben's hand; he'd pressed his mitten against her glove as soon as they walked out the door. Lisa, on the other side, locked arms with Satchel so that the three of them marched up the hill, pressed close together in a line. Josh walked a couple steps ahead, as though on point.

Earlier that afternoon when I got home from the hospital, Satchel had asked, "So who's this guy you went to see?"

I was reluctant to talk about Theodore Dutton but I could hardly avoid it. "He was an English teacher here at Seaton," I said. "Ray and I were both in his class senior year."

"You know, you don't look so hot, Miss Gunnar. Are you all right?"

"Yes. Yes, I'm fine."

She eyed me doubtfully. "So how is he? Your teacher— like, is he going to be okay?"

"Yes. Well, I don't know, really. I think so."

"What's wrong with him?"

"He's in a diabetic coma."

"A diabetic coma? That doesn't sound so good. I guess you're worried about him, huh?"

I nodded while I hung up my coat in the hall closet. I was moving slowly, as though I were pushing against something heavy and viscous.

"Listen, Miss Gunnar, can I get you something to drink? Some water or something?"

"No. Thank you, though, Satchel. Actually, I'm really tired. I think I'll go stretch out on my bed for a while, take a little nap."

"Sure, okay. I think you could use the rest."

"Oh, and Ray's coming tonight with Josh and the kids. He's bringing supper."

"Yeah?" All concern for me vanished as her face lit up. I couldn't help but smile.

Now, as I watched the little band of hikers walking through the snow, I smiled again. It was good to see Satchel enjoying herself as part of a group.

I might have stood there a long time enjoying the moment, but Ray's words pulled me inevitably into the past.

"It's been a long time," he said, "since we walked this campus ourselves at night."

"Yes, it sure has." And those were the days we needed to revisit, because they nagged at us, demanding our attention. I stepped away from the window. "I imagine the coffee's ready."

A pot of decaf was brewing in the kitchen. Ray followed me and sat at the small round table while I poured each of us a mug.

"Black, right?"

"Yeah, that's fine."

I set the mug in front of him and sat down. I stirred some

cream into my own coffee and set the dripping spoon on a white paper napkin. Ray and I both watched as a brown halo blossomed around the bowl of the spoon.

There was so much to be said, and I didn't know where to begin.

Finally Ray broke the silence. "I would have bet my right arm the man was dead."

I raised my eyes to him. "Commander told us he was alive."

"I thought he was lying. Didn't you?"

"Yes."

"I just don't get it."

Commander Pettingill was himself long dead; so was Mildred Bidney. Other faculty members who might have known something about that night had left Seaton years before.

I clutched the mug with both hands and stole a few moments to think by sipping slowly. "Commander was your mom's uncle, right?"

"Uh-huh."

"So maybe he told your parents something."

"Nope. No such luck."

"It wouldn't hurt to ask."

"I already did. I called them before I came over here tonight."

"You did?"

He nodded.

"And they don't know why we were told it was a heart attack?"

"They're as much in the dark as we are," he said.

"Oh." I sipped the coffee. "But then again, it isn't *that* so much that I want to know anyway."

"Then what do you want to know?"

"Why he did it."

"Why Dutton tried to kill himself?"

"Yes."

Ray shrugged. "Now that, I'm afraid, is none of our business."

I set the mug down on the table. My heart was suddenly thumping, and I had to struggle to keep the anger out of my voice. "You know, Ray, we admired Mr. Dutton. We looked up to him. And we were just kids. It was terrible what he did to us."

Ray looked amused, as though swallowing laughter. "What he did to him*self* was terrible. It's got nothing to do with us."

"What do you mean? Are you saying he thought he could just destroy himself and it wouldn't affect us?"

"Listen, Beth. I don't think he was thinking about us at all. I mean, come on. By the time someone puts the blade to his wrist or the gun to his head or whatever he chooses to do, he's not thinking about anything but himself and his own despair."

"But that's just it. Why the despair? And why did we never suspect anything?"

Ray sighed heavily. "People are complicated creatures, Beth. Sometimes, when it comes to what we do, the choices people make, there's just no explanation that anyone can understand. The person himself may not even fully understand his own mind."

"But, Ray," I asked, exasperated, "don't you want to know? Haven't you ever wondered why Dutton did what he did?"

He lifted the mug to his lips, changed his mind, and set it down again. "Not after we graduated, no. I was too busy with life."

"But you were the one who found him, you and Ken—"

"Yeah. So?"

"So how could you just forget about him?"

He shrugged, almost nonchalantly. "What else could I have done? No one was going to give us any straight answers. As far as I knew, the guy was dead, and that was that. End of story."

"But you see, *now* maybe—now that we know he's alive—maybe we can finally get some answers."

He frowned, his whole face folding into a look of distaste. "Listen, Beth, why are you so obsessed with this?"

"I'm not obsessed. I just want to know what happened."

He gazed at me for a long moment. "And just what are you going to do? Ask him when he wakes up? *If* he wakes up. 'So, Mr. Dutton, haven't seen you in a while, not since you tried to kill yourself. And by the way, I was wondering—'"

I held up a hand and shook my head. "I'd be tactful about it."

"And you know what he's going to tell you?"

"What?"

"That it's none of your business."

"But it *is* my business."

"Why?"

Frustration rose full-blown in my chest as I struggled to put the words together. "Because for months he told us that life was good and beautiful and worth living, and I believed him. And then he goes and kills himself—or we thought he did—and that kind of cancels out everything he ever said,

213

doesn't it? It never made any sense."

When I finished, we were both quiet. Ray pushed his mug aside and put one hand over mine on the tabletop. "The man still doesn't owe you an explanation, Beth. So just forget it."

I wanted to tell Ray that I disagreed, that in my opinion Mr. Dutton did owe me—us—an explanation. And I wanted to tell him that I couldn't forget it, even if I wanted to. But before I could say as much, the front door burst open, and the children spilled in, bringing with them a gust of cold air mixed with chatter and laughter. That put an end to our conversation about Theodore Dutton. For now.

CHAPTER 39

Classes resumed the Monday after Thanksgiving. Satchel reluctantly moved back to the dorm. Ray went back to work after having Saturday and Sunday off. Ray's son Josh exchanged addresses with Satchel and drove back to Penn State. And sometime toward the middle of that week Theodore Dutton was released from the hospital and sent home.

He wasn't Ray's patient, and Ray didn't see him again after the day Dutton was admitted. Ray made a point of not following our former teacher's progress and finally learned of Dutton's discharge only when someone mentioned it in passing. He told me about it that night, adding, "So listen, Beth, he's home and he's all right. You don't have to worry about him anymore."

Natalie was incredulous when I called to tell her Theodore Dutton was alive. She was out of town with her family over Thanksgiving, and by the time I carved out a moment to call her, Dutton was already home.

I spilled the news as soon as Natalie picked up the phone, and after a suspended period of silence, she said, "I don't believe it."

"It's true."

"Are you sure?"

"I saw him at the hospital."

"And you're sure it was *our* Theodore Dutton?"

I thought of the scar on his wrist. "Yes."

"Did you talk with him?"

"He wasn't conscious, but I spoke with his wife. She was aware he had taught at Seaton."

"So what in the world is he doing now?"

"They own a bookstore on Lancaster Pike."

"No way!"

"Yeah. It's called Bel's Book Nook. Ever heard of it?"

"No." Another pause. Then Natalie said, "Well, if this doesn't beat all. Commander was telling the truth when he said Dutton was alive."

"Yes, at least part of what he told us was true."

"Well, what do you know? I can't believe it," she said again. After a moment, she added, "And you say he's been right here in Wilmington all this time?"

"Oh no. Apparently he spent a good number of years teaching at a school in upstate New York. His wife said they moved back down here four or five years ago."

"So the old guy got married, huh? What's his wife like?"

"We only spoke for a few minutes, but she seems very nice."

"They have kids?"

"No, she mentioned they don't. But she also said Dutton has always been particularly close to his nephew Lennon. Remember him?"

A long pause, then, "No. Should I?"

"We met him a few times when he was visiting Dutton. You know, long hair, guitar, he used to jam with Ken."

"Oh yeah! I do remember him. Vaguely." She gave a small laugh and said, "Well, whoever would have thought Dutton was alive? At least that answers your question, doesn't it?"

"Part of it anyway."

"What do you mean?"

"I mean, yes, I've wondered whether he was alive, and now I know he is. But what I still don't know is why he did it."

"Why he tried to kill himself?"

"Yeah."

"Forget it, Beth. It happened so long ago it doesn't matter anymore."

Was I the only one who wanted to know? "You sound just like Ray," I retorted.

"Why? What did Ray say?"

"That whatever the reason was, it's none of my business."

"I hate to say it, Beth, but I'm with Ray on that one."

I sighed heavily into the phone. "Come on, Natalie. Don't you want to know what happened to the man you once called Teddy Bear?"

She had to think about that. I heard her breathing on the other end of the line. "I don't know," she confessed. Then she added more firmly, "No, I don't. Like I told you before, I stopped caring about all of this a long time ago, and I'm not about to go dredging the whole mess up again at this point in my life. Forget about it, Beth. Let sleeping dogs lie. Don't beat a dead horse. It's water under the bridge . . . and . . . and every other cliché I can throw at you to convince you to just put it all behind you."

When she finished, I didn't respond. Finally I said, "So I guess that means you don't want to go confront him with me?"

She laughed out loud. So did I.

Forgetting did seem to be the only reasonable option, and I tried. As those first days of December slipped by, I tried to push Theodore Dutton to the back of my mind, someplace dark and preferably bottomless. But the thought of him kept rising up like fog seeping in under the crack of a door. I found myself wondering about him even when I determined to fix my mind on something else. I could not let him go.

Still, I wouldn't seek him out. No, Ray and Natalie had a point. If I sought him out, how would I ever put him behind me?

Ultimately, though, it didn't seem to be up to me. Life caught him up again and rolled him into my path as though he were a bit of unfinished business that I simply had to attend to. I was broadsided, practically knocked windless, when one wintry night not long before Christmas, Isabel Dutton called and said her husband would be pleased if I would come visit them.

CHAPTER 40

The anxiety in the pit of my stomach felt sickly familiar. It was the sensation of going to school on the first day of a new year and wondering what lay ahead.

I took several deep breaths of icy air as I moved up the walkway toward the Duttons' modest clapboard house. The windows glowed with the muted light of electric Christmas candles, and a wreath of fragrant pine boughs hung on the door. The house itself was warm and welcoming, and yet the barbed tangle of nerves kept tumbling around inside of me, leaving me weak and shaky.

I couldn't find a doorbell, but the large wreath circled a brass knocker, which I tapped tentatively. I heard footsteps, heard a lock being unlatched, and then I was face-to-face with Isabel Dutton.

She was smiling. "Hello, Beth. So nice of you to come. Won't you come in?"

I could see at once the woman's touch inside the house. The place was tastefully decorated with an assortment of antique furniture and bric-a-brac. Persian rugs adorned the hardwood floors, and chintz curtains hung in the windows. Paintings, not just prints, filled the walls. All that remained of that little cabin on campus was the books. But now they were neatly arrayed on shelves rather than tumbling all over the tables and floor.

"How is Mr. Dutton?" I asked, handing my coat to Isabel.

"Much better, thanks." She hung up the coat, then said,

"He's anxious to see you." She nodded her head slightly toward the back of the house. "He's in the den."

I followed her down a narrow hall to a room that was unmistakably Theodore Dutton's. All was in disarray, with books everywhere. In the midst of it, in an easy chair with his feet propped up, sat Mr. Dutton himself. His eyes were shut.

"Ted," his wife said softly. "Beth is here."

The figure roused himself then and, blinking a pair of eyes made large by his glasses, looked up at me. He squinted and frowned, as though he couldn't see or couldn't remember who I was.

Then he held out a hand. I stepped across the room and took it. "Beth Gunnar," he said. He held my hand in a firm grip. "I'm so glad you came."

"Hello, Mr. Dutton. It's good to see you. How are you?"

The eyes that searched my face were cloudy and uncertain. "I can't—" he dropped his hand, waved toward a small sofa to his left. "I can't see very well anymore. Did Bel tell you?"

"No." I let my purse slide to the floor and sat down on the couch.

"It's the diabetes. Nasty disease."

"I'm sorry."

He waved his hand again, as though to wave away my sympathy.

"I'll bring us some tea," his wife said.

"All right, dear," Mr. Dutton said. Then he added, "And do we have a little cake to go with it?"

"You know we don't, Ted. Don't even try that with me."

He grinned playfully. Isabel Dutton left the room, and there I sat with Theodore Dutton, the dead man come to life.

I clasped my hands together in my lap to keep them from trembling.

"Beth Gunnar." When he said my name, it sounded like a sigh. "I was delighted to hear you came by while I was in the hospital. And I understand one of the doctors there was also a student of mine?"

"Yes. That's right."

I had promised myself I wouldn't reveal the name, but Theodore Dutton was smiling at me eagerly. "And who was that?" he asked.

I hesitated a moment, then said reluctantly, "Well, you may not remember him. Ray Schmidt?"

"Ray—oh my, yes! Of course I remember him. Wonderful boy, top-flight student. I thought he might pursue the arts, but he opted for medicine, did he?"

"Yes, it seems he did."

"Wise move on his part, I suppose. Not much money in the arts." Mr. Dutton's head moved slowly from side to side. "Still, I'm having trouble picturing that young boy as a doctor."

"Well, he's not a young boy anymore. In fact, he has a son who is older than Ray was when you knew us at Seaton."

The head continued moving like a metronome. "Oh dear. Where has the time gone?"

"I wish I knew." I smiled wistfully.

The metronome stopped counting out the lost years, and Mr. Dutton settled his wide-eyed gaze at me. "Bel tells me you're teaching English at Seaton."

"Yes. I just started this year."

He gave a satisfied nod. "I always knew you would do

well. I was hoping you might pursue teaching. We used to talk about that, didn't we?"

"Yes, we did. You were the one who encouraged me. And now the room where I teach is the room where you taught in Heath Hall."

"Well now, what do you know about that. Funny how things work out, isn't it?"

"Yes, I guess it is."

Isabel returned with three teacups on a tray, along with a creamer and sugar bowl. All were of a hand-painted china. Somehow I wouldn't have expected anything less from her.

I accepted the tea, declining the cream and sugar. Wisps of steam rose from the cup, so I waited for it to cool. I was afraid to lift it to my lips in case the cup itself should shudder, revealing my nervousness.

Dutton sipped his at once. He seemed to relish the warmth of the tea, taking it in as if to stave off the cold of the room, though he wore a heavy cardigan and had a wool plaid blanket covering his lap.

He pressed his lips together, nodded. "Thank you, Bel," he said. "That's just what I needed."

His wife cast him an unspoken word of acknowledgment when he settled the cup in the saucer. Then, as though he were finished with the pleasantries, his face took on a stern expression. "Beth," he said, "I owe you an apology."

At last! I thought. *At last we will talk about that night, get it out in the open, come to some sort of understanding.*

But I feigned surprise. "Oh?"

"Yes. You wrote to me after I left Seaton, and I never responded."

I cocked my head. He wanted to talk about my get-well

card? "You remember that?" I asked.

"Oh yes," Bel jumped in. "As I think I told you, his memory is amazing. He's not doing so well in other ways, but there's nothing wrong with his mind." She smiled broadly, amused by her husband's retrospection.

I attempted to return her smile, then turned what must have been a dubious gaze upon Theodore Dutton. I thought it might be a good thing if he couldn't quite see my face.

"Yes, it was nice of you to write to me, Beth, while I was recuperating. I really should have acknowledged the card you sent, but, you see, my recovery from the heart attack was rather lengthy and . . ."

He went on, but I didn't hear what he said. My mind had ground to a halt at the words *heart attack*. The room seemed to tilt a moment and then right itself. I set my teacup down on a nearby coffee table and gripped the arm of the couch tightly with one hand.

So Theodore Dutton too was willing to take part in this charade? He too believed the student body had been duped into believing he'd had a heart attack?

Most had, yes. Most of our graduating class left Seaton thinking Dutton's heart had somehow gone haywire. Even the substitute teacher they brought in to replace him thought Dutton would be coming back, "once he's recovered from his unfortunate illness."

But what Theodore Dutton didn't know was that a few of us knew better. Obviously no one ever told him who had found him, who had been there. But, of course not. All of that too would be edited out of the revised version of that night's story.

An hour passed, during which time I reconnected with

the conversation. We spoke of Seaton and of my work there, we spoke of their store and of the book Bel was reading to him because he could no longer read for himself. And all the while I thought of the poem by T. S. Eliot, the one I first read in Dutton's class. I heard, from somewhere in my brain, the lines mocking me, *"Should I, after tea and cakes and ices / Have the strength to force the moment to its crisis?"* And I knew that no, no, all was small talk. We walked the surface while the past lay buried just beneath our feet, and I wouldn't speak of it because, like J. Alfred Prufrock, I was afraid.

I would measure out my life in coffee spoons, speaking of small and meaningless things, never daring to ask questions of any consequence. I was Prufrock, listening to my own self-recrimination:

And would it have been worth it, after all,
After the cups, the marmalade, the tea,
Among the porcelain, among some talk of you and me,
Would it have been worth while,
To have bitten off the matter with a smile,
To have squeezed the universe into a ball
To roll it toward some overwhelming question,
To say: "I am Lazarus, come from the dead,
Come back to tell you all, I shall tell you all"—
If one, settling a pillow by her head,
Should say: "That is not what I meant at all.
That is not it, at all."

At the end of the hour the fear was gone, replaced with an unyielding sadness and a withering resignation. I rose to go.

"I'm so delighted you came, Beth."

"It was good to see you, Mr. Dutton."

"You must stop by the store sometime," Isabel added. "We closed it temporarily, but we'll reopen next week."

"I'll try to do that."

"And give our greetings to Ray," Theodore Dutton said.

"Of course."

"Tell him we should like to see him sometime."

"I have heard the mermaids singing, each to each.
I do not think that they will sing to me. . . ."

CHAPTER 41

My Favorite Thing to Do
by Satchel Queen

Ever since I was a little kid, I've liked to look at the old photographs in history books. I like to look at the pictures of men in bowler hats and women carrying parasols and little girls dressed up in pinafores. I like to imagine what it would be like to ride in a horse-drawn buggy or in a Model-T Ford. The old days are totally fascinating to me, because they are a time I will never experience myself.

Sometimes I wish I could step into a photo the way Mary Poppins and her friend Bert and the Banks children stepped into the chalk drawing and it became real. I thought that was the greatest thing in the world when I saw that movie with my dad. Imagine stepping into an old photo and all of a sudden everything is real and people are talking and cars are moving and clocks are ticking, and for a little while you can see what it was like to live in another time. There are so many times and places I would like to see. We don't get to choose the place and time we're born into, and I suppose we should be satisfied where we are, but I can't help thinking that maybe there's a place and time I might like more than here and now. I wish that I could look around and see, and I wish, if I could find such a place, I could stay there.

Another thing I like to do when I look at an old photograph of a group of people is pick out just one person and imagine what their life was like. Sometimes I might pick one young woman and think, What was her name? Who did she marry? Did she have children? Was she happy? The funny thing is, I always imagine happy things for these people, even though I know everyone has problems in their lives. But when I look at an old picture I don't think about the bad things. It's almost as though a story comes into my head, and it's a good story with a happy ending.

It would be interesting to meet these people in heaven, if there is a heaven, and ask them what their life was like and see how far off I was. But maybe some of them really were happy. I hope so anyway. I'd like to think that somebody somewhere is happy.

Then I wonder whether someday my own face might be in a history book, not because I'm famous but because I just happened to be in a photograph that was used in the book. And I wonder whether someone a hundred years from now might look at my picture and ask themselves, Who was she and what did she do and was she happy?

And then sometimes when I start to think about it too hard I get a little scared, even though looking at old pictures is one of my favorite things. I get scared because from one face in one place at one time, the picture starts to expand, and I begin to think about all the other places and all the other times. I might think about a soldier who fought in Vietnam or in the Second World War or in the Civil War. Then from there I'll jump over to think about a slave who worked on a plantation in Mississippi before slavery was abolished. Or an Indian who lived on the land before the white men came. Or a sailor who sailed with Christopher Columbus. Or a handmaiden who waited on Queen Isabella. Or a noblewoman who went to the guillotine during the French Revolution, a Chinaman who helped build the Great Wall of China, a slave who hauled stones to the Egyptian pyramids, a shepherdess who drew water from a well in the deserts of Saudi Arabia, a child sitting in a grass hut in Africa. And after a while I don't see them by themselves anymore, but I start to see them altogether, and that's when it gets to be too big. I'm sitting here in the present and I look all the way back to when those first human beings stood on two feet under the same sun shining on me today, and even though there is a finite number of people who have ever lived, it looks to me to be as infinite as the universe. It just seems like an endless procession of people.

When you think about all the people who have ever lived and all the people who are alive now and all the people who are going to live but just haven't been born yet, you have to stop and wonder, with all those people and all those lives, how can anyone see me? And can even God see me in a crowd like this?

If I'm not careful, my favorite thing to do leaves me feeling small and sad. If I think about everyone at once, I'm totally lost, like I'm drowning. So I go back to a photograph and look at just one person and try to imagine that her life was good and meaningful and maybe even happy, even if she's dead now, and even if hardly anyone knew she was alive when she really was alive. I hope someday someone will do the same for me.

CHAPTER 42

The picture window in my parents' living room looks out over a sea of mountains, each wave solid in its crest, motionless, neither rolling nor waning. Thousands of years ago the earth stopped heaving and laid itself to rest. Now nothing disturbs its sleep. The hills may shiver now and again, as though yawning and stretching. But it would take one huge quake to change the lay of the land, and such a catastrophe isn't likely in western North Carolina. The only things that change in the mountains are the colors, which are as predictable as clockwork. You can stand at the window and say, *Oh, there's Mt. Pisgah,* or *There's the mountain that looks like a man sleeping,* and whether the mountains are in winter or summer or autumn garb, you will be right.

Three days after Christmas the scene was of dark and leafless trees, arms lifted toward an overcast sky the color of a frozen pond. Slowly the ridge of the mountains began to glow as though backlit with fire until the snow on the peaks captured the morning light, tossing it back heavenward in a glimmering volley.

It was a lovely scene, and yet a person feels inescapably small and mortal in the face of the eternal landscape. You say to yourself knowingly, *The mountains were here a long time before I was, and they'll still be here long after I'm gone. They keep going while I'm the one who disappears.*

I thought of Satchel. She turned in her final essay for the semester three days before Christmas break. It was two days

231

late. I told her I would have to deduct half a grade. She said she could accept the lower grade; what she couldn't do was turn the essay in until she had it right.

When I read it, I knew she had it right. When a person considers her place in this wide world, she begins to drown.

I stood at the picture window, feeling the cold seep in through the pane. Even my heavy terry-cloth robe and the mug of hot coffee in my hands couldn't keep me from shivering.

"You're up early, sweetheart." My mother, also in robe and slippers, came and joined me at the window. She too clutched a mug of steaming coffee.

"I thought I'd enjoy the sunrise."

She nodded. "Beautiful, isn't it?"

"It sure is."

"I don't enjoy this view near enough. That's what happens, isn't it? You begin to take the beautiful things for granted until you hardly even see them anymore."

"I'm afraid so, Mom. I wonder why that is?"

"A lack of gratitude, I suppose."

She settled herself on the couch then and sipped pensively at her coffee. After a moment she said, "Well, now that the house is quiet, we can talk."

Both of my sisters and their families had left the previous day, moving on to celebrate the New Year with their respective in-laws. I would be staying with my parents a couple more days before heading back to Delaware.

When Mom said she wanted to talk, I sat down in the recliner across from her.

"Is Dad up yet?" I asked.

"He's never out of bed before nine anymore if he can help it."

"Nice to be retired."

"Hmm." She nodded. "So what about you, dear? What's bothering you?"

"Why do you think anything's bothering me?"

"I'm your mother. I know."

"Uh-huh." I smiled at her. "Well, Mom, there are a couple of things, I guess."

"Like what?"

I stole a moment by taking a long sip of the coffee. "It's the strangest thing, really. Do you remember the English teacher I had senior year, Mr. Dutton?"

"Mr. Dutton?" She looked toward the window, then back at me. "Vaguely."

"The one who had a heart attack."

"Oh yes. I remember that now."

"Well, it wasn't a heart attack."

"It wasn't? What was it, then?"

For the first time I told her the whole story, from the night of April 1, 1977, right up to my visit with the Duttons at their home only days before. When I finished, the sun was considerably higher, the coffee in my mug had grown cold, and Mom's face had passed from rosy to fiery to ashen.

A few silent moments went by before she said, "Why did you never tell me any of this?"

"Well, like I said, Mom, I wanted to, but we had made a promise to Ray and Ken—"

"But you were just children, Beth. You never should have kept all this to yourself."

I shrugged. "What's done is done."

"So all these years you thought he was dead, that he'd killed himself?"

I nodded.

"And now you've found him again, and he's alive."

"Strange, isn't it?"

"Oh, Beth." She leaned forward toward me. "I don't know what to say. I'm sorry. I'm sorry for how this must have affected you. I only wish I'd known."

"You couldn't know, Mom. That's the thing—it was all so quickly swept under the rug."

"But I knew Commander. I knew what kind of person he was. I can't believe he lied about what happened."

"He did what he thought was right at the time. And anyway, it wasn't just Commander. There were others involved. It was just . . . unfortunate. The whole thing was just unfortunate."

"I'm so sorry, sweetheart," Mom said again. "What are you going to do now?"

"Nothing. I mean, what can I do?"

"Will you be able to put it behind you now that you know the man's alive?"

I had to think about that. "Not exactly."

"What do you mean?"

"Bel, his wife, is very busy with the store right now, and she asked me to find a student who might be willing to read to Mr. Dutton on Saturdays. His sight is so bad because of the diabetes that it's hard for him to read anymore. Anyway, I volunteered Satchel, and she's willing to do it."

"Satchel? That little girl who called you here?"

"Yeah."

Satchel had indeed called me at my parents' home on

Christmas Day. I'd given her the number right before she left for White Plains. When she called, she said she just wanted to wish me a merry Christmas, but the constant sniffling on the other end of the line told me she was crying. She tried to pass it off as simply a cold, but when I pressed her, she admitted to the tears. "They don't even know I'm here," she'd wailed. She didn't want to be with her mother and Roger; she just wanted to get back to school. I sympathized with her and told her to find some good books to read. It would help to pass the time. I promised her dinner at Pine Glen as soon as we got back. I promised to have plenty of dried mango on hand that we could eat before or after or during dinner, or all three. That seemed to cheer her up.

"She must be very fond of you, this Satchel," Mom said.

I nodded. "We have kind of a special relationship. She spends a lot of time with me at Pine Glen."

"She no doubt sees you as a substitute mother, judging from what she told you about her own mother when she called."

"I think she does. And that's all right. I like it. I like having her around."

"I'm glad, then. But what else are you worried about? Is it something to do with Satchel?"

"No, not really. I worry about her, but—"

"It's Ray then, isn't it?"

"You can read me like a book, Mom."

"I just know you, honey." She smiled gently.

I sighed. "His former wife, Brenda, is in Delaware visiting the kids for Christmas."

"She is? I thought she was completely out of the picture."

"So did I. Apparently she decided it was time to

reconnect. She called Ray and told him she'd be staying at a hotel in Newport and asked if he could arrange for her to see the children."

"That's a pretty bold move on her part. Did Ray agree to it?"

"He talked to the kids, and they said they were willing to meet with her." I shrugged, trying to sound nonchalant.

"And what does Ray think about all this?"

"Well, that's the thing. I don't know. I'm just not sure he ever really got over her. He says he did, but I don't know. . . ." My voice trailed off. Mom nodded. "So you're worried about the two of them seeing each other again."

"I guess I am. I probably shouldn't be. You know how I've always had to worry about everything."

"Yes." She smiled and nodded. "Of the three, you were always my best worrier. And I understand how you feel, Beth. I really do. But I think you should put it in God's hands and leave it there. He'll know what to do."

"You've always said that, Mom."

"Um-hmm. And I've always believed it too."

"You don't think Ray and Brenda might consider getting back together?"

She shook her head. "I imagine there's very little chance of that."

I wished I had her faith.

"Sounds like your dad is up and puttering around the kitchen," Mom said. "How about some breakfast? Everything looks better when you have a little food on your stomach."

"Sounds good. Maybe we can talk Dad into making his famous chocolate chip pancakes."

"I don't think it'll be too hard to persuade him." She smiled, and we walked together toward the kitchen.

CHAPTER 43

Pine Glen was tucked beneath a three-inch blanket of snow that first Saturday night of the New Year. The usually draughty house was warmed by crackling flames in the fireplace. I wondered briefly why I hadn't bothered to build a fire earlier in the winter, but then, I hadn't built this one either. Ray had hauled some logs from his place, and Josh had opened the flue and arranged the wood and newspaper over the grate. A couple of matches later the kids were roasting marshmallows to make s'mores for our evening dessert.

We had eaten large portions of spaghetti and garlic bread and salad with Italian dressing, the meal I'd promised Satchel we would have as soon as we got home. I hadn't intended to invite Ray and his family—in fact, I didn't invite them at all. Satchel had done it, calling Lisa as soon as she dropped her suitcase in her dorm room and sped down the hall to the pay phone. Ray later called me to verify the invitation, and I, knowing nothing about it, said of course Satchel and I were planning for them to come.

So there we were, looking very much like a contented family gathered around the hearth on a snowy night. And all the while my heart was constricting with a fearful curiosity as to what had happened with Ray's former wife, Brenda.

"Who wants a s'more? You want it, Miss Gunnar?"

"Sure, Josh. Thanks." I didn't much care for s'mores but didn't want to turn it down since Josh had, as he said, "painstakingly roasted the marshmallow to perfection." I took small bites of the gooey graham cracker sandwich. Warm chocolate always tasted bitter to me, like something spoiled. Josh made another for his father, who sat in the wing chair, unusually quiet.

The evening slid by on small talk among the kids, talk about Christmas gifts and New Year's resolutions and the classes Josh would be taking when he returned to Penn State. Satchel hung enthusiastically on every word Josh spoke, and I wondered whether he noticed the longing on her face or the giddiness in her laughter. She was not the same girl who, two months earlier, told me not to play with fire by falling in love.

I glanced at Ray, sensing he was not really there in the room with us, that while he was in the chair only feet from me, his mind was somewhere else.

Ben sat on the floor at Ray's feet, wrapped in the afghan that normally covered the back of the couch. He took large bites of his third s'more, then licked his sticky fingers and dried them on his shirt.

"My mommy showed us how to make these. Aren't they good?" Ben looked at me when he spoke, so I assumed it was from me that he expected an answer.

"They're delicious, Ben," I offered, feigning enthusiasm.

So there she was, right among us. And when Brenda showed up, Ray returned, moving his eyes around the room and settling them on his young son. I couldn't read his face. It was blank and smooth as a communion wafer.

"So, Ben," I ventured, "how was your visit with your mom?"

The child shrugged. "Good, I guess."

"I thought it was weird," Lisa interjected. "I mean, she leaves us and we don't see her for years, and all of a sudden she wants to do Christmas together like nothing ever happened? I don't think so."

"Yeah, well, it probably soothed her conscience or something, coming to see us and giving us a bunch of gifts. Like it would make up for lost time." Josh stretched out on the floor, crossed one foot over the other, and slipped his hands beneath his head.

"She was looking for closure, kids," Ray said quietly. Finally saying something. Finally joining us.

Josh laughed. "Sure, Dad. First of all, that word is only so much psychobabble. And second, I highly doubt that she's really interested in us. She's only interested in you. Or, I should say, your money. After years of trying to make it on her own, she realizes what she had wasn't so bad."

"That's not fair, Josh, and you know it."

"I agree with Josh, Dad," Lisa said. "She's tired of having to make it on her own. She figures she had a pretty good deal before, so why not try again?"

Ray glanced at me, then away. "Let's drop it, kids."

"At least I'm out of here in a few more days," Josh said. "Just in time not to have to deal with her when she comes back."

"Lucky you," Lisa said.

"She's coming back?" It was Satchel who asked what I was afraid to ask.

Josh nodded. "She's moving back to Wilmington. Says she's got some sort of receptionist job with DuPont. She's already signed a lease on an apartment somewhere."

I felt myself stiffen, muscles pulling taut against the news. I looked at Ray. He stared at the fire.

Satchel, meanwhile, was watching me. I knew she was; I

could feel her gaze. And I knew what she was thinking. It was the same thing I was thinking. I glanced at her, tried to smile, glanced away.

In spite of the heat of the snapping fire, I felt chilled to the bone.

CHAPTER 44

"Ted, your company's here." Bel laid a gentle hand on her husband's shoulder. At her touch he drew in a breath, lifted his head from the back of the chair, and blinked several times. Then he smiled.

"I must have drifted off," he explained unnecessarily. He elbowed his way out of a slump and straightened the buttons of his cardigan. "This chair is worse than a sleeping pill, Bel. We ought to just get rid of it. Well, Beth, so good of you to come and to bring, um . . ."

"Satchel," I reminded him. "Satchel Queen. A lover of literature and one of my best students."

Satchel smiled shyly, pleased at my introduction. She took Theodore Dutton's outstretched hand and squeezed it self-consciously before pulling away.

We were in the back room of Bel's Book Nook, a spacious but windowless room with a concrete floor painted gray and a variety of built-in bookshelves that weren't painted at all. Up against one wall was a small kitchen area: sink, counter, cabinets, refrigerator, microwave, coffeepot, and hot plate, as well as a small Formica-topped table and chairs. Mr. Dutton's overstuffed chair sat a few feet from the kitchen in the center of an area rug the color of red clay. All in all, the place put me in mind of Mole's underground dwelling in *The Wind in the Willows*, that "lowly little house with its spirit of divine discontent and longing."

Bel dragged a couple of the chairs away from the table and

waved us into them. "I don't mean to be impolite," she said, "but with Selma out sick today, I've got to stay out front. We really need to hire one more person." She paused a moment and laughed lightly. "As soon as our ship comes in."

"I'm sure that'll be any day now, dear," Mr. Dutton said.

I had a feeling I'd just been privy to a standing joke between them.

"Selma's been a godsend," Bel went on. "Selma Rainbo. She's been with us from the get-go, and I couldn't manage without her. You'll meet her next time you're here, Satchel."

"Her last name's Rainbow, like a rainbow?" Satchel drew an arch in the air with one index finger.

"No *w* on the end," Bel explained.

"No lie? Selma Rainbo? That's cool." Satchel nodded.

Bel smiled. Turning to me, she said, "There are some cold drinks in the fridge. Just help yourselves. And holler if you need anything. I'm not far away."

Bel left and Satchel wandered to the refrigerator where she pulled out a can of Coke. "You want anything, Miss Gunnar?" she asked.

"No thanks, Satchel. What about you, Mr. Dutton? Would you like something to drink?"

Dutton frowned a moment. "Is there any coffee in the pot?"

Satchel looked at the coffeepot. "Yup, a little."

"Still hot?"

She felt the pot with the back of her hand. "Yup. You want some?"

"Half a cup, please. Just black. There are some mugs in the cabinet right above the pot."

Satchel returned with the Coke and the mug of coffee,

which Mr. Dutton accepted gratefully.

"I can use a shot of caffeine right about now," he said.

Satchel sat and squirmed a moment, searching for a comfortable spot in the rigid, upright chair. Finally, she pulled the tab on the can of Coke. After a long sip she said, "You don't have any dried mango, do you, Mr. Dutton?"

I couldn't help laughing at the look of bewilderment on Mr. Dutton's face. To Satchel, I said, "I don't think he has any mango, but you can have some later at my place."

"Dried mango?" Dutton asked. "Am I missing something?"

"It's Satchel's favorite food. She'd practically live on it if she could."

"Well, then, Satchel, next time you come, I'll be sure to have some on hand."

"Hey, thanks. That'd be cool."

With the pleasantries completed, Satchel looked expectantly at the ailing man cushioned in the cradle of the overstuffed chair. He returned her gaze, his eyes oversized marbles behind the thick lenses of his glasses. Now I remembered how blue his eyes were.

"Tell me, Satchel," he asked, "who are your favorite authors?"

Satchel shrugged nonchalantly, though her voice held an air of confidence. "I have a lot of favorites. Thornton Wilder, Charles Dickens, Willa Cather. People like that."

"Really?" Mr. Dutton was wide awake now, and I guessed it had more to do with delight than caffeine.

"Sure. And that Irish guy—what's-his-name. The one that wrote *Angela's Ashes*. I really liked that book."

Theodore Dutton smiled broadly. "You can tell a lot about

a person from the books they read. Did you know that?"

Satchel shrugged again. "I guess so." She lifted the aluminum can to her lips, tilted her head back slightly, and took another drink. One corner of her mouth was visible to me, and it was curled up in a tiny amused smile.

"I understand you're willing to spend some time reading to me."

Satchel nodded.

"My eyes—" He waved a hand toward his face. "The diabetes has done a number on them."

"Yeah. Miss Gunnar told me."

"It saddens me. For one thing, I'm not much use around the store anymore. And for another thing, I'm hardly able to read to myself. I have to have a lot of light and use a rather large magnifying glass, and it all gets rather cumbersome. But I don't want to stop reading."

Satchel looked around the room. The many shelves were brimming with used books. More books grew up like stalagmite from the floor, forming stacks that seemed precariously high. One false move and I could well imagine the domino effect of volumes tumbling all over one another from one end of the room to the other. This was obviously where Bel and Selma sorted the inventory before placing the books out in the store to be sold. And here Theodore Dutton sat comfortably in the midst of them in an overstuffed chair next to a table that was itself covered with books.

"If you stopped reading, you might as well be dead, huh?" Satchel asked.

Mr. Dutton laughed loudly. "I think we're going to get along very well, Satchel. We understand each other already."

Satchel smiled, then momentarily hid again behind the

Coke. I could tell she was starting to enjoy herself.

"Do you like Thackeray?" Mr. Dutton asked.

"Don't think I've read him."

He exchanged his coffee mug for a thick volume from the pile beside his chair. "*Vanity Fair?*"

"Nope." Satchel shook her head. "I've heard of it, but I never read it."

"Delightful story," Dutton exclaimed. "Bel's been reading it to me for some time now, and we've almost reached the final chapters. Of course, having read it several times already, I know how it ends. So you and I, Satchel, can either pick up where Bel left off, or we can start with something new. Whatever you like."

Satchel's shoulders went up again. "It doesn't matter to me what we read. You're the one who has to listen."

"Well, then, why don't we go on with *Vanity Fair*. Next time you come, that is. For now, let's just talk some more, get better acquainted. Do you have any questions for me?" Dutton put the book aside and laced his fingers together over his waist.

Satchel thought a moment. She looked around the room again, then back at Dutton. "Just one," she said.

Dutton smiled placidly, a smile that invited her to ask what was on her mind.

She pointed toward the ceiling. "What's that?"

Not sure Dutton could see as far as the ceiling, I scrambled to help out. "It looks like the entrance to an attic. You know, Satchel, you pull on that rope, and the stairs come down."

"Ah yes." Mr. Dutton nodded. "That's just the attic. We use it for storage."

Satchel shot another glance at the attic door. "Don't tell

me. The place is full of books."

Another booming laugh. "Delightful girl," Mr. Dutton exclaimed, looking at me. Then to Satchel, "Guilty as charged, I'm afraid. I've spent my life collecting books, and now I'm drowning in them."

"Yeah." Satchel nodded knowingly. "It's the only way to go."

Mr. Dutton screwed up his eyes and nodded enthusiastically. "Yes, you and I are going to get along just fine, Satchel. I knew Beth wouldn't disappoint me when we asked her to pick out her best student for us."

My student and my former teacher exchanged a smile then, obviously pleased with each other. I sat on the periphery watching—and hoping I hadn't made a mistake.

CHAPTER 45

"Penny for your thoughts."

Joel Sexton's voice pulled me out of the bewildering maze my mind was wandering and brought me back to our office in Heath Hall. I looked over at Joel and tried to offer him a smile.

"I'm not sure they're worth that much."

"I don't know, Beth. You spend an awful lot of time gazing out the window. You must be pondering something big."

I shook my head. "No. I just like to watch the snow fall."

"But it's not even snowing."

I glanced at the window again. He was right. The afternoon sun shone unimpeded across an open sky. The temperature had risen enough to melt the snow and ice that had covered the fire escape the day before.

"Listen, Beth," Joel said gently, "if something's bothering you, I'd like to help."

I closed the grammar book I'd been pretending to read and pushed some papers aside on my desk. "Thanks, Joel. I appreciate it. Really. But I'm fine."

He gave me a look that told me he didn't believe me. "You're not happy here at Seaton, are you?"

"No," I protested. "I mean, I am. I'm happy here. It's just—"

I stopped and looked at Joel. He raised his eyebrows to flag me on.

"Well, okay. I'm not sure I should have accepted this job. I'm not sure I'm right for it."

"Not right for it? Are you kidding? You're a fabulous teacher, Beth."

"Well—"

"You're great with the kids. You really know your stuff, and on top of that, you make it interesting for a bunch of teenagers who basically couldn't care less about reading or writing."

"Well, thank you, but I'm not so sure about all that."

"Just look at Satchel. You've taken her under your wing, and she's thriving. She really seems happy."

I nodded. "Yeah, you're right about that. But I'm afraid I can't take all the credit for her happiness. Satchel happens to be infatuated with a certain young man, for one thing, and—"

"Really? Someone here at school?"

"No, he's a student at Penn State."

"Ah, an older man, is it?"

I laughed lightly. "They're not exactly dating, but—I think she wishes they were. So you've got the endorphin effect going on there, and you know a little of that goes a long way. And then she's really enjoying her work with Theodore Dutton."

Joel cocked his head. "Name sounds familiar, but I can't place him."

"He was an English teacher here when I was in upper school."

"Really? I never had him for English."

"He wasn't here very long. He had to leave suddenly near the end of my senior year."

"Oh? What happened?"

I looked at Joel, then out the window. "Heart attack," I said.

"Bummer. And he never came back?"

"No. But he and his wife own a secondhand bookstore over on Lancaster Pike now. Bel's Book Nook. Ever heard of it?"

"Don't think so."

"Satchel's working there part-time. She's been there about three weeks now. She was supposed to spend a couple hours on Saturdays reading to Mr. Dutton, but Bel needed help in the store, and Satchel just kind of ended up filling in."

"And she likes it?"

"Loves it. And, you know, one of the best things about it is the Duttons trust her. She's allowed to help customers find what they're looking for, and then she rings up the sales at the cash register. They've even given her a key to the store. She's the first one there every Saturday morning, running the vacuum cleaner before they open up the shop."

"How's she get there? Her folks give her a car?"

"No. She catches the bus right at the south entrance to school. Tuesdays and Thursdays too. She catches one of the afternoon buses and goes in to work for a few hours. She had to get special permission from school to leave campus on weekdays, but Farrell gave it to her, thankfully. I think for the first time, she really feels . . . I don't know . . . grown-up, important. Needed. And wanted too. They like her and they want her there, and she knows that."

"That's great, Beth. And she gets paid for this, right?"

I nodded. "A little bit of cash and a whole lot of dried mango."

"Dried mango?"

"Her favorite food."

"Oh. Okay." Joel shrugged. "Well, anyway, it sounds like

a good deal for Satchel. You arrange this job for her?"

"Sort of. The Duttons were looking for someone, and I recommended Satchel."

"And to think at the beginning of the year I had Satchel pegged as a troublemaker."

"So did I."

"She might have been if you hadn't taken an interest in her."

I thought a moment. "Maybe."

"Maybe, nothing. It's true. So you see, you're needed around here."

"I hope so."

Joel scratched the back of his head, then looked at his watch. "Ho, boy, time for my favorite class. Freshman English."

"Do I detect a note of sarcasm in that?"

"Is the Pope Catholic?"

"Do you teach the freshmen what a cliché is?"

Laughing, Joel pushed his chair back from the desk and stood. He gathered up the books and papers he would need for the class and headed for the door. "So listen, Beth," he said, turning back a moment, "are you sure that's all that's bothering you? Just insecurities about the job?"

"Yeah." I shrugged. "I guess that's it."

"You got nothing to worry about," Joel offered. "In my opinion, you're right where you should be, doing exactly what you should be doing. And next year I'm going to give you the opportunity to teach the freshmen classes. That should provide ample opportunity for challenge and reward."

"Thanks, Joel. I appreciate that."

CHAPTER 46

Throughout the long gray month of January, Ray and I saw each other from time to time. We met for coffee after he got off work. He stopped by Pine Glen briefly once or twice. We talked on the phone. But just as on that first Saturday night after Christmas break, he wasn't really there, and our conversations were stilted and awkward. Every time we were together, he grew more and more translucent, until at length I could scarcely see him anymore. Finally he no longer met my gaze or held my hand or kissed my cheek good-night.

Satchel said that when you love someone, you have something to lose. She was right about that.

I didn't want to love Ray Schmidt. I really didn't. But like Satchel also said, we don't have any choice when it comes to whom we love. It's something that happens to us, like getting a door prize or getting a jury summons or getting cancer. Good or bad, there it is, and we can't help it.

While I had denied to my friends and my family—and even to myself—that there was anything other than friendship between Ray and me, my heart knew otherwise. I have to wonder how the mind and the heart can live out two different stories at one time. Yet they can and do.

I allowed myself to realize what I felt for Ray only as I watched him growing distant. It may have been his backing off that opened the channel between my heart and mind so that the message could get through, and I could comprehend what I was feeling. I knew I loved him because there was so much pain involved in watching him fade away like some sort of apparition vanishing at dawn.

On the first of February, a Sunday afternoon, the phone rang at Pine Glen. "We need to talk," Ray said, and I thought, *No, I really don't think we do. The not talking was enough.*

But he came over anyway and sat in the chair that Satchel always sat in when she was there, and he looked as though he hadn't slept since sometime before Christmas, which may have been very close to the truth.

"I don't know how to begin," he said.

I wished he wouldn't begin at all, because I didn't want to hear it. "It's all right, Ray," I told him. "I know what you want to say."

"But I want to explain."

I nodded. "All right."

He looked stricken. My heart pounded. "Brenda and I have been . . . talking. She's—I don't know how to describe it, but . . . she's changed. She really has. I know that sounds trite, but it's true."

His eyes pleaded with me to believe him. He waited for me to respond. I said nothing.

"I care about you, Beth," he went on. "I thought maybe you and I . . . that maybe this time we could—"

He stopped. He seemed not to know how to go on.

And so I finished for him. "But Brenda's coming back changes everything," I said.

"I guess so."

"Do you still love her?"

The question appeared to startle him. "No. I don't know. She was my wife."

"She deserted you. And your children."

"Yes." His knuckles turned white and taut as he squeezed his hands together. "I hated her for a long time. But I hated her, you see, because I loved her. Does that make sense?"

I felt myself turning to stone. "Yes, I understand."

"She wants me to forgive her."

"Can you?"

"I don't know. But I believe I ought to try. I want to try."

Silence. Then I asked, "And she wants to reconcile?"

He shook his head firmly. "We haven't talked of that."

But they will, I thought. *They'll talk of it.*

"I need some time," Ray said.

I nodded, a small stiff nod.

"I don't want to lose your friendship, Beth. And I'm not saying . . ."

Not saying what? Oddly, he got that far and then didn't say anything more. He just looked at me with such a pained expression that I very nearly felt sorry for him.

"I just need some time," he repeated.

I told him I understood. What else was there to say? She was, after all, his wife. She had claimed him long ago, made a marriage with him, had children. If they should be reconciled, who was I to interfere? Doesn't a wife have first rights, even a former one, and even if it meant that, once again, your own dream was coming true for someone else?

At the door he took my hand and said quietly, "I'm sorry, Beth."

The air outside was cold and full of snow. When Ray was gone, I shut the door. I would not cry this time. I was too old and tired for all that. Young women cried and railed and cursed, calling life unfair. I wouldn't do that anymore; the years had taught me better.

I went back to the living room—empty now except for my friends. My faithful, ever present, unchanging friends. Rows upon rows of them, all in a line, welcoming me.

We're the one thing that will never leave you, they said.

I lifted my hand to touch them. Jane Austen. Charles Dickens. Thomas Wolfe. Dostoyevsky. Tolstoy. Solzhenitsyn. Oh, and the poets! T. S. Eliot. Butler. Yeats. Keats. Emily Dickinson.

We're all here. Everything you know of truth and beauty and even of love lies in us.

I pulled them from the shelves, one book and then another and another until my arms were full. I thought of the words, the passages, the verses I had known all my life. Still here, unchanged, more alive to me than any living soul. I took them to the couch where I sat and opened one. I began to read. I didn't know and didn't care which book it was; all I wanted was the words. Like a lush, I drank them in, drinking until I drifted into that place of forgetful sleep.

CHAPTER 47

My Dream Job
by Satchel Queen

Before I write about my dream job, I have to tell you a true story. It was a conversation with Mr. Theodore Dutton that got me thinking about what I'd like to do with my life, if I could.

For several Saturdays now I've been reading to Mr. Ted from the book Vanity Fair *by William Makepeace Thackeray. Finally last weekend we finished the book. Well, the book ends with these words: "Ah! Vanita Vanitatum!" (That's Latin for vanity of vanities.) "Which of us is happy in this world? Which of us has his desire? Or having it, is satisfied?"*

When I read that, Mr. Ted and I just kind of sat there without saying much. I guess we were both thinking about those words.

Finally I said, "Do you think he's saying that no one's happy in this world?"

Mr. Ted shook his head. "That seems to be what he's saying, doesn't it?"

"Do you think it's true?"

Mr. Ted took such a long time to answer I thought maybe he didn't hear me. But finally he said, "What do you think, Satchel? Are you happy?"

I had to think about that before I could answer. Then I said, "Sometimes I am. What about you, Mr. Ted? Are you happy?"

Mr. Ted smiled a little. But it was kind of a sad smile. "Sometimes," he said.

"I wish everyone could be happy all the time," I said.

"I think that's what we all wish, Satchel."

"Do you think it will ever be like that?"

"No, I'm afraid not. Not in this world anyway."

That's when I decided if I could do anything I wanted to do, I'd build a machine that would suck all the sadness out of people and replace it with happiness. It would work the same way a dialysis machine works. See, one of my mother's boyfriends, before she married Roger, was a man named Evan, and Evan had a problem with his kidneys and he had to go to dialysis three times a week. I asked him once what happened when he went for his treatment and he said the nurses hooked him up to a machine that took the blood out of him, washed all the poisons out of it, and then put the clean blood back into his veins. It was the machine that kept him healthy and alive.

When you consider the word "sanguine" you realize there is something important about our blood. The dictionary gives three definitions for sanguine:

1. of the color of blood; ruddy; said esp. of complexions

2. in medieval physiology, having the warm, passionate, cheerful temperament and the healthy, ruddy complexion of one in whom the blood is the predominant humor of the four

3. cheerful and confident; optimistic; hopeful.

It makes a person wonder whether happiness is flowing through our veins just like red blood cells and platelets. And maybe somehow sadness gets in there like a sickness and starts to crowd out all the hope. So I'd like to build a machine that can separate the happy blood from the sad poisons and siphon off the bad part while putting the good part back into the human body.

Only with my machine, unlike with dialysis, you'd only have to have your blood washed one time. Only once, and then you're set for life. I'd also let everyone have it done for free so even people without health insurance can get the sadness taken out of them. Imagine what the world would be like if everyone everywhere were happy and satisfied.

P.S. Miss Gunnar, you said to use our imaginations and write about anything, even if it's something we don't think we'll really end up doing. So that's what I did. I'd like to make everyone happy, the way I feel when I'm with you or Mr. Ted or when I get a letter from Josh. That's my dream job. I hope I didn't botch this assignment. Sincerely, your friend, Satchel Queen.

CHAPTER 48

There truly must be some correlation between blood and emotions, because as I sat in the back room of the bookstore reading Satchel's essay aloud to Theodore Dutton, I suddenly understood the expression, "It made my blood boil." I was angry with Dutton, though I was trying hard not to show it.

When I finished reading, Dutton said happily, "That child does have quite an imagination, doesn't she? Whoever would have thought of something like that—a machine to wash our blood of sorrow. Leave it to Satchel." He shook his head while offering me an amused smile.

"She *is* just a child, Mr. Dutton," I said with strained politeness. "I certainly don't think you should tell her that no one is ever happy in this world."

He looked at me a long moment through those disarmingly thick glasses, the lenses like two magnifying glasses enlarging his eyes. Then he said, "First of all, I really do think you should call me Ted. Our relationship isn't one of teacher and pupil anymore, now is it? We can simply be friends, I hope."

I wasn't interested in being his friend. My allegiance lay with Satchel; I had an almost maternal desire to protect her. "I know we can't shield children from all the hard things in life," I went on, "and I also know that the present generation is especially worldly wise as well as cynical, but I still think one of our duties as adults is to at least offer them some sort of hope."

"Oh, I couldn't agree with you more, Beth, I—"

"To prepare them for the world is one thing, but to purposely discourage them is something else altogether. I mean, when you were a teacher . . ." I couldn't go on. I didn't want to think about what he had done to his students when he was a teacher.

He leaned forward in his chair. He seemed to be studying my face.

"When I was a teacher, what, Beth?"

Silence. Then, "Nothing. Nothing, really. It's just that I recommended Satchel for this position thinking it would be good for her."

"And she seems very content to be here."

"But you're only feeding into her cynicism when you tell her no one is happy. She trusts you, and she's going to soak up everything you say and do like . . . like . . ."

My breath caught in my throat, leaving me speechless. We sat there without moving, an old-fashioned tableau, a scene depicting—what? Two bewildered people unable to bridge the gap with words?

"Beth," Dutton said quietly, "what is it that's really bothering you?"

I couldn't say. I could only choke out one whispered sentence: "Please don't hurt her."

Dutton leaned back in the chair, obviously dumbfounded. "I have no intention of hurting Satchel. I don't understand what you're getting at. She comes and reads to me, she works around the store, she sits and eats her dried mango quite happily. We laugh together. I believe she enjoys being here."

"Her father committed suicide."

The words jumped from my mouth, seemingly of themselves, hitting Dutton hard like a punch between the eyes. He looked startled, and the color drained from his face. "When?" he asked. "You mean, it's just happened?"

"No. When Satchel was eight or so."

"I'm sorry to hear that. I didn't know." He put a hand to the side of his head, as though he was in sudden pain. He rubbed circles into a small spot above his right temple while his eyes roamed the room. "But that has been some time now, hasn't it? She seems to have adjusted well. What does that have to do with today or with this essay?" He looked up at my face then. "Or with me?"

I folded Satchel's essay and tucked it into my purse, then rose to go. "All I ask is that you let her have what's left of her childhood."

"Of course, Beth. Listen, I think you misunderstand. Satchel didn't write about our whole conversation in that essay. She didn't write the half of it. Why don't you sit back down and let me explain?"

"Well, I—"

"Uncle Ted, do you happen to know where—oh, excuse me. I didn't know anyone was with you."

Turning toward the voice, I saw a man who looked eerily like the Theodore Dutton I'd known in high school, except a little older. He wore jeans and a flannel shirt over his tall and lanky frame, and his dark hair was disheveled, as if he'd tumbled out of bed only moments ago. He had a rugged look about him, but his eyes were intelligent and his smile engaging.

"Len, come on back. I'd like you to meet Beth Gunnar. She's Satchel's teacher, the one Satchel talks about. Beth, this is my nephew, Len. He's just back from Europe. He's been on sabbatical from Quentin College in upstate New York, and he decided to come here and spend some time with Bel and me before he returns to teaching. Wonderful, isn't it?"

The man stepped toward me, hand extended. "Very nice to meet you, Beth."

Lennon Dutton. The long-haired boy with the guitar. But that was long ago, and in the intervening years he seemed to have left all that behind and grown into the image of his uncle. I started to tell him we had already met, years ago in Cabin 1, but I suspected he wouldn't remember. "Nice to meet you too," I replied, accepting his outstretched hand.

"So you're the Miss Gunnar that Satchel goes on about," he said, pumping my arm enthusiastically.

"Does she?"

"Oh my, yes," Theodore Dutton laughed. "Miss Gunnar this and Miss Gunnar that. She adores you, you know."

"Does she?" I asked again.

Mr. Dutton waved a hand, and his nephew seemed not to hear my question. Len said, "So you teach where Uncle Ted used to teach, right? Over at Seaton?"

"Yes. Yes, English. Over at Seaton." I was flustered, seeing Lennon Dutton unexpectedly after so many years, flustered by the family resemblance. I reclaimed my hand and pushed my sweaty palm into a pocket of my slacks. "And you're teaching at a college?"

He nodded. "I'm taking a break from all that, though. I've been doing some research in Europe, like Uncle Ted said, and now I'm going to spend some time here helping out around the store. Actually, I've been wanting to do this for a long time—just come down here and work among the books. Academia can be a bit stuffy, even at a small private school like

Quentin, and . . . well, this comes as a welcome break."

"Do you teach English?"

A shake of the head. "History," he said. "Medieval history is my primary interest. That's what I've been doing in Europe, studying the church in the Middle Ages and the effect the Protestant Revolution had on—well, never mind. I won't go into all that."

"Oh no, really. I'd like to hear about it sometime. It sounds very—"

"Well, what's going on back here? Having a party and you didn't invite me?" Bel entered the room, laughing. "Beth, I trust Ted introduced you to our nephew, Len."

"Of course. Len was just telling her about his time in Europe," Mr. Dutton replied.

"Wonderful, isn't it? London, Brussels, Frankfurt—imagine! Then last Saturday he took a flight from Frankfurt to Philadelphia, and here he is. He called us from the airport and said he'd come to help."

Len smiled sheepishly. "I'll be more help around here once I'm past the jet lag."

"The price one pays for traveling the world." Mr. Dutton laughed and looked up at us from his chair.

"Beth, can you stay and have lunch with us?" Bel asked. "I've just stocked up the fridge, now that Len's here."

"You didn't have to do that for me, Aunt Bel."

"Oh yes I did. Look at you, skin and bones. Did you forget to eat while you were in Europe? Well, never mind. You won't be going hungry as long as you're staying with us. I can't do much cooking here at the store with only a microwave, but there's plenty of fresh fruit and frozen dinners, and I'll be bringing in leftovers from home. Speaking of which,

I've got last night's chili for lunch today. Can you join us, Beth?"

"Thanks, Bel, but I've got a one o'clock class. I'm afraid I've got to go."

"That's too bad. Well, come back another time, and we'll all have lunch together."

"All right. Yes, that would be fine."

"By the way, Satchel's coming in tomorrow, isn't she?"

"Let's see, tomorrow's Tuesday. As far as I know, she's planning to be here."

"Do you suppose she could stay until closing? Usually Selma's here, but her husband is having hernia surgery, and she's asked for a couple days off."

"I think that should be fine. I'll talk with the principal about getting her permission to stay late. You close at nine, right?"

"Yes, nine o'clock."

"All right. I'll come pick Satchel up so she doesn't have to take the bus back to campus."

By the time I said good-bye to the three of them, I had almost forgotten why I'd come. But as I reached into my purse for my car key, I felt Satchel's essay tucked in there beside my wallet. Then I remembered.

I looked at Theodore Dutton and found that he was already looking at me, his face a picture of entreaty. He seemed to have suddenly realized, as I did, that something had been left unsaid, that we had been interrupted before we had reached an understanding. But it was too late now. Bel had laced her arm through mine and was walking me toward the door, away from her husband and whatever it was he had wanted to say to me.

CHAPTER 49

The next evening I drove back to Bel's Book Nook to pick up Satchel. The night was clear and unusually mild for February, and the black bowl of space overhead was brimming with stars. When I pulled into the small lot in front of the store, I could see Lennon Dutton through the plate-glass window, going over some receipts at the register.

The bell tinkled quaintly when I opened the door, and I was greeted with the musty odor of aging books. Len looked up at me and smiled. "Hello, Beth. How are you tonight?"

"Fine, thanks. And you? A little more rested?"

Still smiling, he shrugged and gathered the receipts into a pile on the counter. "I suspect I'll be on Europe time for a few more days. But that's all right. I'll adjust."

"Where's Satchel? In the back room?"

He shook his head. "No, she's taken Uncle Ted out for a walk."

"They're out walking? It's cold out there."

"It's not so bad. Besides, they're all bundled up. I insisted they go because Uncle Ted needs the exercise. He and Aunt Bel intend to fatten me up, and I intend to slim Ted down. It gives us something to work toward while I'm here." He laughed an amused little laugh, then picked up an armload of books and stepped out from behind the counter. "They're just going down the street a short ways. They should be back any minute, and then you might as well take Satchel home. It's been a quiet evening; it won't take us long to close up."

I looked around the store. It was empty of customers. "Is Bel here?" I asked.

He nodded toward the back room. "She's puttering around back there. We **got** a lot of books in today on exchange, so she wanted to start going through them." He dropped the load he was carrying onto a cart, which he then pushed slowly down one of the aisles while his eyes scanned the shelves. "Go on back if you'd like. I know she's got a pot of decaf brewing."

"All right," I said. But I didn't go. I randomly pulled a book from the shelf and pretended to look at it. After a moment I said, "Len, you know we met before, don't you? Years ago."

He stopped pushing the cart and turned back to look at me. "Did we?" he asked.

"I don't expect you to remember. It was when your uncle was teaching at Seaton. Sometimes you'd visit him, and there'd be a group of students there in his cabin. . . ."

My voice trailed off. He seemed to be trying to remember, and I wanted to give him a minute to think. I reshelved the book and waited.

"Hmm . . ." he said finally, shaking his head.

"You used to bring your guitar and play with a boy named Ken. I was there and my friend Natalie and our friend Ray."

"Yeah?" He frowned. "I haven't picked up a guitar in years. I used to really enjoy it, though."

He didn't remember. That was all right. "It was a long time ago."

"Well, now that you mention it, I do remember that cabin on campus where Uncle Ted lived. I guess I visited him there a few times. That was back when he was batching it, before he met Bel, right?"

I nodded. "He wasn't married yet. They usually stuck bachelors in those cabins back then, and your uncle was one of the few unmarried teachers at school that year."

"Yeah? I guess I'm not surprised. We Dutton men aren't known for marrying young." He pushed the cart a foot or two, stopped again, shelved a book where he decided it belonged. "So how long was Uncle Ted at Seaton?"

"Not long. He had to leave before the year was over."

"Oh yeah. That's when he had the heart attack, wasn't it?"

I almost believed that story myself now. A widespread lie eventually takes on the sheen of truth. "Yes," I said. "In April of our senior year."

His eyebrows rose in surprise. "You have a good memory. I had almost forgotten Uncle Ted was at Seaton when he had the heart attack."

"Well, we were all very fond of Ted." The last word sounded strange as it dropped from my tongue. I had so far avoided calling him Ted, as it was too familiar; I simply couldn't think of him that way. "He was a favorite teacher for many of us. It came as a shock when he had to leave."

Len nodded. "He's been a remarkable teacher all his life. Well, just a great person, really. He's the one who encouraged me to study history when my own dad said I'd never make a decent living with a degree like that. Dad wanted me to follow in his footsteps and become a dentist." Len laughed loudly. "The last thing I wanted was to spend my days poking around in people's mouths. Nope, fighting tooth decay just didn't do it for me, you know? So I'm glad I listened to Uncle Ted when he told me to pursue my interests. My dad and

Uncle Ted are brothers, but they're as different as night and day. Kind of funny how that happens, isn't it?"

Before I could respond, the bell over the door tinkled, and Satchel and Dutton slipped in on a gust of laughter.

"It's cold out there!" Dutton cried merrily. "Len, you're going to be the death of me."

"Don't listen to him, Len," Satchel said. "It's just fab out there! Oh, hi, Miss Gunnar. Hey, you know what? You could see about a billion stars in the sky. Mr. Ted showed me Orion's Belt. You know, those three stars lined up in a row. I never saw it before. It's so cool!"

"There you two are," Bel said as she approached from the back room. "Did you manage to stay warm?"

She started unwrapping the scarf from around her husband's neck as Dutton said, "We survived, dear. But if the temperature drops any lower than it is right now, Satchel and I will have to become mall walkers."

"All right!" Satchel exclaimed, her eyes widening. "I'll do the mall with you anytime you want, Mr. Ted."

"A little cold isn't going to hurt you, Uncle," Len said. "It gets the circulation going."

"Says you." Mr. Dutton smiled playfully. "Meanwhile you stay indoors where it's warm."

"Len's right, dear," Bel insisted. "You haven't been getting the exercise you need. Remember what the doctor told you last time we saw him?"

Mr. Dutton ignored her. "So, Beth, you've come to take Satchel away from us, have you?"

"I'm afraid so. We both have early classes in the morning."

"Well, then, we reluctantly surrender her to you, though we always hate to see her go."

"I'll be back Thursday, Mr. Ted. Don't worry about that. Maybe we can get another walk in."

"And maybe Mother Nature will be kind enough to send a blizzard so we can all stay indoors."

"Now Ted, quit complaining and come warm up with a nice cup of hot coffee." Bel linked arms with her husband and started to lead him off but turned back long enough to say good-night to me and Satchel.

"Ready to go?" I asked Satchel.

"Just a minute. I'll be right back." She rushed off toward the back of the store.

Len smiled after her. "Uncle Ted is really enjoying her company."

I had to agree. "He seems to be good for her too."

"Yes. Well, I guess they're good for each other. Maybe she can inspire him to take better care of himself. I worry about him, with the diabetes and all. That's really why I'm here. I decided I'd come when I heard he was in a coma."

"But they have that under control now, don't they?"

"If you mean that Bel is watching his diet and making sure he takes his insulin, yes. But when your health is as frail as his, you never know."

"Hmm." I nodded. "Let's hope he lives to be old."

Len smiled. "I suppose he's got enough stubbornness in him to keep him alive a good long while yet."

Satchel reappeared chewing on a piece of mango. She carried several more pieces in a plastic bag. "Okay," she said, "I guess this'll last me till we get back to campus. I'm ready to go."

CHAPTER 50

"Happy Valentine's Day."

"Thanks, Natalie. Same to you."

I had hoped, when I picked up the phone, that it might be Ray. When I heard Natalie's voice, I was disappointed but not surprised.

"So what's up?" she asked.

"Not much, other than the usual Saturday morning chores. I just finished washing and waxing the kitchen floor."

"Why?"

"Why what?"

"Why were you washing and waxing the kitchen floor?"

"Um, because it was dirty?"

"You know I've always said that a clean house is the sign of a life misspent."

"So I should be doing something else?"

"Yes. Anything else but that."

"You're a liberated woman, Nat."

"I just know how to use my time wisely, and washing and waxing are not on my to-do list."

"Okay, well, so what are you and Ron doing for Valentine's Day?"

"We've decided we're actually going to treat ourselves to dinner out tonight."

"Nice."

"But we're taking the kids too."

"Better yet."

"That's what you think."

"Listen, consider yourself lucky. I'd love to be going on a family outing."

Silence. Then Natalie said, "I guess that's why I called, Beth. I hate to think of you alone on Valentine's Day."

"No big deal," I said. "I'm staying busy."

"There's got to be something better to do than clean the house."

I laughed a little for her sake. "Nat, you're a good friend, but you don't need to worry about me."

"Listen, why don't you come to dinner with us tonight?"

"What?"

"I mean it. Come with us."

"Oh sure. Ron would love that."

"He'd be fine with it. Like I said, we've already got the kids tagging along."

"Thanks, but no. Anyway, there's a Valentine's dance here on campus tonight, and I've volunteered to help chaperone."

Another silence. Then tentatively, "Have you talked to Ray recently?"

"He called a few nights ago."

"What did he have to say?"

"Not much after he said hello."

I heard her sigh through the telephone line. "I'm sorry, Beth. I was really hoping—"

"Never mind, Nat. It's all right. Oh hey, you'll never believe who I ran into at the bookstore this week."

"Yeah? Who?"

"Lennon Dutton. Remember him?"

After a long pause Natalie said, "No. Should I?"

"He's Mr. Dutton's nephew. We'd see him sometimes

272

when he stayed with Dutton in the cabin."

"Yeah?"

"You know, kind of a shy kid with long hair."

"We knew about a thousand shy kids with long hair when we were in high school, Beth."

"Yeah, I guess we did. Well, anyway, he ended up a history professor at some school in New York. He's on sabbatical, and he's helping out at the store."

"Oh? I wish I could remember him, but it doesn't ring a bell."

"Never mind, then. It's not important."

"So how's our friend Ted doing these days?"

"You could find out for yourself if you'd ever come to the bookstore with me."

"No, thanks."

"I can't believe you don't want to see Theodore Dutton."

"You should believe it by now, since I've already turned you down a dozen times."

"But why don't you want to see him?"

"Because I don't believe in dredging up the past. There's only one way I'm going to look, and that's forward."

"Well, you're probably right, Nat."

"I know I'm right. Besides, I liked Dutton better when he was dead. I didn't have to think about him. If I saw him now, I'd probably strangle him for what he did."

I laughed out loud. "I know how you feel. I really do."

"You mean you feel like you want to strangle him sometimes?"

"Yeah, I do."

"So why are you bothering with him? Why don't you just distance yourself from the guy?"

"For one thing, he's good with Satchel. Both he and Bel have been good to her."

"And? Anything else?"

I thought a moment. "I guess that's kind of like asking the question, why does someone climb a mountain?"

"And now I'm supposed to say, 'Because it's there,' right?"

"That's right."

"Well, the Atlantic Ocean's there too, but you won't find me swimming across it. Face it, Beth, you're still hankering to find out why Dutton attempted suicide, as if he's ever going to tell you."

"I can't just bury the past the way you do."

"It's called minding my own business, moving on with my own life, which I did a long time ago, thank heavens. You know what happens to most people who climb mountains just because they're there?"

"What?"

"They fall off. The body may or may not ever be recovered."

"Okay, so maybe the mountain thing was a bad analogy."

"I don't know, Beth. I'm just saying, you do what you want, but I have no desire to see Theodore Dutton. I don't trust him, and why you ever allowed your student to get involved with him is beyond me."

I was stunned. "Really, Nat? You really think I've done the wrong thing?"

She sighed deeply. "I don't know. I hope not. You say she's happy working for him, so maybe it's all right. Does she know what happened our senior year, what Dutton did?"

"No, I never told her."

"That's just as well, I imagine. Let her think he's some nice old man who's half blind and needs to be read to."

"But that's exactly what he is, Natalie."

"Yeah, right. According to what you told me yourself, he had no qualms about handing out the beer and getting smashed with Ray and Ken when they showed up at his cabin. And let's not forget that bit of insanity the night the boys found him on the bathroom floor."

"That was a long time ago. People change."

"Are you sure Dutton's changed?"

"Yes," I answered tentatively. Then I added, "He's hardly the hard-drinking bachelor he was when we knew him. I mean, no . . . no, he's not like that at all. If you saw him, you'd see what I mean. He's just a harmless old guy now who can't really do all that much for himself, and—" I stopped then and took a deep breath. "Okay, Natalie, it's true I've had my doubts. I've thought maybe I should never have introduced Satchel to Dutton. But it's too late now. You might say they've bonded."

"Well, listen, Beth," Natalie said, "my personal dislike for the guy doesn't really count for much. For all we know, he's been resurrected a better person and only good can come of Satchel knowing him. Let's hope so. But anyway, I didn't call you to talk about Dutton. I just wanted to wish you a happy Valentine's Day."

"Thanks, Nat. I appreciate that."

"Sure you won't join us for dinner?"

"I'm sure. But thanks."

That night I went to Hawthorne Gymnasium to help chaperone the Valentine's Day dance. Satchel wasn't there. She had called from the bookstore and asked me to see if the principal would allow her to stay at work until closing. Because she was holding down a responsible job, Mr. Farrell had no problem granting her permission. I had hoped she would come to the dance, where I could see her. But these days she was spending far more time with the Duttons than she was with me.

CHAPTER 51

A month later the Duttons invited Satchel to stay with them during spring break, but her parents insisted she spend the week with them in White Plains. I flew to North Carolina to visit my folks and to watch the warmer season ease in over the mountains. When I got there, spring was already arriving in hints, with shades of green slowly uncoiling over the dark landscape and tentative blossoms breaking up through the brown earth around the yard where my mother had planted tulips and crocuses.

In my suitcase I'd smuggled a half dozen companions for the trip—books I'd been wanting to read for months but hadn't yet found time for. I knew I wouldn't read them all in the span of seven days, but I wanted them with me anyway. Three novels, two biographies, and one slim volume of poetry, the latter an aging hardcover collection of nineteenth century verse written by American women. Theodore Dutton gave it to me just before I left town.

"When somebody brought this in on exchange, I put it aside for you," he said. "I remember how you used to enjoy poetry whenever we read it in class."

I accepted the gift gratefully. "I can't believe you remembered, Mr. Dutton."

He laughed. "In all my years of teaching, only a handful of students have really appreciated poetry the way you did. It's a little hard to forget something like that."

I stacked the books on the table beside the guest bed.

Every morning I took the volume of poetry to the living room and read it by the picture window while sipping a cup of coffee. The verses brought a sense of quiet to that first hour of dawn, setting the tone for the day. It was a restful week, refreshing in the solitude it offered and in the chance it gave me to separate myself from Seaton and teaching and the Duttons and, most of all, from Ray.

On my final morning in Asheville I sought out, as usual, the recliner in the living room but was surprised to find my father already in it. He wore a plaid bathrobe over a pair of pajama pants and a T-shirt. His feet, in fur-lined slippers, were propped up on the recliner's footrest. His hair was disheveled from sleep, and his face was dotted with whiskers, and he was reading through a pair of dark-framed glasses that badly needed cleaning.

"What are you doing up so early, Dad?" I asked, settling on the couch across from him.

He shrugged. "I couldn't sleep, so I decided to go ahead and get up."

"Anything wrong?"

"No, not really. I just get a bit of insomnia now and again. I don't like lying around in bed when that happens, so whenever I can't sleep, I get up and get busy."

I glanced at the open book on Dad's lap. "Reading through the Bible again?"

He nodded. "Genesis straight through to Revelation. No matter how many times I go through it, I'm always amazed at what I learn with each new reading. It seems to be completely inexhaustible."

"I suppose it must be," I agreed. I had read the Bible through myself, years before. Now I couldn't remember the last time I had opened one. "So where are you now?"

"The book of Hosea." He tapped the Bible with an index finger. "This one has always baffled and comforted me at the same time."

"How so?"

"You remember the story of Hosea and Gomer, don't you?"

"Yeah, I think so," I lied.

"You know, she was a prostitute. Here's Hosea, a prophet, a man of God, and what does God tell him to do? Marry a prostitute!" Dad shook his head and gazed briefly out the picture window. The corners of his mouth turned back in a smile of bemusement.

"That does seem strange," I said. "You'd think God would want him to marry someone a little more . . . well, pure, I guess."

"You'd think so, wouldn't you? I always kind of felt sorry for Hosea. Here's this poor guy just trying to be obedient, and for that he's saddled with a cheating wife. She didn't suddenly decide to become monogamous when she married him, you know. She went on carrying out her profession as if Hosea wasn't even there. So when the children came along, Hosea didn't know whether half of them were his or somebody else's. He just kept taking old Gomer back, though. Sometimes he even went out looking for her and brought her home."

I drank from my mug of coffee, then wrapped both hands around it again for the warmth. "It all seems out of character for God, doesn't it?"

"Well, yes and no," Dad said. "You have to consider the fact that God is always trying to say something."

"What do you mean?"

"It's all symbolic, of course, this marriage between Hosea and Gomer."

"Is it?"

"Well, yes. It's the picture of God and His people. God is Hosea, and the rest of us, well, we're Gomer, I'm afraid. We leave, we drift away, we turn our attention to other things. We *love* other things to the point of more or less ignoring God. But in spite of all that, God always takes us back. Comes after us, even. That's what's comforting."

I inhaled deeply. Dear Dad. I was beginning to see what he was getting at. We hadn't mentioned it all week, and he wanted to talk about it before I went home again. I smiled gently and said, "You're trying to talk to me about Ray and Brenda, aren't you?"

He looked at me with eyebrows raised. "Am I?"

"Well, sure. You know, Brenda left him and went out to play the field, or whatever it was she did, and now she's shown up again, and he's forgiving her and he's willing to take her back. So it's like Hosea and Gomer, right? Thanks, Dad, but don't worry. I already know Ray's doing the right thing. I don't like it, but I accept it."

Dad closed the Bible and laid it aside. He looked genuinely perplexed. After a moment, though, his face opened up, and he said, "I really hadn't thought of that before, but Ray and Brenda would be kind of a modern day Hosea and Gomer, wouldn't they? At least in the fact that she strayed and he took her back. But that didn't occur to me until you mentioned it just now."

"Really?"

"Really." He shrugged. "So no, I wasn't trying to talk to

you about Ray. I see you as capable of handling that yourself. I will say, though, that I think you've handled the situation with grace, and I'm proud of you."

"I don't know about that, Dad, but thanks. I know Mom is disappointed. Again."

"Don't worry about your mother. She'll get over it."

"Poor Mom. I bet she's got a hope chest stashed away for me somewhere, and she's still adding to it."

Dad laughed loudly. Then he said, "All she really wants is for you to be happy. You can't fault a mother for that."

He pushed the handle on the side of the recliner that dropped the footrest. "I think I'll get some more coffee," he said, picking up the empty mug. "By the way, what book have you got there? A book of Psalms?"

I held it up so he could see the cover. "No. Poetry. Mr. Dutton gave it to me. I often read poetry in the morning because it—I don't know—centers me or something."

"Centers you? What does that mean?"

"You know, makes me feel peaceful, helps me transcend the world and all its problems for a little while."

I smiled at Dad and thought he might smile in return, but he didn't. Something like concern flashed across his face, but before I could ask him what was wrong, he said, "The Psalms are beautiful poetry too."

I blinked and shook my head. "I know, Dad. Sure, the Psalms are beautiful."

"Well, then—" he looked at the mug in his hand—"can I get you some more coffee?"

"No, thanks. I'm fine."

He leaned over and kissed my forehead. "I love you, Beth."

"Love you too, Dad."

Then he smiled and went to the kitchen to replenish his drink.

CHAPTER 52

I sat at my desk in my classroom in Heath Hall, watching the students trickle in after morning assembly. It was our first day back from spring break as well as the start of a new semester, the final stretch of the school year. My first class of the morning was a one-semester course called Drama as Literature. Eight students had signed up for the class. When the ritual claiming of the desks was completed and a quiet had settled over the room, seven students sat facing me.

"Where's Satchel?" I asked. "Has anyone seen her?"

A girl who lived in the dorm raised her hand. "Tess told me at breakfast this morning that she didn't come back."

For a moment I couldn't respond. I held the girl's gaze as though daring her to defend herself. Then very quietly I asked, "Are you sure?"

"Well, yeah," she retorted. "That's what Tess told me, and she should know. She has to room with her."

"Did Tess say why Satchel didn't come back?"

The girl shrugged complacently. "No. She said she didn't even hear anything from her. Satchel just didn't show up yesterday when the rest of us came back."

"All right." I glanced out the window at the metallic March sky, trying to process what this student had just told me. "She might have gotten sick or something and just couldn't get back yesterday. But maybe she'll show up today. Let's hope so anyway."

As I scanned the vacant faces before me, I knew I was

talking to myself. It didn't matter to them where Satchel was or whether she was coming back. It mattered only to me.

I pushed my chair back from the desk and walked to the blackboard. I had to will my feet not to go any farther, not to go out the door and down the stairs to the office to see what the secretary could tell me about Satchel. I had a class to teach.

I wrote the name Thornton Wilder on the board. "How many of you were in the fall production of *Our Town*?"

The hour dragged by on leaden feet. I found myself repeatedly glancing at the clock. More than once I had to ask a student to repeat a question or comment because my mind was somewhere else. My mind was with Satchel. Wherever that was.

When at last the clock's minute hand moved far enough to release us, the students jumped up from their chairs and fled the room. I was close behind. Descending the musty stair-case, I almost tripped over the long adolescent legs of boys and girls reclining on the steps between classes. "The staircase isn't a lounge, you know," I huffed. But I didn't stop to shoo them elsewhere; I was too intent on reaching the administrative offices on the first floor.

Delia Simpkins was just hanging up the phone when I reached her desk. "Do you have any word on Satchel Queen?" I asked her.

She pointed at the phone. "I was just talking to her father."

"Stepfather," I corrected.

"Whatever. They're withdrawing her from school."

"What? Why?"

"They need her at home."

"They can't do that."

Delia Simpkins looked at me askance. "Yes, they can. Any parent has the right to—"

"But why? What did he say? What does he mean, they need her at home?"

The secretary picked up a pencil and starting turning it over on the desk the way Mildred Bidney used to do just before she read the barn duty list in morning assembly. "Apparently," she said, "the mother is pregnant and not feeling well. They want Satchel at home to help her around the house."

"But they can't do that."

This time she didn't bother to respond. She simply looked at me while the pencil turned point to eraser and back again.

Finally I said, "So they can pull her out of school this late into the school year?"

"Sure. They're enrolling her today in the public school there."

"But they can't do that," I said one more time.

The pencil stopped. Delia Simpkins looked up at me with something like confusion and something like concern. "Listen, Beth. I don't know what planet you woke up on this morning, but around here it works this way: She's their kid. Her parents can do whatever they want, and like it or not, we can't do anything about it."

CHAPTER 53

Night after night as I worked at the dining room table, I'd lift my head toward the window, expecting any minute to see Satchel strolling down the hill from the dorm. She'd be coming to talk about what we were discussing in class or to chat about life in general. Or maybe she wouldn't want to talk at all, but rather sit quietly in her usual spot by the fireplace, an open book in her hands.

Then I'd remember. Satchel was gone, yanked out of school to fulfill a role her parents required of her. They had made their plans believing that the school was a faceless institution. They didn't know that I was here, yearning to talk with the child. I hadn't even had the chance to say good-bye.

I thought of the Duttons and how they had shared my distress over Satchel when I stopped by Bel's Book Nook to tell them the news.

"How can they do this?" Bel had exclaimed, slapping the counter with an open hand. "That isn't what's best for Satchel. Don't they know—"

"Are you sure, Beth?" Mr. Dutton interrupted. He sat behind the counter on a stool, looking up at me with muddled eyes. "Are you sure she won't be coming back?"

"I'm sure. The secretary has already started the paper work—"

"They're keeping her home," Bel said, "to play nursemaid to her pregnant mother?"

"Apparently the mother has always been somewhat dependent on Satchel, and—"

"Then why did they send her to Seaton in the first place?"

"I'm not sure, exactly, except that Satchel's mother and stepfather were only recently married and—"

"Yes, yes. We know all that. Satchel told us all about them. And frankly, I'm not impressed."

"Can we call them?" Mr. Dutton asked. "Do you suppose we could try to reason with them, see if they won't allow her to at least finish out the school year?"

The three of us fell silent, studying each other, hoping one or the other of us would come up with an answer. Mr. Dutton's pale skin turned crimson as he waited. Bel dabbed with a tissue at eyes that threatened to spill over.

At length I said, "No, we can't call them. It's no use."

"But—"

"I asked the same question of our principal. He said no. It's the parents' right to take a child out of school, and there's nothing we can do about it."

Lennon Dutton entered the shop while I was speaking. He met us at the counter and, after looking pensively at each of our faces, asked, "What's wrong?"

"Satchel's gone," Bel said.

"What do you mean?"

I explained, and as the four of us talked about Satchel, the air became heavy with a palpable sadness. Len said in the end, "I think the three of you were really her family. More of a family to her than her own parents anyway."

He was right. Satchel Queen was a child of my heart.

After a dozen days and nights of gazing out the dining room window, watching for her to appear on the crest of the hill, I pulled the drapes.

CHAPTER 54

Dear Miss Gunnar,

I've been thinking about calling you, but I decided I better not. If I did, the call would show up on the phone bill, and Mom would have one huge hissy fit about me spending too much money, and Roger would give me the lecture about having to work to learn the value of a dollar. As if he's not Mr. Moneybags and they didn't spend last fall tramping all over Europe at hundreds of dollars a day. I thought about calling you collect but—no offense—I know you don't make a whole lot of money doing what you do, so I didn't feel right reversing the charges. So I finally decided I'd write to you because Mom and Roger don't have to know, and I can afford a stamp on my own.

I just want to say I really miss you, Miss Gunnar, and I miss the Duttons, and I even miss Seaton. When Mom and Roger told me they were pulling me out, I couldn't believe it. First they sent me to boarding school when I didn't want to go, and then when I was finally happy there, they pulled me out. That night when they told me, we had a huge fight about it, with Mom and Roger and me all screaming, and I just kept telling them I hated them because I thought maybe then they'd want to get rid of me again and send me back to Seaton. But no such luck.

They're keeping me home because Mom's got morning sickness real bad. The doctor says maybe she's having twins. Mom says that's okay as long as it's twin boys. And I keep thinking, yeah, because you were never happy with the girl you had. Only Dad was happy about that.

So anyway, they have this housekeeper that comes in every day but only part-time. She takes care of everything while Mom lies around in bed watching TV or shopping online on her laptop. I think she's using this morning sickness business as an excuse to lie around all day. When I get home from school, the housekeeper leaves and I take over. I guess I'm needed, but I'm not wanted, and I sure would rather be wanted. Roger doesn't do anything to help around the house. I think he figures he brings home the bacon and that's enough. I think he's happy about the baby (or the babies) because he doesn't have any other kids, but who knows for sure. It's not like we're all touchy feely around here and having heart-to-heart talks all the time. If Roger tells me he liked the tuna casserole I made for dinner, that's a red-letter day. Yeah, I'm the cook around here, if you can believe it.

I've been at the public school for a little more than a week now, and I hate it. It's pretty much made up of Goths, drug addicts, and a whole bunch of other slime bags, and that includes the teachers. My English teacher must have been hired off the street just because nobody else would take the job. He doesn't know one thing about poetry or literature. Remember that poem by Christina Rossetti you and I talked about once called "The Dirge"? Well, I mentioned that in this guy's class the other day, and he thought I was talking about some song written by The Grateful Dead. Sheesh. I mean, how am I going to learn anything from him? He's just not like you at all, Miss Gunnar.

Have you seen Mr. Ted and Miss Bel and Mr. Len? I guess they know by now what happened. Please tell them that it wasn't my choice, though. I really liked working for them. Tell them when I get out of high school, I'll come back and work for them again. I'll be eighteen then, and I can do what I want. It's really not that far away, is it, even though it seems like a million years. When I think about all of you, I start to cry. I've been crying a lot these days.

Another rotten thing is that Josh and I aren't really talking anymore. I guess I'm not too surprised. I kind of expected it. But *still, it hurts. He's dating someone at Penn State now. Did you know that? Maybe not, because I know you don't talk to Dr. Schmidt that much anymore, so there wouldn't be any way for you to get the news. I think about all of us when we were toasting marshmallows at your house, remember? And it all just seems like a really good dream, and then you wake up into real life and suddenly everything stinks. I wonder why real life can never be as good as dreams.*

I know you've told me about a million times you think Dr. Schmidt is doing the right thing, and I guess I have to accept the fact that that's how a grown-up might look at it. But for myself, I still think he ought to be with you instead of trying to make it up with someone who dumped him. But you know, really, I'm finding out that more and more of life just doesn't make sense.

I guess that's it for now. I'll write again and I hope you'll write me. I know I'll see you again someday because, like I said, eighteen isn't all that far away. I'm not going to stay in this house one minute past high school graduation.

Sincerely, your friend forever,
Satchel Queen

CHAPTER 55

I wrote to Satchel at the return address on the envelope, but I don't believe my letter ever reached her. The day after I dropped the letter in the mailbox, Jack Farrell called me into his office.

"Have a seat, Beth," he said. The somber look on his face told me he was about to tell me something I didn't want to hear.

He waved me into one of the wing chairs situated by the window; he sat across from me in the other. He fidgeted a moment and ran an index finger across his lips before he began to speak.

"Harlan Quinn got a call from the White Plains police this morning," he said. "He routed the call to me."

The place that was my heart immediately became a well of fear. Why would the White Plains police be calling our headmaster? "It's Satchel, isn't it?" I asked. "Is she all right?"

Jack sighed heavily as he leaned forward in the chair. "She's run away, Beth."

"What?"

"Her parents reported her missing yesterday morning. Her mother's car was missing too. Apparently Satchel found the key and just drove off."

"Have the police put out a bulletin on the car?"

"Yes, and it was found last night—"

"And Satchel?"

Jack Farrell opened his hands and turned his palms toward

me. "The car had been abandoned by the side of the interstate in Jersey, just south of Newark. It was out of gas."

"So Satchel probably took off from there on foot?"

"Presumably so. She may not have had the cash to fill up the tank."

"Does anyone have any idea where she might be headed?"

"Yes. That's why the police called Harlan. Her parents feel certain she's headed here. She was driving south on 95, and that's a straight shot into Wilmington."

"But the car ran out of gas."

"Yes."

"And now she's out there by herself. How can she walk all the way—"

"She'll most likely try to hitch a ride, don't you think?"

"But that's the worst thing she can do."

Jack leaned back again in the chair and frowned. "Beth, we have to hope she shows up here. And when she does, the minute she does, you'll have to let me know."

"You think she'll come to me?"

"I think that's exactly what she'll do. When she does, don't let her out of your sight. Call me, anytime, day or night. You have my cell number, right?"

"Yes."

"Good." He looked at me intently a moment, his dark eyes questioning. "You will call me, won't you, Beth?"

"Of course."

"We've got to do everything we can to get that child home to her family."

"Of course," I said again. Reluctantly.

"Well." He stood, signaling the end of our conversation.

Following suit, I got up from the chair. "Thank you for letting me know, Jack."

He nodded. "It's a sad situation, but let's hope it gets resolved quickly and easily."

"Yes, I hope so."

He walked me to the door of his office. More gently now he said, "Try not to worry too much, Beth."

I nodded. But it was advice I couldn't take. "Do you know what happens to young girls when they run away from home?"

Jack Farrell laid an unfamiliar but comforting hand on my shoulder. "For now, we're going to assume that Satchel is heading straight for you."

I ascended the stairs to my classroom, only half aware of my surroundings. My mind wanted to be with Satchel, to will her to keep coming, to help her reach me before anything might happen to her. But as I entered my classroom I was greeted by the questioning glances and barely concealed disappointment of a dozen sophomores. Had I been gone five minutes more, they could have, by school rules, left the room and considered Sophomore English canceled for the day. But, too late. Here I was. I told them to open their textbooks to chapter 10.

Satchel would have to find her way to me on her own.

CHAPTER 56

"I hope you don't mind my just stopping by."

"No. Of course not, Ray. Come on in. The house is a mess, but—" I shrugged and stepped aside to let Ray enter the front hall. "Actually, I was just making myself some chamomile tea. I thought it might help me sleep. Come on back to the kitchen."

"I won't stay long. I know it's getting late."

He followed me to the kitchen where a glance at the clock told me it was almost nine thirty. I'd planned to spend some time reading and drinking tea and was, in fact, just heading upstairs to put on my pajamas when the doorbell rang.

When the tea was done steeping I poured two cups. As I poured, I watched the teapot shiver from the tremble in my hand. Though we'd spoken on the phone, I hadn't seen Ray for many weeks.

"So are you just getting off work?" I asked as I set the teacup before him on the kitchen table.

"No." He pulled the cup toward him but didn't drink. "I was putting Ben to bed when I decided I had to come and see you. I'm sorry. I should have called ahead."

"It's all right. You're always welcome to stop by." I laughed a little, but it sounded unconvincing.

"I was worried about you, Beth, because I heard about Satchel."

"You heard she was pulled from school?"

"Yes, and that she has since run away." He sipped the tea,

then looked at me sheepishly. "Natalie called to tell me. She said she thought I might like to know. She was right."

I nodded. I'd called Natalie early that evening to tell her about Satchel. She must have called Ray as soon as we hung up. I stirred my tea with a spoon to cool it down. The spoon made small rippling circles in the tea as it clinked against the sides of the porcelain cup. "Thank you for being concerned, Ray."

For a moment neither of us said anything. I almost wished that the radio was playing or that the phone would ring—anything to fill the void.

Finally Ray said, "Have you gotten any word from the police?"

"Nothing since the call to Harlan this morning."

"And how long has she been gone?"

"Two days." I looked up at the clock again. I could actually hear it ticking. "They think she's making her way back to Delaware. Without the car, of course."

"So I understand."

"They're guessing that she wants to make her way back to me."

"That's probably a good guess."

"I'm not so sure. She might try to contact the Duttons instead."

"Let's hope she contacts someone."

"Yes," I agreed. "But if and when she does, we'll just have to turn her in. I hate to think of sending her back to her mother and stepfather."

"Are they abusive? Is there something social services should know?"

I shook my head. "No, it's not what you'd call an abusive

situation. There's just . . . I don't know. A lack of love. I guess that's the best way to describe it."

"But she's safe there?"

"Oh yes. I think so. Just not happy."

"Then you have to notify the police if she shows up here. What else can you do?"

"I know." I finally stopped stirring the tea. But I didn't trust my hands to carry the cup the brief distance to my lips. "There isn't anything else I can do."

While my eyes were on my hands, I heard Ray sigh. "Are you doing all right, Beth?"

I didn't want to cry. I took a deep breath. "I'm worried. I wonder where Satchel is, where she's sleeping, whether she's cold . . ."

Ray nodded as I spoke. "I know. I'm worried too."

"You don't suppose," I said, looking up at Ray, "she'd try to go to Josh instead?"

Ray considered that for a moment, his face tightening into a frown. "No, I don't think so. There's really nothing between Josh and Satchel. Josh says they've always been just friends."

"I suppose you're right," I said. "She'd have no reason to go there. I just hope she shows up *some*where. I don't care who finds her, as long as somebody finds her."

"I know, Beth. I hope so too."

He finished his tea, and I offered him more but he declined. Again, the room was heavy with silence, a silence weighted with words that neither of us seemed able to speak. I expected any second to hear him say he had to go, but the clock ticked on, and he remained.

"So how are you doing, Ray?" I asked reluctantly.

"I'm doing well." He rubbed an index finger along the

rim of the saucer. He didn't look at me.

"And the kids?"

"Doing great. Yeah, doing great."

I thought I might attempt to lift the teacup to my lips but decided against it. Not now. Certainly not right now. Fortifying myself with a deep breath, I asked, "And Brenda?"

His eyes came up, met mine, went back down. He seemed to have to think about his answer for a while. "We're, um, we're seeing each other. You know, getting reacquainted."

I watched his finger caressing the saucer. "That's good, Ray."

"Yeah." It was more of a sigh than a word.

"So maybe it'll work out again?"

"Maybe."

I swallowed, moistened my lips. I startled even myself by saying, "I think you still love her, Ray."

He looked up at me then and held my gaze. How, I wondered, could anyone look so infinitely sad and so marvelously happy at one and the same time?

"I don't think I ever really stopped loving her, Beth."

All the air escaped my lungs in one long sigh. "You can forgive her, then?"

"Yes. Yes, I think I can."

"That's good, Ray, really—"

"I'm just sorry, Beth—I never meant to hurt you—"

I cut him off. "Stop, Ray. Don't apologize. I'm happy for you. I really am."

The sadness that I had seen clinging to him for months seemed to slip away then. A small and tentative smile settled on his face. "Did anyone ever tell you that you are one rare lady?"

I nodded slowly, as though in thought. "I think you did once, many years ago."

"Well, if I did, I was right."

"Thanks."

He smiled fully then and nodded. He pushed his chair back from the table and rose to go. At the door he said, "I almost forgot to tell you. When I put Ben to bed tonight, he prayed for Satchel, that she'd be safe."

"Tell Ben I thank him for that. And tell him to keep it up."

"I will. And we will. We'll both keep praying for her."

When I shut the door behind Ray, I went to the dining room and pulled open the drapes. I watched the taillights of Ray's car disappear out of campus. When all I could see was my own reflection in the dark window, I realized with shame that I had myself not prayed one prayer for Satchel's safe return. I wanted to now. I wanted to put her into the hands of a loving God, but as I tried to gather up my thoughts and fashion them into a prayer, I discovered that the words were rusted and wouldn't break apart into meaningful sentences. How long had it been since I had prayed about anything at all? What had happened to the God I had known, the one who had come to me in those moments of being?

I turned from the window and walked to the living room. My eyes roamed the shelves, seeking out the all-familiar books. I scanned the spines; I read the titles. I lifted a hand to take a volume from the shelf, but then I stopped, letting my hand fall to my side. Because I suddenly knew what I hadn't known before.

Not every altar in this world is made of wood and stone.

CHAPTER 57

That night I dreamed I was in the eighth grade again. Our class had gathered in the assembly hall to practice for our Reader's Theatre performance of "The Highwayman." My part was coming up, those three little words, "with her death." I was ready for it this time. I could say those words and be heard. The highwayman was galloping toward the inn as the class recited in unison: "Then her finger moved in the moonlight, / Her musket shattered the moonlight, / Shattered her breast in the moonlight and warned him—"

Stop. Silence. That was my cue. "With her death." That was all I had to say. It was so simple.

But the words weren't there, because *I* wasn't there. I could not be seen, and neither could I speak.

As I moved about the school from there unseen, I felt on the one hand a great sense of relief. I could float freely, watching. I could simply observe without participating. I didn't have to prove myself. I didn't have to be good enough. No sitting down to sweaty palms at final exams. No running on the hockey field and bungling a goal. No passing through the smoking lounge on my way to my locker and hearing the occasional snicker that followed me. Nothing.

On the other hand I felt an almost sickening sense of isolation. I had no name, no face, no identity. The vacuum in which I moved was enormous, a black hole from which I couldn't escape. I could not step out of the hole and into a place in the world. I was invisible. I existed only to the point of knowing that I didn't exist. I wanted to scream, but I had no voice; I couldn't make a sound. The black hole pulled me farther in, sucking me up and sending me tumbling through lightless space, an endless free fall through an empty universe.

I awoke suddenly in a dark room. It was morning but not yet daybreak. I lay in the bed staring up at the ceiling, feeling my heart knocking up against my rib cage. I listened to myself breathe. I became aware of the soft weight of the linens against my skin. Slowly the terror passed. The bed felt warm and comforting. The room was there with everything in its place—the chest of drawers, the rocking chair, my desk. The familiarity cradled me.

This was my home. Outside the window was the campus of Seaton School. This place rested on the soil of a state called Delaware. The First State. The first state of a new nation, one nation under God.

I smiled, remembering the question from my childhood. *Could anything at all come out of Delaware?*

How did that Bible story go? Philip told Nathanael they'd found the one the prophets wrote about. It was Jesus of Nazareth, the son of Joseph. And Nathanael said, "Can any good thing come out of Nazareth?" Philip invited him to come and see.

So Nathanael went. And even before he had quite arrived, Jesus saw him coming and called out to him.

Nathanael didn't understand. "How do you know me?" he asked.

Jesus answered like it was commonplace, like everyone could see people who weren't even there. While Nathanael was out of sight, while he was still standing under the fig tree where anyone with human eyes wouldn't have seen him for the distance, Jesus claimed to have seen him anyway. That's what He told Nathanael: "I saw you."

I remembered that now, the words coming to me the way the morning sun tapped at my bedroom windows. As a child, I had known those words, had known that story by heart. In my moments of being I had felt those same benevolent eyes on me, confirming my created presence within His sacred presence, affirming His love for even me. But I had forgotten. Not all at once, but through slow distraction and inattentiveness I lost the ability to know the one real thing beyond appearances. I could not see, because I thought I could not be seen.

Dear God, I thought. *God of the moments, God of the bells, God who sees me and comes to me, could it be that you too know what it is to love and not to be loved in return?*

"Forgive me," I whispered.

Two small and barely audible words, but I knew they had been heard.

The day was waiting; I had classes to teach, students to see, papers to grade. I got up and slipped on my robe, wiggled my feet into my slippers, headed for the stairs. Those words, "I saw you," and those same gentle eyes followed me down.

At the bottom, in the hallway, instead of turning right to go to the kitchen as I usually did, I turned left, inexplicably, into the living room. I took only one step, then stopped short.

There on the couch, wrapped up like a gift in the knitted afghan, lay Satchel, fast asleep.

CHAPTER 58

I kept one eye on the clock as Satchel pounced hungrily on the plate of scrambled eggs and toast I'd placed before her. In another few minutes I'd call the office in Heath Hall and ask Joel to dismiss my eight-thirty class. I wasn't ready yet to call Jack Farrell. I wanted to talk to Satchel first.

After she cleaned the plate, she finished off a glass of orange juice in a couple of swallows. She settled the empty glass on the table and wiped her mouth with a paper napkin.

"You were hungry," I said.

She nodded. Pushing her chair away from the table, she got up and carried the dirty dishes to the sink. There, she stood with her back to me looking out the kitchen window.

"Where have you been the last couple of days?" I asked.

She turned around slowly, sighing. "Trying to get here."

"They found your mother's car."

"I figured they would. Little hard to miss a car on the side of 95. I ran out of gas."

"I know. What did you do then? Walk?"

"Some. Then I finally hitched a ride."

"That was dangerous, Satchel."

She shrugged. "I made it, didn't I?"

"Thank God, you did."

She looked at me, saying nothing.

"How'd you get into the house?"

"Easy. You really should get locks on your windows."

"You just crawled in through a window?"

"Yeah, that big one in the living room."

The thought unnerved me a little. "All right, I'll get locks." Then I added, "But I'm glad you got in."

She leaned back against the counter and crossed her arms. Two dark crescents hung beneath her eyes like shaded moons, while her eyes themselves looked large and luminous against her colorless skin. Her unkempt hair was loose and stringy on one side, matted from sleep on the other. She wore a dark knitted sweater over a button-down shirt, the tails of which hung out over the belt loops of her tattered jeans. After just a few days the look of the streets had rubbed off on her.

"I don't want to go back," she said firmly.

"I know you don't."

"Let them hire a maid. That's all they want me around for anyway."

"I know, Satchel," I said again.

"I want to stay here."

I glanced at the clock. "Listen," I said, "let me call Mr. Sexton and have him cancel my first class. Then we can go into the living room and talk."

"You're not going to tell him I'm here, are you?"

"No."

She looked at me warily.

"Honest, Satchel. I just want to ask him to cancel the class. Can you hand me the cordless?"

She did, and I made the call without giving Joel a reason for my being late.

In the living room Satchel and I sat down beside each other on the couch. She pulled the afghan around her, holding the front closed like a cloak. She inhaled deeply, as though she were pulling the warmth into her lungs. For several days she had been cold and hungry—that much I knew.

"I'm glad you're all right, Satchel. I was worried sick," I said.

"Really?" She seemed surprised, and pleased.

"Of course. What do you think? That you might be lost out there and I simply wouldn't care?"

She looked at me sheepishly then. "I'm sorry I worried you."

"Oh, Satchel." I sighed heavily. "It was wrong to run away. Everyone was worried—the Duttons, the people here at school, your parents—"

"Mom and Roger don't care about me."

"Of course they do."

An expression of anger crossed her face but only briefly. As soon as it passed, Satchel said quietly, "Can I stay here with you, Miss Gunnar?"

I wanted to say yes, of course she could stay with me. Instead, I shook my head. "No, Satchel. You can't. Your parents have taken you out of Seaton, and it's not up to me to keep you here."

"So you'd make me go back?"

"I don't have any choice. *You* don't have any choice. Where you go—well, it's your parents' call."

"But . . ." She gazed at me a long moment with wide eyes. "Being here with you and the Duttons, this is the only place I've ever really been happy since Dad . . ."

She covered her face with the afghan then and began to weep. I put an arm around her and pulled her close. "I'm sorry, Satchel," I said. "I really am. If it were up to me, I'd let you stay here. I want you here. But it simply isn't up to me."

"But you could talk to them," Satchel wailed, her words

muffled by the afghan. "You could talk to Mom and Roger and see if they'd let me finish out the year here. Maybe if you tell them you want me here . . ."

"I don't think it would be much use. They've already made up their minds."

She lifted her head and looked at me accusingly. "You don't want me either, do you?"

"Oh, Satchel. That isn't it at all. I wish you could stay here. I wish you were my own child—"

I stopped. Satchel and I looked at each other.

"Won't you talk to them, Miss Gunnar?" she asked finally.

I sighed heavily once again.

"Bring me the phone," I said.

CHAPTER 59

Satchel punched in the numbers herself, then handed the cordless back to me. As I listened to the ringing on the other end, I was keenly, almost shamefully, aware that I shouldn't be doing this, that I should be calling Jack Farrell instead. After half a dozen rings I began to feel confident that no one would answer. With relief I moved an index finger to the Off button. But too late. In the next moment I heard a click and a woman's weary voice saying, "Hello?"

"Mrs.—" I stopped, unable to remember Satchel's mother's name.

"Leeson," Satchel whispered.

"Leeson?" I repeated.

From the other end of the line: "Yes?"

I cleared my throat and tried again. "Mrs. Leeson, this is Beth Gunnar, Satchel's English teacher at Seaton School."

A long pause. Then another uncertain, "Yes?"

"Well, I'm calling because Satchel's here, and—"

"Satchel's there?"

"Yes, she showed up—"

The woman cried out, then said away from the phone, "Roger! Roger, it's Satchel! She's showed up." Then back into the mouthpiece, "Put Satchel on the line, will you? Let me talk to her."

Satchel, able to hear her mother through the phone, drew back and shook her head.

"Well," I said, "first I'd like to talk with you about—"

"I said, let me talk to Satchel!"

"She doesn't want—"

"Please put my daughter on the line."

Satchel, frowning, took the phone and said, "Mom, I'm here at Miss Gunnar's house. I want—"

"How could you do what you did, Satchel? How could you just take my car like that and run away?" Like Satchel a moment ago, I had no trouble hearing the woman's voice as it came through the phone line.

"I told you I wouldn't stay. I told you—"

"You're coming home as soon as—"

Satchel narrowed her eyes and angrily tossed the phone down on the couch. I picked it up. Mrs. Leeson was still talking.

"—and Roger can get down there and—"

"Mrs. Leeson. Mrs. Leeson, it's Beth Gunnar again."

"What? Where's Satchel?"

"I called to talk with you about—"

"What is it, Judy?" The voice in the background belonged to a man, presumably Roger. "Who are you talking to?"

"It's Satchel's teacher at Seaton."

"Let me have the phone."

"No, Roger, I'm—"

"Judy, give me the phone."

"But I'm—ow, that hurt my hand—"

"Hello? Who is this?" asked a Brooklyn accent.

"This is Beth Gunnar, Satchel's English teacher," I said again.

"Oh yeah. How are you, Miss Gunnar?"

"Um, I'm fine. I'm calling because—"

"Is Satchel all right?"

"Yes, she's fine. She's here with me, at my home."

"Thank God," he said, sounding genuinely relieved.

"Yes. Yes, well—she asked me to call and talk with you. If it's at all possible, she'd like to finish out the school year here—"

"That's out of the question," Satchel's mother interrupted.

"Judy, hang up the extension. Let me handle this."

"No, Roger, she's my daughter, and I want her here."

"Judy, hang up the phone."

A long pause followed. Then I heard the sound of a phone being hung up.

"So," Mr. Leeson said, "Satchel thinks she wants to stay at Seaton for the year?"

"Yes, she'd at least like to finish out this year. There are only a couple of months left."

"Yeah? The school here in White Plains isn't good enough for her?"

"I don't know about that, Mr. Leeson, I just know—"

"Let me talk to Satchel."

One thing I could say about Satchel's parents—they weren't very good at holding a conversation. I handed the phone to Satchel.

"Yeah?"

"So, kid, you all right?"

"Yeah, I'm all right."

"What's the matter? You don't like it here in White Plains?"

"It isn't that, Roger, it's more like—"

"Your mother—she thinks she needs you right now, you know? You don't want to be around to help her out?"

"No. I mean, yeah, but—"

"But you'd rather be down there."

Satchel nodded. "Yeah."

Another long pause. Satchel looked up at me, her eyes two pools of anxiety.

"Tell you what," her stepfather said. "Put your teacher back on the line, will you?"

Satchel handed me the phone. "Yes, Mr. Leeson?"

"Listen, I've got nothing against the kid finishing out the year there—"

"Roger!" From somewhere in the background.

"Let me finish, Judy." Then back to me: "Tell you what," he said again, "Judy and I, we'll come down there and talk this thing through, all right?"

"Sure. All right."

"Roger, I—"

"Be quiet, Judy." To me: "All right, then. I can't make it down there today because I've got to be in the office. In fact, I should be there right now. But tomorrow I'll take the day off, and we'll come down. You arrange a meeting with the principal and yourself and the two of us, all right?"

"Yes, I'll do that."

"We'll see if we can't talk this thing through."

I smiled up at Satchel. "Great, Mr. Leeson. Yes, that'll be great."

"In the meantime, can Satchel stay with you?"

"Absolutely."

"Don't let her out of your sight."

"No, I won't. I promise."

"All right, then, we'll be there sometime tomorrow afternoon. Judy, she's not doing so good in the morning, but she's better by afternoon. I'll call from the road, let you know how we're doing time wise."

"Good, good. I'll call Mr. Farrell right now and arrange the meeting."

"Thank you, Miss Gunnar. And I'm sorry for any imposition."

"Not at all. Don't worry."

After we disconnected, I stared at the receiver for a minute. Then I said, "I think maybe you've got Roger on your side."

Satchel smiled, but the relief was short-lived. "Now all we have to do is convince Mom to let me stay," she said. "And that's not going to be easy."

CHAPTER 60

Jack Farrell called in a substitute to cover my classes while I stayed home with Satchel. She slept a good deal, and when she was awake, she ate a good deal. In the late afternoon she showered and changed into a pair of loose-fitting jeans and a sweater that I let her pick out of my closet. She had packed a suitcase when she ran away but left it in the trunk of her mother's Infiniti G Coupe when the gas gauge hit empty and the car sputtered to a stop. The only thing she carried on the road with her was a backpack with a few dollars, a hairbrush, a pair of sunglasses, a leather key ring with her keys to the dorm and to Bel's Book Nook, a bag of dried mango, and a paperback copy of George Eliot's *The Mill on the Floss*. Theodore Dutton had given her the book shortly before spring break.

We spent the entire day at Pine Glen. I thought we might call the Duttons to tell them she was here, but she wanted to wait until after the meeting with her parents. She was hoping, after the whole thing was settled, to go to the Duttons and tell them the good news in person.

I hoped that would be the case as well, that somehow Roger would persuade Satchel's mother to let her finish the year. While Satchel appeared calm about the meeting, I felt like a defendant awaiting a verdict. I wanted Satchel to stay, for her sake and for my own. I steeled myself against the thought that she might be carried back to White Plains no later than the next afternoon.

When an early dusk settled in, I realized Satchel needed a more comfortable place to sleep than the couch in the living room. I rummaged through the linen closet in the upstairs hall, then carried a couple of pillows and clean sheets to the second bedroom, a spacious sunny room that might have made a nice guest room or an office if I weren't using it for storage. It had come furnished with a daybed and a chest of drawers, something left over from one of the previous occupants of Pine Glen. Since my move, though, the room was cluttered with odds and ends normally relegated to the basement or garage, neither of which I had. A stationary bike, a couple of unused floor lamps, boxes of kitchen items and knickknacks and memorabilia I intended to sort through but hadn't so far. And books. Mostly books. Some shelved, some in piles on the floor, some still in unopened boxes left over from the move. I had too many books. Clearly, it was time to get rid of some of them, not because I didn't love them, but because I loved them too much.

I would do that soon, I resolved, but first take care of Satchel. I put the clean sheets and a comforter on the bed for her and even fluffed up the pillows. Then I headed to the kitchen, where I roasted a chicken for dinner and made mashed potatoes while Satchel cut up vegetables for a tossed salad. We ate, we watched the news, she read in the wing chair with her feet propped up while I sat on the couch going over my lesson plans for the next day. Once when I looked up, I noticed that the book was in Satchel's lap and her eyes were closed. I smiled and went back to my papers.

A few minutes later I looked up again and said, "Satchel, why don't you go on up to bed? You're falling asleep."

She shook her head but didn't open her eyes. "I'm not asleep."

"Then what are you doing?"

"I'm asking God to let me stay."

"You are?"

She nodded. She opened her eyes and looked at me. "I think He wants me here."

"You do?" I was afraid she was projecting her own desires onto God and would be severely disappointed if her parents took her back to White Plains. "Why do you think that?"

"Well," she said, drawing her legs up into the chair and tucking them beneath her. "Do you remember that story about the bells in the church you told me about?"

"Yes, I remember."

"It's something like that, I guess."

I waited for her to go on, but she appeared deep in thought. "What do you mean?" I prodded.

She came back then from wherever she had been and said, "I hated being in White Plains. I hated every minute of it. I was so mad." She shook her head slowly. "I told God I hated Him for giving me such a lousy life."

"So what happened?"

"I cried a lot. I got mad a lot. I got in trouble in school for fighting with other kids." Her eyes darted toward me as she rushed to add, "Not fistfights. Just yelling, screaming—that kind of thing. I couldn't seem to help it. I just had to yell at somebody."

I nodded. "That's understandable."

"Then one morning I woke up and I didn't feel angry anymore. I didn't feel anything—but in a good way, I mean. It felt good not to feel mad. So I was lying there in bed, and

I turned toward the window, and there was the most beautiful pattern of frost on the glass. I couldn't believe it. I got out of bed and went to the window so I could look at it closer. And you know, if you looked real close, every little speck of frost was shaped like a snowflake, like there were a zillion little tiny snowflakes that had formed a pattern on the window. My dad used to tell me that Jack Frost came around in the winter to paint the windows, but I knew this wasn't the work of any Jack Frost. And then while I was kneeling there looking at it, the sun started coming up, and when it hit that frost on the window, it just about blinded me. It was like a star exploding or something. And it was like God telling me everything was going to be all right. That's when I decided to come back here. The next day I ran away."

I hesitated to respond. Finally I said, "I thought you weren't sure you believed in God."

"I do now."

"Because you saw the frost?"

Satchel shook her head. "It wasn't so much seeing something as knowing something. Like when you heard the bells, and you knew God was there."

I nodded, unsure of how to respond.

"It's not the frost or the bells or anything like that," Satchel said. "The way Mr. Ted put it was . . . well, he had a name for it. Something Latin. *Sensus divinus*, or something."

"*Sensus divinitatis?*" I asked.

Satchel's eyes widened. "I think that's it. It means people can sense the divine."

"And Mr. Dutton told you this?"

"Yeah." Satchel nodded. "We were talking about it before

spring break. Before that too, I guess. We kind of talked about it a lot."

"You did? What did he say?"

"Um, well . . ." She put a hand to her head and rubbed her temple with an open palm, as though to loosen the thoughts at the back of her mind, to bring them up to the light where she could see them. "He said a lot of people have written about it. You know, a lot of the poets and the saints." She paused and smiled. "Because it's a universal thing, you know? Though some people see it as one thing, and some people see it as another, and some people just don't see it at all, even though it's, like, something we're born with."

"I'm not sure I'm following you, Satchel."

Two lines formed between her eyes as she frowned. "Mr. Ted said Virginia Woolf wrote about it, even though she didn't know what it was."

"Virginia Woolf?"

"Yeah. He said she wrote about those times when she sensed something, and she really felt like she was alive or like she was connected to something, or something like that. I think he said she called it her 'moments of being.' Mr. Ted said he had a student once who wrote a paper about it, who said, you know, that those moments of being were when God came to Virginia Woolf, and she sensed him, but she just couldn't figure out what it was."

I scarcely breathed. With some difficulty I asked, "Did Mr. Dutton tell you who that student was?"

"No." She shook her head. "Why?"

"Nothing. I was just wondering."

"Oh. So anyway, Mr. Ted said it took him a long time to realize maybe there was something to that. I mean, something to the idea of God coming to people. He said he believes it now, though."

"He does?"

"Yeah." She sounded far away and dreamy. "Yeah, he does. And I think he's right, because to me, Mr. Ted's a poet and, you know, I think he may even be a saint."

"A saint?" I whispered.

"He understands things, like you do, Miss Gunnar. He's a lot like you, or maybe you're a lot like him because he was your teacher. I don't know. But anyway, that's what I like about you and Mr. Ted. You understand things. Not like my mom and Roger. They're like, well . . . they're like cardboard or something, like they're just made out of cardboard. My mother thinks beauty is a perm and a wax job, you know? I don't think she's ever read a poem in her life. And Roger— he's nothing like what my dad was like, which is probably why Mom's crazy about him. I mean, to him, everything's about money, you know? He's checking out the stock market before he even has his first cup of coffee in the morning. Know what I mean? And . . ."

Satchel went on and I listened, though barely, catching only fragments of what she said. I was preoccupied with the pendulum of my emotions swinging rashly between awe and anger. Theodore Dutton seemed to me an ever-deepening enigma, a riddle without an answer, and I didn't like being left dangling and frustrated. I didn't like it at all.

CHAPTER 61

Judy Leeson, Satchel's mother, was a petite woman who looked scarcely out of high school, though she must have been in her late thirties. She had bottle-blond hair and painted acrylic fingernails, and she wore a stylish maternity pantsuit that downplayed her newly swollen belly. Her husband was an older man, graying but distinguished, his smooth skin tanned in spite of the season, his Gucci suit murmuring wealth.

At first glance they appeared a pleasant enough couple though somewhat reserved, maybe a bit standoffish. Roger Leeson managed a smile and a respectable handshake when I met him in Jack Farrell's office. Judy Leeson offered a hand as lifeless as a sock monkey and half as warm. I knew I was in trouble when she met my gaze with a brief reluctant glance.

Neither hugged Satchel, who entered the office on my heels and stood silently while Jack introduced me to the Leesons. After the introductions, Mrs. Leeson looked at her daughter as though the girl seemed vaguely familiar, but she couldn't quite place her. Again, it was Roger Leeson who smiled and made an attempt to greet Satchel, though his "Hello, kid" was met with a grunt as Satchel dropped her eyes to her shoes.

Jack Farrell invited us to sit. We settled ourselves into the chairs placed around his office, then bounced awkward glances off one another for several unnerving seconds. Finally Jack cleared his throat and said, "Our headmaster—ah, here he is now."

Harlan Quinn rushed stiffly into the room, his aging limbs like rusty pistons reluctant to work. "You must excuse me for being late," he said breathlessly. "I can't seem to make a simple trek across campus without being waylaid by questions. As though I'm the only one with any answers around here—"

"You're not late at all, sir," Jack interrupted. "We were just getting started."

"Ah, good, good. That's fine, then."

"I'd like to introduce you to the Leesons."

Roger Leeson rose quickly and shook the old man's hand. Judy Leeson remained seated and lifted her limp hand, briefly allowing her painted fingertips to touch the old man's weathered skin. Her marriage to Roger had lifted her from poverty to plenty, and she wore the arrogance of the *nouveau riche* very well. These few minutes were enough for me to understand why Satchel didn't care to return to White Plains.

"So," said Harlan Quinn, settling himself in the last available chair in the room. "We're here to discuss the matter of . . ." He glanced around, apparently looking for someone to finish his sentence.

Jack stepped up quickly to fill in the blank. "Our former student, Satchel Queen. The Leesons are her parents. They've withdrawn her from Seaton, though Satchel would like to finish out the year."

"Ah yes."

I watched the old man's head bob in reply, and I wished he would do us all a favor and retire.

"Satchel ran away from home," I volunteered, "but she has in a very real sense turned herself in. She's willing to talk with her parents and see if they can't compromise somehow."

"I see." The head bobbed again. "Yes, I remember." He

324

turned his gaze to Roger Leeson and asked, "You prefer to have the child at home?"

"Well, you see—" Roger began, but his wife cut him off, saying, "Of course we do. What kind of question is that?"

"Now, Judy, we agreed that I would do the talking—"

"You decided that, Roger. I didn't agree to anything—"

"Mr. and Mrs.—" Harlan began.

"—she is my daughter, after all, and if I want her home, she should be home—"

"Mr. and Mrs. Leeson," Harlan tried again. "If I may interrupt . . ."

Surprisingly, the Leesons quieted, turning in unison to face the headmaster.

"Now then. You sent the child to us in September, asking us to provide her with a quality education. I wonder, has there been a problem in that regard?"

"Oh no, Mr. Quinn," Roger rushed in to say. "No, it isn't that at all. Seaton is a fine school, top-notch. It's just that Judy here is expecting and could use some help around—"

"I just want my daughter with me," Judy interrupted. "Is that too much to ask?"

Beside me, Satchel said under her breath, "Yeah, right."

Harlan said, "Perfectly understandable, Mrs. Leeson. Of course you do. Your daughter should be with you. But perhaps you would be willing to wait just a couple of months—"

"But I need her—I want her home now."

"Judy, you said you'd be willing to think about—"

"Don't put words in my mouth, Roger."

"On the way down, dear, you said you'd consider—"

Satchel jumped up. "She just wants me around to wait on her hand and foot!"

"That's not true!" her mother protested.

"Yes it is, and you know it."

"Satchel, darling—"

"Darling? Oh, that's good, Mom. Put on your best show for these people."

I tugged at Satchel's sleeve. "Satchel, this isn't helping," I pleaded.

She yanked her arm away without looking at me. "If Dad were here, he'd let me stay, because he'd know that was best for me."

Judy blanched while Roger shifted in his seat, crossing and uncrossing his legs. An electrified hush passed through the room, shocking us all. But it took Satchel's mother only a moment to snap back, and when she did, she was calm and cold. "Well, your father isn't here, is he?" she said evenly. "So it's up to me to decide what's best for you."

Satchel narrowed her eyes. "Yeah, right," she said defiantly, the words drawn out.

I tugged on her arm again. She sat.

Roger Leeson sucked in air and said, "It seems your mother has made up her mind—"

"So what about you, Roger? You'd let me stay, wouldn't you?"

Her stepfather looked at Satchel with amazingly apologetic eyes. For a moment I almost felt sorry for him.

"Satchel, listen, I think it's best—"

Satchel exhaled loudly, shook her head, and dropped her gaze to her shoes again. In doing so, she conceded defeat.

Jack, who'd been quiet up till now, said awkwardly, "I think I speak for Headmaster Quinn, Miss Gunnar, and myself when I say we're sorry to lose Satchel. She was an excellent student and an asset to Seaton. But of course we defer to the family in these rare situations when—"

Satchel interrupted Jack's soliloquy by leaping up and dashing from the office. I looked across the room at Roger and Judy Leeson, trying to gauge their reaction. They sat ashen, wide-eyed and silent, as though too stunned even to move. Mumbling some words of excuse, I ran after Satchel, catching up with her at the crest of the hill leading to Pine Glen. I pulled the child into my arms and held her as she sobbed into my blouse.

"It's going to be all right, Satchel," I said helplessly, not believing it myself.

"No it isn't, Miss Gunnar. It isn't." Her words were muffled, and her head rocked on my shoulder as she spoke. "I know I'm supposed to be here, and they just don't understand."

"Maybe they'll change their minds over the summer. Maybe they'll let you come back next year."

"But I'm supposed to be here now. Why can't they just let me stay?"

Twenty minutes later I watched Satchel climb into her stepfather's BMW, her backpack slung over her shoulder. I blew her a kiss as the car pulled away, but she didn't respond— not a wave, not a smile, nothing. She looked as though she had turned to stone.

Late that night I got the call from Jack Farrell. When the Leesons had stopped for gas somewhere in the middle of New Jersey, Satchel headed for the ladies' room at the station and didn't come back. For whatever reason, her parents had trusted her out of their sight, and when they weren't looking, she ran. This time no one assumed she was making her way back to Seaton.

CHAPTER 62

Theodore Dutton, for all his love of words, couldn't seem to find a single one with which to respond after I told him about Satchel, how she had been found, and how she was lost again. He tried once, twice, and then again to grab at something floating through his mind, but it must have been as fragile as gossamer, because when he opened his mouth, there was nothing there.

Finally Len Dutton spoke. "Does anyone have any idea at all where she might be headed?"

"None," I said.

We sat around the small table in the back room at Bel's Book Nook. It was just the three of us, as Bel had left to run errands an hour before I arrived. Selma Rainbo was out front manning the cash register.

"And you say this happened yesterday?"

"Yes. They were driving back to New York late yesterday afternoon when Satchel ran off."

"This wouldn't have happened at all if her parents had simply let her finish out the year," Len said.

I nodded. "It's really all so senseless. And unnecessary. Her stepfather might have let her stay, but her mother refused."

Mr. Dutton clenched his hands together on the table. He squeezed until his knuckles turned pasty, and then he released the grip like a sigh. He looked older than I had ever seen him. I knew there was something he wanted to say, and so I waited. Len sat quietly too, his fingers a tent over his lips.

At last Mr. Dutton said, "We can only do one thing." His voice was raspy and faraway, like a scratchy record on an old Victrola.

"What's that, Uncle Ted?" Len dropped his hands and leaned forward.

"Pray." He nodded slowly as his lips grew taut and his eyes moistened.

I looked at him fully, and he met my gaze. "You speak of prayer, Mr. Dutton, as though you think it might help."

"It's the only thing, Beth, that can help. It's all we can do for Satchel now."

"You told her . . . about my essay. Virginia Woolf . . ."

"The moments of being."

"Then you know?"

"Yes, now I know."

"What happened?"

"I finally listened." He leaned forward, bringing his face closer to mine, as though to make sure he could see me. "I had always sensed it, you see—what person doesn't? But for a long time I didn't understand. That thing beyond the appearances that Woolf wrote about—we give it so many names, or we say it is nothing at all, choosing to live as though it isn't there. But it is insistent, so maddeningly insistent, and I finally listened. . . ."

Bel's sudden appearance in the doorway interrupted him. "Beth, Selma said you were here. Have you had word about Satchel?"

"She has, Aunt Bel," Len said. "Come on, have a seat and we'll fill you in."

She joined us at the table, and I repeated the events of the previous day. By the time I finished, Bel was weeping quietly.

"Dear Satchel," she said, "I'm so afraid for her."

"Listen, Aunt Bel, why don't you and Uncle Ted go on home for the day. Get some rest. I'll stay here with Selma, and she and I can close up shop tonight. As it is, you're not going to be good for much around here."

Bel nodded and wiped her eyes with a paper napkin from the pile on the table. "I think you're right, Len. Thank you . . . thank you for staying and taking care of things."

"That's what I'm here for," Len said. "Go get some rest, and I'll see you at home tonight."

Obediently, Bel and Dutton pushed their chairs back from the table. As Dutton stood, he faltered, as though his legs were weak. Bel caught his arm on one side; I caught his hand on the other. For a long moment Theodore Dutton held on to my hand. He looked at me, and something passed between us, a communion of sorts, an understanding.

"I believe she got it wrong, you know," he said.

"Virginia Woolf?"

"Yes. In the end she thought it all came down to us. 'We are the words,' she said. 'We are the music; we are the thing itself.'" He shook his head slowly. "But it isn't that at all."

"It's God, of course," I whispered.

A small smile formed at the corners of his mouth. "It can be nothing else."

"Thank you," I said, "for praying for Satchel."

He squeezed my hand gently. "Thank you," he said, "for . . . everything."

Bel looked at us quizzically but said nothing. She helped her husband put on his jacket, then took his arm and led him to the door. I watched them leave, the two of them walking slowly, like people bent over by grief. I thought of how

Satchel had wanted to come herself to tell them the news that she was back. Instead, I had come with the news that she was gone.

Turning back to Len, I was struck again by how much he looked like the Theodore Dutton I had once known. He more closely resembled my former English teacher than the elderly man who just left the room.

Len met my gaze. "You know," he said, "they almost came to think of Satchel as a daughter."

"I feel the same way," I admitted.

Len nodded. "I don't know Satchel as well as you do, but in the little time I spent with her, I grew to care about her. I want you to know that. As a teacher, I've known a lot of kids over the years, but with Satchel—I don't know, there was just something different about her."

"Something special," I agreed. "She kept saying she was supposed to be with us—with me and the Duttons—but I guess that was wishful thinking."

I started to rise from the table then, but Len stopped me by placing a hand on my arm. "Beth," he said, "I don't want to offer empty words or false hope, but I want you to know that I think, somehow, Satchel is going to be okay. I don't think she's going to go far."

I tried to smile. "I hope you're right, Len."

He gave my arm a gentle, comforting squeeze. And then I rose to go.

CHAPTER 63

Spring flowed into the Delaware Valley with a rush of warm air, bringing with it the newborn colors of the year's early foliage. Seaton's campus became green again, the hills carpeted with grass instead of snow and mud. A myriad of leaves unfurled everywhere, cluttering the treetops and casting shadows on the ground. Soon Chapel Valley would be filled with daisies, a sight that, in my childhood, had never failed to fill me with joy.

I wasn't sure, though, that this present season would hold such promise. My one comforting thought was that with the passing of winter, Satchel would no longer be out in the cold.

Almost every day now, after school, I went to the bookstore. At first I visited briefly and left, but slowly I fell into a routine of voluntarily helping out, doing some of the odd jobs Satchel had done. Bel needed the help, and I needed to be doing something that made me feel connected to Satchel. Each day when I arrived, Mr. Dutton or Bel or Len would ask, "Has there been any word?" and every day I said no, the police had no leads as yet. We'd let the dread and disappointment pass inevitably through us, some of it settling once again into that empty place in our hearts, and then we'd go to work.

I gained a certain solace from being with the people who loved Satchel as I did, the people who missed her, who feared for her, who prayed for her. We didn't even have to say her name; a certain look might pass between us, and we knew that it was Satchel we were thinking of, her name that we were silently lifting to the One who could see her wherever she was.

The last weekend in April was a long weekend for the students at Seaton, which allowed the boarders time to go home. I should have used that Friday to grade papers and catch up on lesson plans, but I didn't. For the first time in my life, I was very nearly neglecting my job and my students. I was too distracted by thoughts of the one student who was lost.

I spent that Friday at the bookstore, shelving books, working the cash register, helping customers. The Duttons weren't there in the morning because Mr. Dutton had a doctor's appointment, and afterward they stopped to pick up groceries on the way to the store.

At nearly noon the two of them came in the back door carrying paper sacks. I was already in the back room, searching the refrigerator for something cold to drink. When Bel saw me, she said, "The cupboard is bare, I know. Honestly, I think Len's stomach must be a bottomless pit. I can't keep anything on hand anymore, not since he arrived. But, bless him! What would we do without him?"

I laughed and took the sack she handed me. "Good," I said, looking inside. "You got more cranberry juice. Just what I was looking for."

"Help yourself," Bel said. "There should be plenty of ice unless Len's used it all up and didn't make more."

I set the sack on the table and pulled the juice from it. "Are there any more bags in the car?" I asked.

"Just a couple."

"I'll get them." This was from Len, who was suddenly striding into the back room on his long legs. He passed us and disappeared out the door.

Mr. Dutton was busy at the counter, putting food away. I watched as he pulled a glass, bell-shaped cookie jar down from the cupboard. Inside were a few scattered pieces of dried mango. He set the jar on the counter, then untied the twist tie from the neck of a plastic bag.

In spite of the obvious, I asked, "Mr. Dutton, what are you doing?"

He paused and turned to me. "You really should call me Ted, you know, Beth. I'd prefer it."

I frowned and shook my head. "But why are you filling that jar with mango?"

"It's for Satchel when she comes back." He emptied the plastic bag, then put the lid on the jar and lifted it to the cupboard again. "It's just—I don't know—it makes me feel hopeful."

"I see." My response was weighted with uncertainty.

"If you're going to be perfectly honest, dear," Bel chided, her head in the fridge as she rearranged items on the shelves, "you might as well admit that you're the one who's eating it in the meantime."

"Yes, well, I'm afraid I've taken a liking to it."

"As long as you don't eat too much, Ted. Your diet, remember?"

"Speaking of which," Len said, coming inside and dropping the last two grocery sacks on the counter, "how does the doctor say the old man's doing?"

"Amazingly well, for someone in such poor health," Bel quipped.

"He says," Dutton added, "I can expect to live a little while longer. Though I plan to do better than that, of course."

"You will if you watch what you eat," Bel said. "You can't

do like Len here—eat everything you want and expect to get away with it."

"Now, Aunt Bel, I'm not such a bad eater."

"Just a big one, which is as it should be."

Len started to say something, shrugged instead, then began pulling groceries from the sacks.

Mr. Dutton pushed a button on the stove to start the tea-kettle boiling. By the time the last groceries were put away, he had poured himself a mug of tea and settled into his over-stuffed chair. He sank into the cushions with a heavy sigh. "Well, if the rest of you don't mind, I think I'll wait right here for a while."

"That's fine, dear," Bel said absently.

Len gave his uncle a bemused look. "And if you don't mind my asking, Uncle Ted, just what are you waiting for?"

Mr. Dutton looked up and blinked at Len from behind his thick glasses. "Why, I'm waiting for Satchel to come back, of course. Aren't you?"

Len, Bel, and I exchanged glances. Mr. Dutton was right. While on the surface of things we appeared to be going about our lives, our primary activity was waiting. Above all else, we were just waiting for Satchel to come home.

CHAPTER 64

While we waited, something entirely other was happening. In this unexpected and unwelcome place, Len and I were thrown together like two ticket holders watching for an overdue train. We found ourselves, in a sense, sitting side by side on a bench in the station, glancing at our watches, wishing the train would come, tossing comments to each other to commiserate. But eventually we found the comments leading to genuine conversation, until finally our thoughts flowed easily, as though we'd never been strangers at all but had always known each other.

In fact, he did remember us as kids, he said—remembered those nights in his Uncle Ted's cabin when a group of students came around to hang out with Mr. Dutton. "I'd mostly forgotten about those visits," he confessed, "but being here in Delaware again—I don't know—kind of brings it back."

We were taking a break in the back room, drinking raspberry tea from glass bottles and nibbling on mixed nuts Bel had dumped into a candy dish. I leaned forward over the table and looked at Len intently. "What do you remember?" I asked.

"I remember you," he said. His bottle of tea hovered momentarily between the table and his mouth. "And another girl, a blonde—"

"Natalie."

"Yeah, I guess so."

"She was my best friend. Still is."

He nodded. "She was dating Ken, right? The guy that played the guitar."

"Yeah."

"And you were dating the other guy—what's-his-name."

I gave a small laugh. "Ray."

"Uh-huh." The bottle finally reached his lips, and he took a long swallow. After a moment he said, "So what happened to him?"

"Ray? Oh, he became a doctor, got married, had kids."

"Uh-huh." Another swallow, another nod of the head. "But you never did?"

"Get married? No. And you?"

"Came close once. She broke it off."

"I'm sorry."

"Oh, don't be sorry," he lobbed back at me. "I'm not." He laughed and shook his head. "Not at all."

After that, when I was in my classroom in Heath Hall, I realized I was counting down the hours until I could leave Seaton and go to the bookstore. Sometimes when I arrived, Len was at the door watching for me. He'd open the door and welcome me, and we'd go on glancing at our watches and waiting for that train, but at the same time we talked and laughed, and sometimes we got so wrapped up in the moment we very nearly forgot we were waiting for anything at all. It's funny how something bad and something good can be happening at the same time, and even be related, one event springing up out of the other. And I guess that's the funny thing. If the train had not been waylaid, Len and I might never have known each other.

That last Friday in April, the Friday Mr. Dutton replenished the jar with mango, I stayed at the store until about five o'clock. I might have stayed longer, but Natalie had invited me to meet her at a coffee shop for sandwiches and dessert. Since Satchel ran away the second time, Natalie had been taking special care to be in touch with me daily, which I appreciated.

As I was preparing to leave, I carried one last stack of books from the back room to the front counter to tell Len they'd been inventoried and were ready to shelve. Len leaned on the counter, reading the newspaper.

"Any good news?" I asked as I dropped the books beside the cash register.

Len looked up at me and said, "I guess that depends on how you define good." He smiled, and I returned it.

"I suppose you're right," I said.

He tapped an index finger on the open page. "Did you know the U of Delaware is hosting a series of readings by local authors?"

"No. Guess I missed that. I haven't read the paper in a few days."

"The first one's tomorrow night, a guy named Russell Barrett. Ever heard of him?"

I shook my head. "I don't think so. What's he write?"

"Poetry."

"Really? And it got published?"

"Apparently. It says here he'll be reading from his newest release, *Blue Moon Over Autumn*, which is his second volume of poetry. He's a professor at the university."

"I wonder whether anyone will go."

"His students will if they know what's good for them."

"Spoken like a true teacher." I laughed.

"But who knows, maybe the guy's actually good." Len

shrugged, then frowned at me. "Hmm . . . you look doubtful. What? You don't like poetry?"

"Me? I love poetry. It just seems like very few people do these days."

"I do," he said.

"Yeah?"

"Yeah, I do." He folded the paper then and put it aside. "Well, would you like to go, then?"

"To the reading?"

"Yes."

"Do you mean . . . with you?"

"Well . . . yes."

I was flustered, and the words felt slippery on my tongue, like a school of minnows that I couldn't wrap my hands around. At the same time I considered responding with that old cliché, *I thought you'd never ask,* because all along I'd been waiting for this too. Satchel, yes, of course, but this too.

"Yes," I said when I finally said something. "Yes, I'd like to go."

Len smiled once more, and I had an odd sensation that Satchel Queen was looking on and laughing.

CHAPTER 65

After the poetry reading we stopped at a restaurant in Newark to grab something to eat. As Len took a bite of his hamburger, he shook his head and laughed silently.

"It wasn't that bad, Len," I said.

"It was awful," he countered. "And the worst part was that everyone in the audience acted like he's some ancient sage spouting off pearls of wisdom."

"Well, he had a few nice images—"

"But did you understand a single one of his poems?"

I sighed in defeat. "No, not really."

"No, and neither did anyone else. But people want to pretend to understand so they don't look like fools. Classic case of the emperor's new clothes. No one will admit the stuff is drivel."

"The book actually got some good reviews . . ."

"Yeah, which is a sad commentary on those particular literary critics." Len devoured a dill pickle spear in a couple of bites and followed it with a large swallow of iced tea. "Though I have to say—and I hate to admit it—but I kind of envy the guy."

I felt my eyebrows reach for my hairline. "How so?"

"Well, here he was up there reading from his own work, you know? I mean, he's holding in his hands a book he'd written himself."

"You want to write poetry?"

"Great Scot, no," Len exclaimed. "I like poetry, if it really is poetry, but I'm not going to try to write it. No. I want to write history."

"You do?"

"Well, yes. That's why I was in Europe, you know, doing research into the medieval church and the Protestant Reformation. I suppose it sounds like a complete bore—"

"Oh no, not at all."

"But I'd like to write a book about it. Actually, I've been planning to write about it for a long time."

"Really? I think that's wonderful."

He looked at me and smiled. "You do?"

"Yes, I really do."

He nodded as though in satisfaction, then went back to work on his hamburger.

"Well, what's keeping you from doing it?" I asked.

He looked thoughtful a moment. "Nothing, really. Now that I've done the research, I just have to find the time to do it. I've got to somehow carve out time in my teaching schedule, and that isn't going to be easy."

"No, I imagine not. You're going back to Quentin College in the fall, aren't you?"

"Oh yes. I'm afraid so. Don't have much choice about that. Not with a mortgage and a car payment. But like I say, I'm going to get that book written somehow."

Our waitress appeared and poured us both more iced tea. "Can I get you anything else?" she asked.

Len looked at me. "Beth?"

"I'm fine for now, thanks."

The waitress left, and Len poured a couple packets of sugar into his drink. He stirred the grainy cloud of sweetener until it dissolved into the tea. "Guess I should really cut back on the sugar," he said. "I don't want to end up like Uncle Ted."

"I don't think you will."

"No, probably not. He had a huge jump start toward diabetes that I never had."

"What do you mean?"

"Just that he may not have ended up a diabetic if not for all the drinking in his early years. Or at least that didn't help." He looked up at me suddenly and said, "You probably weren't aware of that, were you? I mean, did you know he was an alcoholic when he was teaching at Seaton?"

"Not at the time, no. But Ray recently told me about it."

"Really? You still in touch with Ray?"

"I saw him at homecoming last fall. You know, that's how I got back in touch with your uncle. He ended up in the hospital where Ray works."

"Oh yeah? Small world, isn't it?"

I nodded. "Sometime after that, Ray told me he and Ken used to go over to the cabin once in a while and share a few beers with Mr. Dutton."

"No kidding." Len pushed his empty plate aside and curled both hands around the glass of iced tea. "I'm not surprised, but I hate to hear that."

"Yeah, well, they were young."

"Uncle Ted wasn't. He should have known better. But he was pretty far gone by then."

"You know, Len, what amazes me is that I had no clue."

"A lot of alcoholics are good at hiding it."

"But Mr. Dutton seemed to have it so together."

He shrugged. "Typical."

"Did you know at the time that he was drinking?"

"Sure. I mean, I'd stay right there in the cabin with him

whenever I came down to visit. It was kind of hard to miss all the bottles everywhere. I'd get up in the morning and go looking for corn flakes and find Jim Beam in the cabinet instead."

"He didn't try to hide it from you?"

"Not very hard. Listen, tell you the truth, I drank with him sometimes. I thought it was cool. He was so different from my dad—Mr. Shirt-and-tie Conservative. You know how parents look to teens."

"I guess so."

"I just didn't know *how* far gone he was," Len continued. "Talk about not having a clue."

I stopped picking at my grilled chicken salad and looked intently across the table at Len. "What do you mean, you didn't know how far gone he was?"

He glanced sideways. He looked uneasy, but when he turned his gaze back to my face, he tried to smile. "I trust you, Beth," he said. "Listen, Uncle Ted didn't have a heart attack. He tried to kill himself."

The fork I'd been holding landed on the table with a loud clang. "You know that?"

"Of course." He studied me, his eyes narrowing. "You act as if you know it too."

I looked at him hard. "I do know."

Silence. Then, "How? How do you know?"

"I was there."

I told him the whole story then, while he looked incredulous one moment, grieved the next. When I finished, neither of us spoke for what seemed a long time.

Finally he said, "I can't believe you've known what happened all these years."

"Yes. It's never left me. The only thing I don't know is why he did it."

Len shook his head slowly. "I don't know that either, Beth. I've never really understood. But—" He took a deep breath and sat up straighter, as though he'd just snapped out of a trance. "It was a long time ago, and Uncle Ted has really changed. I mean, he stopped drinking, got his act together, and went on to live a productive life. So, happy ending. What more can you ask for?"

I didn't respond. Suddenly I was thinking of Satchel. I turned to the window and saw my own reflection in the glass. The night outside was dark and overcast, and the clouds had begun to spit rain that looked like scattered gemstones in the lamplight.

"She'll be all right," Len said.

"What?"

"Satchel. You were thinking of Satchel, weren't you?"

I drew in one quivering breath. "Yes, I guess I was. I hope she's . . . inside somewhere, out of the rain."

His hand found mine on the tabletop; his skin felt warm and reassuring. "One thing I can say for sure about Satchel," he said. "She knows enough to come in out of the rain."

He was right, of course. I nodded, squeezed his hand, offered him a smile. "Thanks, Len. I'm glad you happened to be here now while all of this is going on."

"So am I."

We sat quietly then, not needing to talk. We seemed to understand something without saying the words aloud. He'd be going back to New York before too much more time had passed, but that wouldn't be the end of things. His hand in mine was both strange and not strange, unexpected and yet somehow expected. Like a piece of a puzzle finally fitting snuggly into its companion piece. *Of course,* one thinks. *This piece goes with that one. I should have seen it long ago.*

When Len asked me out and the pieces fit, there arose that sense that this was somehow where we'd been headed all along, even when he was a long-haired dreamer and I was an invisible child.

After he drove me home to Pine Glen, he put his arms around me at the door and held me, and he kept on holding me until I felt solid and whole and warm and seen. He didn't let go until I knew that I was there. And then he said goodnight and told me he would call me the next day.

So that when, on Sunday afternoon, the phone rang and the caller ID gave Dutton's home number, I thought surely it was Len. But it wasn't. The voice on the other end of the line belonged to Theodore Dutton. He had never called me before, and I didn't expect him to call me now, so the first words out of my mouth were, "Is everything all right?"

"Oh yes," he assured me. "Everything's fine. It's just that—" he stopped a moment and lowered his voice—"I believe I know where Satchel is. I can't tell you where, Beth, but I want you to know she's safe."

CHAPTER 66

"Why can't you tell me where she is?"

"If I do, you'll go after her, and we can't go after her, Beth. It won't work that way. She'll have to come back to us on her own."

"But—how do you know where she is?"

"I'll explain everything to you later."

"When?"

"After she's back."

"And what if she doesn't want to come back?"

"I think she does. Yes, I think she will."

"But you can't be sure!" The shrillness in my voice was rising along with my anger. Theodore Dutton was a master of frustration, and he had kept me frustrated to varying degrees for a good portion of my life. I took a deep breath to calm myself. "All right, so you think you know where she is."

"Yes. And if she's where I think she is, she's quite safe."

"But you're not sure?"

"As sure as I can be."

"Listen, will you tell me where she is if I promise not to go after her?"

"I think it best not to say right now."

"But Mr. Dutton!"

"You will have to trust me on this, Beth."

"Trust you?" My voice was shrill again. "How can I trust you?"

"It's best that no one knows where she is. I wanted to tell

you she's safe just to put your mind at rest, but I can't tell you any more than that. And I'm not saying a word about any of this to Bel or Len."

"But why? I don't understand."

"Like I said, we can't force her to come back. She'll have to want to come back. Otherwise it's no good. We'll just lose her again. All we can do is let her know we love her, and then wait."

"Let her know we love her? But how on earth are we supposed to do that?"

"She'll know, if she listens."

"Listens to what? You're not making any sense."

"Never mind that. Trust me. Everything's going to be all right. Like I said, she's safe at the moment."

"But is she with somebody? Is someone taking care of her?"

"Well, yes and no."

I wondered then whether he had lost his mind. I thought it might be his illness talking, or maybe he had even relapsed and gone back to drinking.

"Just tell me, is she in a shelter, some sort of place for runaways?"

"Well, in a manner of speaking. Though I advise you not to start making the rounds of the local safe houses. That would only be wasting your time."

"Look, Mr. Dutton, Jack Farrell tells me Satchel's parents are beside themselves with worry. If you know something of her whereabouts, I think you owe it to them to speak up."

"No, Beth, no. They're exactly who she's hiding from. You know that as well as I do. They will simply have to be patient along with the rest of us."

"Where's Len?" I demanded.

"Out running errands. He'll be back soon."

"And Bel?"

"Upstairs napping. Which gave me the opportunity to call you."

"Listen, I don't know why you're doing this, and I'm not even sure you really know where Satchel is—"

"Beth!" He sounded genuinely hurt. "I'd never lie to you."

But my experience with him told me otherwise. Why had I tried to forge a friendship with the man after I saw him at the hospital? I should have listened to Natalie. I should have been satisfied to know he was alive while resolving to stay away. And certainly I should never have sent Satchel to work alongside the Duttons in their store.

"So how long do you intend to just wait for her to come back on her own?" I asked.

"As long as it takes."

I wanted to scream. Instead, I said with as much composure as I could muster, "And what if she moves on from wherever she is? What if we lose this opportunity to go after her?"

"I don't think she's going to move on."

My hand was beginning to cramp from my hold on the phone. "If she does, though, and if we lose her, I'm blaming you."

His voice was amazingly calm. "I believe what I'm doing is right, Beth. And I also believe that Satchel is going to come home. Now, Len has just gotten back so I'm going to hang up. But don't worry. Trust me."

CHAPTER 67

But I didn't trust him. And it was a distrust that went back decades. It was a doubtfulness born on an April night when a young girl's heart was broken by her hero. Maybe he had changed. Maybe, as he claimed, he had heard the call of the moments and recognized the voice of God, and it may be that he had paused long enough to listen and respond. Still, something was broken and hadn't been made right.

I stayed away from the bookstore for three days. Because of the depth of my anger, I was afraid of how I would respond to Theodore Dutton if I should see him.

Len called to ask where I was, why I wasn't coming in to the store. I told him I was busy at school and couldn't spare the time. He wondered, I knew, whether it was something between us—between me and him—but I couldn't explain. Not without telling him about the mysterious conversation with his uncle, which I didn't feel free to talk about.

For three days my stomach turned, and I swallowed the anger that burned my throat with bile. Assailed by images of what happens to young girls on the streets, I scarcely ate or slept and thought of little else other than Satchel and her whereabouts. I wondered whether Dutton really knew where she was, and if he did, I wondered at his insistence on keeping me from her. Once again, he was the man who owed me answers but refused to give them.

On the fourth day I couldn't stand it anymore. I drove to the store at closing time. When I pulled into the lot, Selma

Rainbo was getting into her car to go home. She tossed me a pleasant wave, then signaled a right turn and pulled out into a lull in traffic. I was glad she was leaving. One less person to deal with.

I parked my car and went inside. Len stood at the front counter looking over receipts. His face lit up when he saw me. "Beth!"

"I need to talk to Mr. Dutton," I said.

"What? Is something wrong?"

I shook my head, unable to speak.

"He's in the back room with Bel. We're just closing up for the night, you know."

"I know."

"Are you sure you're all right, Beth?"

I didn't answer. I turned away from Len and walked through the musty aisles toward the back of the store. Bel was wiping down the kitchen counter with a dishcloth while Mr. Dutton sat at the table looking over a pile of books.

"Why, Beth!" Bel said cheerfully. "I'm so glad you stopped by."

"I need to speak to Mr. Dutton, Bel."

"Well, all right."

"Alone."

She looked questioningly at her husband. He pushed the books aside and nodded at Bel. "Why don't you and Len go on home. I'll stay and chat with Beth, and then when we're finished I'll call Len to come pick me up."

"No," I said. "I'll take you home, Mr. Dutton. Len doesn't have to come back."

Mr. Dutton looked at me while adjusting his heavy glasses on his nose. "All right."

"Well, then." Bel tried to sound agreeable, but I could hear the hesitancy in her voice. "I'm ready to go home and put my feet up anyway." She looked at the dishcloth in her hand, seemingly not quite sure what to do with it. She settled on rinsing and wringing it out, then hanging it over the faucet. She did this slowly, as though hoping I would change my mind and tell her she could stay.

I didn't. I waited quietly for her to leave. Finally, with a dubious smile for me and a kiss for her husband, she left the room.

As soon as she was gone, I said, "I suppose you know why I'm here."

Mr. Dutton reached over to the chair beside him and pulled it away from the table. "Why don't you sit down, Beth."

I didn't sit. "Where is she, Mr. Dutton?"

The room became quiet, and I heard the tinkle of the bell over the front door, then a key in the lock, signaling Len's and Bel's departure.

Speaking quietly, almost in a whisper, Mr. Dutton said, "I know you're worried."

"I'm way beyond worried at this point. The not knowing is killing me."

Mr. Dutton leaned back in the chair, glanced up at the ceiling, looked back at me. "I can tell you she is safe, and you will only make matters worse if you don't give it some time." He continued to speak in low tones, as though he were afraid Bel and Len were hunched at the back door, listening.

I started to pace then, a few steps back and forth in the small space that was the kitchen. If I didn't move, I thought I might explode. I heard Mr. Dutton say my name, but I didn't respond. I was suspended between that moment and a long-ago night when Ken Cunningham stood under a starry sky running an index finger over his wrist. I heard Natalie scream, saw her fall to the ground, felt again my own grieved astonishment as a distant siren faded into the dark.

I stopped pacing and swung around toward Theodore Dutton. "Why did you do it?" My voice trembled, and my eyes felt like they were on fire, but it was only the tears that had been pressing against them for days, for years.

"Why did I do what?" Mr. Dutton looked up at me dumbfounded, blinking behind his glasses.

"Why did you kill yourself?" I cried. And then I asked it again. "Why did you kill yourself?" It made no sense, asking that question of a living soul, but for me he had been dead for years.

Once the words were out in the open, I found myself gazing upon the face of a man who seemed to be breaking apart into a thousand tiny pieces. I watched as his skin changed hues from red to pink to chalky gray. His eyes widened, his mouth came unhinged, his jaw trembled. He lifted one hand toward me, and it fluttered in the air between us like a wounded bird.

His lips moved. He was trying to say something. I waited and watched as he choked out the words, "What do you know about that?"

Cold tears rolled down my cheeks. "I know everything, Mr. Dutton."

"How?" He shook his head; it seemed a great effort. "How long?"

"I was there that night."

"What do you mean?"

"It was Ray and Ken who found you. They found you on the floor, in the blood . . ."

"Dear God," he breathed, shutting his eyes, and I thought he was indeed addressing God and not me. "They told me it was Fosset. They said Clarence Fosset found me . . ." After a moment he looked up again. "Tell me what you know." He touched the empty seat beside him, and this time I sat.

"Tell me what happened," he repeated.

I told him the story of that April Fool's night, of going to his cabin with Natalie, of the ambulance and the police and the look on the boys' faces as they stood in the chilly air under the midnight sky. I told him the story that Commander Pettingill spun at assembly on Monday morning, casting it out over the student body like a fraudulent blessing. I told him about the lies and the secrecy and the years I thought he was dead, and how I had grieved for him, and how I had wondered what awful thing would make him want to end his life.

When I finished, he had to moisten his lips before he could speak. He winced as though his tongue were made of sandpaper. "You've lived with this a lifetime, and I never knew."

"I just don't understand what happened, Mr. Dutton, why you'd want to do such a thing."

"I . . . I was a fool, Beth. A drunk and a fool."

"But that doesn't tell me anything. It doesn't tell me *why.*"

"How can I explain?" he said, his face wrinkled with pain, his eyes moist. "I really—I had no reason to die. No reason at all. And I think in the end, that's what it came down to. I had nothing to die for. No noble cause, no lofty ideals, nothing like what the poets talk about, like I talked about in class day after day. Not love of God, because"—he waved a hand—

"there was no God, you see. Not love of family, because I was alone. Not love of country—certainly not that, not after Vietnam. You're too young to remember, I know. You're too young to understand how we were sent to die in a losing battle, and if we came home we were crucified for going, crucified by the very people we were supposed to be defending. That did something to me, Beth, something irreparable, and though I tried to forget about it all and just go on with my life, something inside of me was lost, or hardened, or changed in some way I couldn't understand. After 'Nam, I had no goals other than getting as drunk as I could as often as I could. And I'll tell you, when you're looking at the bottom of an empty bottle and you start realizing there's nothing worth dying for, you finally decide there's nothing worth living for either."

When he finished, we looked at each other for a long time. He wanted me to understand, but I didn't. I said, "But you were the one who told us life was a gift. You were the one who took us out to the valley and told us to feel what it was like to lie under the sun, to be alive on the earth."

"I wanted you to believe that, even if I couldn't."

"But I trusted you. We all did. We all . . ." I stopped, pressing my mouth into a small tight line.

"What, Beth?"

"We loved you. Didn't you know that?"

He closed his eyes, shook his head. "No." The word was a choked whisper. "No. I couldn't see beyond my own misery. That was all—"

"We loved you, and you betrayed us."

I put my face in my hands and wept. I felt Mr. Dutton gently touch my shoulder. "Beth," he whispered, "my dear Beth. Can you ever forgive me?"

For the first time, I knew that I wanted to. But I couldn't stop crying long enough to find the words. Minutes passed. I took deep shuddering breaths and tried to look at the man sitting beside me at the table. When I finally thought I could speak, I opened my mouth, but before I could begin, I was interrupted by a pounding overhead. I looked at Mr. Dutton, then at the ceiling where the clattering came from. I gasped and started to rise, but Mr. Dutton held me firmly by the shoulder, as though telling me to sit. I watched in surprise as the attic door fell open with a crash. A pair of delicate hands opened the stairs and sent them unfolding toward the floor.

Then a figure emerged from the ceiling, climbing backward down the ladder, stopping at the bottom and staring at Dutton and me with an expression of bewilderment, compassion, and love.

And then Satchel Queen came and put her arms around both of us and, without a word, drew us into a place as tender as mercy and as clean as grace.

EPILOGUE

Satchel stands at the open front door of Pine Glen, looking out. I wonder whether she sees that certain light that settles over Delaware on summer nights, that sigh-of-contentment light that warms you even while it's fading. I think she must. Because it's there for all who look and listen, and Satchel is listening.

She lives here now with me in Pine Glen. She has been here all summer and will remain right here throughout her senior year at Seaton. It is an informal foster parenting situation of sorts. I don't know what happened behind closed doors between Roger and Judy Leeson, but once Satchel came down out of the attic, they agreed to let her stay at Seaton for her remaining year of high school. Their one request was that she live with me rather than in the dorm. Jack Farrell told me later about his phone conversation with Roger Leeson.

"I guess it's an unusual thing to ask," Satchel's stepfather had said, "but that child—she's been through a lot in her life, you know? Now, I just want her to be happy. Yeah, I can speak for her mother too. We want Satchel to be happy. We think the best situation for her would be to live with Miss Gunnar and not in the dorm. It'd be, you know, kind of like having a home. Would you consider allowing her to do that?" Jack Farrell didn't have to consider the request for long. As soon as he hung up with Roger Leeson, he called to let me know I was about to become something of a surrogate mother. I couldn't have been happier.

As for Theodore Dutton discovering Satchel's whereabouts, it was the mango that gave her away. "I kept filling up the jar only to find it empty," Ted said. "Someone was eating the mango, and it wasn't me. I can't stand the stuff myself. And Len can't either."

Satchel had a key to the store, so she simply let herself in and went into hiding. At night she came down from her hiding place and rummaged for food.

"Didn't you think the Duttons would suspect something when there was food missing?" I asked when she told me the story of how she came to live in the attic.

"Naw. Bel kept blaming Len for eating everything. I figured I could let him take the fall. I didn't know he doesn't like mango."

"So how long did you intend to stay up there?"

She shrugged. "I didn't bother thinking about that. I was just kind of enjoying it while it lasted."

"Enjoying it? What on earth did you do up there all that time?"

"Slept. Read. There were plenty of books, and I found a flashlight down in the store so I could read even when it was dark. And then I spent a lot of time listening to Mr. Ted."

"Listening to Mr. Ted?"

"Yeah, he'd sit down there in the back room reading the Bible out loud. Yeah, at first I couldn't believe he was reading. I mean, that was my job. I was supposed to read to him. But then I saw the Bible where he left it on the kitchen table. It was large print, and he was reading it with a magnifying glass. And then he prayed a lot."

"Did he pray out loud too?"

"Yeah. And he asked God to keep me safe and bring me home. He said, like, 'Please bring her home, because we love her.'"

Her eyes glistened as we exchanged a smile. That very day I started getting rid of the extra books in the guest bedroom to prepare a place for Satchel. This was before I even knew for sure that she'd be living with me. Something just told me things might end up that way. I taped up some boxes and carried the books out to the car and carted them off to Bel's Book Nook. It took three trips. Whether Satchel stayed with me or not, I needed to get rid of the books. And in the end Satchel did stay.

Now she turns away from the screen door, her whole face radiant. "Where's Len taking us to dinner tonight?"

"I don't know. He says it's a surprise." I'm sitting on the couch watching Satchel, content simply to be with her. "All I know is he said to dress in something nice." Which we have done—new clothes for both of us from Lord and Taylor, courtesy of Roger Leeson. He gave Satchel a generous financial gift, telling her to buy what she needed for school. Then he added, "Buy yourself some new clothes, will you? Something that doesn't have holes in it. And Miss Gunnar too— buy her something nice." He's a happy man these days, the father of twin boys. He has given his wife the gift of a full-time nanny. I've decided he's not such a bad fellow after all.

Satchel moves across the living room and sits down in the wing chair. Wide-eyed, she says, "Maybe Len's going to give you the ring tonight!"

A small thrill of excitement runs through me. "That would be something, wouldn't it?"

"But then . . . maybe I shouldn't be there. If he does, I mean. Maybe you'd rather it just be the two of you."

"Oh no. I want you there. I really do."

Satchel smiles. "It's kind of like we're family, isn't it?"

"Yes," I say, nodding happily, "it's just like that, Satchel."

For a moment she looks dreamy. "You know, it's going to be really cool to be in your wedding. I've never been a brides-maid before."

"You'll be beautiful," I say. "And I can't think of anyone I'd rather have with me than you and Natalie."

Dear Natalie. She's beside herself with excitement, insist-ing that we start planning the wedding right away. I tell her there's plenty of time, as it's at least a year off. Len is going back to Quentin College for another year of teaching. He promises, though, to visit me and Satchel as often as he can. Satchel has already begun working on her application to Quentin. When I move to upstate New York, she plans to be there too.

I will spend this upcoming year teaching at Seaton. Satchel will go on working at Bel's Book Nook. It will be a good year for us both, I think. Pine Glen will be a true home, and we will miss it when we go. But we will leave it in good hands, relinquishing the house to Joel Sexton and his family with the promise that they will never again wake up to find a car in their living room. Joel says he will keep his fingers crossed and hope for the best until then.

Before Satchel and I move to New York, there's another wedding we'll be attending. Ray and Brenda are getting remarried over Thanksgiving weekend. I would tell you that story of love restored, but that is for another book. Suffice it to say that I rejoice for them, knowing that the returning to one's first love doesn't happen very often.

I learned about Ray's impending marriage when he answered Theodore Dutton's request to stop by the store and visit him. Ray did so reluctantly but told me later he was glad.

While he was there, a weight he didn't even know about suddenly rolled off his back. It was the rolling off that let him know the burden had been there for years, and he had simply grown used to carrying it. He said the weightlessness was amazing, right up there with being in love again with his wife. He said sometimes restoration comes to us as a gift when we didn't even know it was possible and haven't done a single thing to deserve it.

Ray went on to tell me Ted thanked him for saving his life. "If you boys hadn't come by the cabin," Ted had said, "I most likely wouldn't be here now. I should think I'd have bled to death."

Ray said he deserved no thanks, that he and Ken had gone to the cabin only to pull an April Fool's joke. Ted waved a hand and said no matter the boys' intent, it became an intervention. "A divine appointment," he'd said, "to keep this old fool alive."

Satchel leans her head back against the chair and shuts her eyes. She is smiling pensively, as though at some secret thought. But I can read her mind. It is a sense of satisfaction that leaves her at rest.

I think I hear a car approaching, so I rise and go to the door. A car passes by, but it isn't Len. He'll be here soon, though. Meanwhile, I will take a moment to stand here and drink in the light, for it is full of life.

Which leads me to the final thing I want you to know. It's a small place, this state called Delaware. Small and rather insignificant and often overlooked. Invisible, even. Kind of like me. Maybe like you. But this is where God met me, raining down goodness on humble ground. So I want you to know that if you stop and listen to the moments, you might realize

He is in them, calling your name. And if you're like Nathanael, and if you're like me, you might be surprised and ask, "But Lord, how do you know me?" And He will answer you the way He did Nathanael, and the way He did me, "When you thought you couldn't be seen, I saw you."

Len's car is coming down the lane now toward Pine Glen. I open the screen door and step onto the stoop, waiting for him there with open arms.

DISCUSSION QUESTIONS
for *Every Secret Thing*
Written by Danica Abisror

1. "When it comes to Delaware, you don't really hear much of anything . . . the state itself is not so different from most of us . . . Very few people know that you exist, or that I exist. . . ." (Prologue). Have you ever felt this way about your existence? What situations brought about these feelings? What does Scripture say about our being known by God? Consider Psalm 139: 1–6; 13–18 and Matthew 10:29–31.

2. The concept "moments of being" is a continuous thread in Beth's experience. Describe the concept from her point of view. Can you identify with her experience? If so, how?

3. There are many teens today who are seemingly "lost" and "invisible" just as Satchel seemed to be. What factors in our world do you think contribute toward their feelings of isolation and despair?

4. "School was a testing ground, and it was here my worth as a person would be determined," remembers Beth in Chapter 7. How would you encourage Beth if you were discussing this with her as a teenager?

5. When she heard the bells in the basilica (Chapter 17), it was both a revelation and a turning point in Beth's life. What was the essence of this experience? Have you ever had a similar experience?

6. As high school students, Beth and her friends felt betrayed by their beloved teacher's "suicide." Have you ever been devastated by a person you trusted? How did you react?

How does it affect you today?

7. What were the "lesser gods" in Beth's life that are shown throughout the story? What are some "lesser gods" in your own life? What should be your response to these things? Read Exodus 20:1-4 and Acts 17:29-31.

8. At the end of Chapter 33 Satchel and Beth discuss whether or not it is worthwhile to love in spite of pain. Read the passage again and describe the mindset behind each character. Have you ever had either of these two perspectives?

9. After reading Satchel's essay "My Favorite Thing to Do" (Chapter 41), Beth comments, "When a person considers her place in this wide world, she begins to drown." Think of several Scripture passages that could encourage a person contemplating the immensity of the universe and his or her place in the world.

10. Trace the concept of love throughout the story. Bring out conversations in the book that discuss this concept. Finally, form a one-sentence conclusion that describes what you think the novel is trying to portray about love.

11. In Satchel's essay "My Dream Job" (Chapter 47) she talks about the "blood-cleaning" machine she would like to create. As you think about Satchel's desire to bring joy and happiness to people, consider the ultimate cleansing of blood. Read Mark 14:12-25 and contemplate these verses in relation to Satchel's dream.

12. Look at the conversation that Beth and her dad had about the book of Hosea in Chapter 51. What was her dad actually trying to talk to her about when she thought he was discussing her situation with Ray?

13. At the end of Chapter 56 Beth asks herself, "What had

happened to the God I had known, the one who had come to me in those moments of being?" What do you think is the answer to her question? Support your answer with Scripture.

14. By chapter 67 Beth still did not fully trust Mr. Dutton. Do you think he earned her complete trust by the end of the story? If so, how? If not, why?

15. Beth closes her story with some final words to the reader: "I want you to know that if you stop and listen to the moments, you might realize that He is in them, calling your name. . . ." As you contemplate this and other lessons learned by the characters in this book, what impact could you let them have on your own circumstances?

Be the first to know

Want to be the first to know
what's new from
your favorite authors?

Want to know all about
exciting new writers?

Sign up for Bethany House newsletters at
www.bethanynewsletters.com
and you'll get regular updates via e-mail.
You can sign up for specific authors or
categories so you get only
the information you really want.

Sign up today